BLOOD toy

B.K. Raine

Published by Benevolence Books

ISBN (paperback): 978-0-9964212-2-5
ISBN (hardback): 978-0-9964212-0-1
ISBN (digital): 978-0-9964212-1-8

Cover Design by: Donna Harriman Murillo

Edited & formatted by: Michelle Josette

To Ron Lindahn, my first editor and mentor, for giving me honest criticism and speaking with a soft voice.

To my parents for believing in me even when I was the 'weird girl in the trench-coat.'

To my friends and first readers, past and present, for getting my vision—Sam, Celena, Karry, Pepper, and Marsha (my inspiration for Renn, may she RIP).

To my husband for taking care of everything else so I could write, and my daughter for being proud of a book she's not even allowed to read.

To Michelle Josette, *Blood Toy*'s editor, for helping me finish this damn thing!

And finally, to my 'Big Grandma' for teaching me that "Everybody needs a little help sometimes." If not for hers, the life my family has now would not be possible.

ℒROLOGUE

The worst and last thing the twins ever did was a consequence of reality TV and a thirty-year-old metal detector collecting rust in the barn next to their dad's nautilus machine. Tate got the idea from a show starring a certain former wrestler turned treasure hunter. Noah went along because he had nothing better to do.

The house had stood at the top of Serpent Mountain — the Snake — forever, as far as forever goes. It was older than Benevolence Baptist, which meant it was older than the name of the town. Benevolence natives gave the place a wide berth for the most part. Even vandals and teenagers were usually gentle about their business. Not the mountain, though. The creeping vines that claimed so much of the wild places in these parts scaled at least six trees to gain access to the roof over which they now draped in profuse curtains. Wood siding, once white, now shone the color of red clay and peeled like a curling half-empty book of matches.

Noah took a long drag, then passed the pinner to Tate. "I don't get it," he said without exhaling.

Tate drummed his fingers on the car door and yawned. "Yeah, what don't you get?"

"The big deal about this place. It's just a house."

"An old ass house."

Noah shrugged. "Still just a house. You know it's been picked clean already."

"You got anything better to do?"

"If I did, I sure as hell wouldn't be here."

Tate flipped up the ashtray door. "You wanna hit this one more time?"

Noah considered it. "Nah, I'm good."

He stubbed out the joint and checked his phone, half charge. "Alright, let's do this."

"I always forget how creepy this place is. I still say it's been picked clean already."

"The good stuff is going to be buried on the grounds anyway."

Four hours later, after digging up their forty-seventh aluminum pull tab, the effort seemed to outweigh any prospect of reward. They would have given up in another five minutes, their only valuable discovery a broken knife with a single purple jewel set in the blade. Thirty yards west of the house, a frenetic series of beeps led them to a narrow concrete stairway covered up with kudzu. Noah fell into it like a snow drift.

Tate scrambled to the spot where his brother disappeared and spread himself out on the ground, grabbing fistfuls of greenery as anchor. "What the hell? You OK?"

Noah crouched on the bottom step over a metal door recessed into the lower landing. "Yeah, but this thing is toast." He held up the metal detector, its handle snapped in two places.

"You could've broke your damned neck."

"Take a look at this though," he said, indicating the door. "It still has a lock on it."

Tate joined him in the stairway. "This is what I'm talking about."

"My guess is we're going to find barrels of two-hundred-year-old turnips behind that door. If we're lucky, maybe a few bottles of wine that haven't turned to vinegar."

"Hell yeah. Free booze. Go get us something to get this lock off."

Noah climbed to the top of the stairs and hesitated. "You wanna come with?"

"Nah, I'll be fine." Tate hunkered down to wait, back against the concrete wall. Sunlight filtered through the kudzu in webs, stenciling the corridor with an intricate pattern of light and shadow that looked something like words. He got the feeling he could read them if he tried. Trailing vines tickled the back of his collar, imaginary spiders to slap away. Dried leaves whispered around him. Had something moved under them? Despite the shade, the metal door radiated heat, absorbing every bit of sun that found its way down. It would make a sweet copperhead den.

"Let's make it quick." Noah ducked into the stairway with his Winchester in hand. "I don't like this place."

"Don't puss out on me, bro. You don't reckon a thirty-aught six will kill a ghost?" He pulled up the flashlight and video apps on his phone, turned both of them on, and motioned for Noah to get on with it.

The rifle butt did a fine job on the lock, and the door opened with a requisite creak. The cellar opened to a wooden ladder, which led down into a foyer just about large enough to fit six full-grown men standing shoulder to shoulder. Another door stood on the far end of the room, this one barred with a slab of wood about the size of a railroad tie.

"This is some medieval shit," Noah said, his voice sounding too loud in the narrow confines. He propped the rifle up against a wall, and they muscled the bar from its hangers to reveal a box-lock with a skeleton keyhole.

"Damnit." Tate pocketed his phone. "Somebody was awfully proud of whatever is in this room. Stand back." He picked up the Winchester and drilled a bullet between the latch and strike plate.

He passed the rifle back to Noah, who dug into his ear with his pinky finger and made a face. "Shit, you don't reckon that was overkill?"

"Overkill is my middle name." Tate pulled out his phone again, and shined its light into the room as he opened the door. Hundreds of answering torches shined back.

"What the...?"

Mirrors filled the triple-locked room, which was about double the size of the one they stood in now. They covered every wall, the ceiling, even the floor. Shards of glass from the ones on the back of the door fanned out across the width of it.

Noah whistled and said, "Sucks to be you. That's seven years of bad luck."

Tate stepped inside. He couldn't see any rhyme or reason for the mirrors' arrangement. An ornate one here that may have hung over a dresser or a bathroom sink, a plain panel there that could have been taken from a barber shop, and dozens of hand mirrors everywhere.

As if from far away, he heard Noah say, "We should get out of here."

"What? No. This is what we came for, bro. There must be over a hundred mirrors in here, like two-hundred-year-old mirrors. They've got to be worth something."

"We can come back."

Tate swiveled his head in Noah's direction. Every now and again he got this twin vibe and could sort of feel his brother's emotions. Right now, Noah was straight up freaking out. "Yeah, OK. Sure. I'll just grab one of these little ones and we'll Google it." He started to pry a petite silver compact off the wall when he saw something move behind him in the reflection. He dropped his phone and spun around with a sharp expletive.

"What is it?"

The mirrors were empty again. "Nothing. Just got spooked is all." When Tate crouched to retrieve his phone, he saw a man standing over him in the fragmented reflection. "Noah, go. Right now. Get the hell out of here."

When he hesitated, Tate yelled, "Run!"

They scrambled up the ladder to the kudzu-shaded staircase and began to climb. And climb. And climb. But no matter how many stairs they put behind them, there were never any fewer above. After minutes, maybe hours, Tate stumbled, fell, looked back into the gaping maw of the cellar...and screamed.

CHAPTER 1

I heard he had a foot fetish. That's why I was standing barefoot in the elevator, a pair of nine-hundred-dollar stilettos with vamp red soles in one hand, a purse too small to hold any weapon deadlier than my dagger in the other. As the car made its slow ascent, I tapped my fingers on the handrail and wished I had taken the stairs. Two men and a woman shared the space with me, all of us observing prevailing elevator etiquette, which meant we stared straight ahead and minded our own business. One of the men checked out my unpainted toes while the other frowned at my hand like he hoped the weight of his gaze would hold it still, but nobody asked, and I didn't oblige.

The men got off five stories before my stop, muttering "Have a good one" to the woman, whose employee badge read: Cindy. I wondered what it would be like to work there, to ride the elevator every day to and from some mundane office job and make small talk with strangers between floors, to tip my head at the security guard every morning and drink too much spiked punch at lame company parties.

Cindy made eye contact with me for a split second and smiled before looking at the floor again. After a pause, she said, "Excuse me, but the price tag is still on your pants. Do you want me to get it for you?"

I tugged my blouse out of the way and arched my spine in search of it, but ended up just nodding. "If you don't mind."

She grasped the tag and hesitated. "I'm afraid I'll rip the seam."

"Don't worry about it." I was only going to wear them once anyway.

"Are those Louboutins?"

I wedged my feet into the heels, scowling. "Whatever they are, they're evil."

"I've always wanted a pair."

"Well, you can have them when I'm done."

She tittered behind her hand and nodded goodbye when the doors opened again, one floor below my stop. I wondered what it might be like to have a friend like Cindy, to borrow each other's clothes and grab coffee together after work.

Twenty minutes earlier I had walked into the upscale boutique next door wearing off-the-shelf jeans and combat boots. I feared the sales associate might pass a kidney stone just looking at them. I was also pretty sure she burned them as soon as I left.

Now, along with my usual slim white button-up and camisole, I wore black skinny pants that showed off pale ankles, and five-inch heels that made my legs look seven feet tall. I had coiled my coffee-brown braid into a low bun and donned lipstick as red as the soles of my shoes. My neck and collar bones were bare. That's what I hated most.

The doors opened on a stark white lobby and reception desk. Do or die time. I reminded myself to make noise when I crossed the room. The receptionist smiled, so I matched her expression. "Harlin is expecting me."

"Sure. Your name please?"

"Stacy," I lied.

"Just a sec." She picked up the receiver and dialed an extension. "Mr. Barnes, your 11:00 is here." To me, she said, "He'll be right out if you want to have a seat."

I didn't, but it was the expected social protocol, so I sat. Five minutes later, a dark-haired man in a beige two-button suit appeared. He reminded me of a politician when he smiled. "Stacy, so sorry to keep you waiting."

I wagged my leg at him before uncrossing it to stand. In those heels, I was six-foot-two, Amazonian compared to Harlin. "No trouble."

He led the way to an office with windows that framed an oppressive view of the city, jagged spires of concrete and steel lacerating the sky. I sat down again, this time in a low-backed chair upholstered in stiff, green leather. I expected him to put his feet up on the desk, but apparently that only happens in movies. "Tell me about your portfolio. I understand you are looking to diversify."

Whatever that meant. I gave him the same smile I'd given his receptionist and peeked at him from beneath a heavy fringe of lashes. "I have a confession to make."

"What's that?"

"I didn't come here for investment advice."

He ran a well manicured finger over his lips. "I do hope you aren't a process server. You are far too pretty to turn over to security."

Imitating Cindy's giggle, I asked, "You think I'm pretty?"

"Of course."

"Good." I tried for a seductive grin as I stood, an expression at odds with my reeling insides. Taking slow, deliberate steps to his side of the desk, I contemplated his receding hairline. He had been on the bad side of middle age when he got brought over, but was still handsome in a Lands' End catalog-model kind of way. I perched myself on the edge of his desk, crossing my legs and my nine-hundred-dollar shoes toward him. "I hoped you wouldn't think I was a stalker."

"Why would I think that?" He draped a hand across my knee. I resisted the urge to slap it away.

"You know, Harlin, you are a hard man to get alone."

"I didn't realize you'd been trying."

"I've seen you in the building, and I thought we could be friends."

"Friends?"

"Buddies," I clarified.

"We can be buddies."

He stood, invading my space to show he caught my meaning. After coaxing my legs apart, he drew an ankle up to his waist. His thumb traced the veins that ran along the inside of it. I wanted to ask him if the action was intentional. Instead, I dug my spiked heel into his side, possibly with more force than necessary, though Harlin didn't seem to mind. He unbuttoned my pants while I opened my purse.

"I'm clean. Trust me," he said.

I withdrew a tin of mints, popped one in my mouth and offered another to him. "Humor me."

He did. Then he kissed me. It was wet and sloppy, but it worked. I pushed my own mint into his mouth and kept my lips pressed to his until he swallowed that too. As soon as he did, he pulled away, his eyes turning the color of cherry Kool-Aid. He was a young one.

"What was that?"

"That was candy-coated amethyst." From between my breasts, I withdrew a syringe and thrust the needle into his jugular. "This is saltwater."

I didn't quite make it out of spitting distance before he started to die. While he puked blood, I locked the door, stripped off my blouse and slacks, and changed into the thin jersey skirt and ballerina flats I had rolled up in my purse. My backup syringe fell out with my clothing and cracked on the corner of Harlin's desk. *Good thing I don't need it now.*

After wiping off all traces of lipstick, I took down my braid and finger-combed my hair into ripples that fell to my waist. I wiped off my prints and stuffed everything but the Louboutins in Harlin's trash can. Those I would leave at the security desk for Cindy. It was really just a courtesy cleanup. When people like Harlin die, cops are seldom involved.

I remembered the emergency exit was located next to the elevator, so I would have to go out the way I came in. The receptionist was gone when I entered and the lobby almost vacant, except for the dark-haired man seated in the very same chair where I had waited to meet Harlin. He claimed a wide territory, arms spanning the backs of two chairs, legs spread, keys and cell phone arranged on the coffee table on top of aging copies of GQ and Money magazine. He leaned forward when I entered and fixed me with a hard stare that made the room feel too small for both of us.

He stood when I passed him and cornered me at the elevator. I considered the stairs, but decided against them. What if he followed? I didn't have a backup syringe, not to mention I was underdressed. I made a mental note to be better prepared in the future. Always carry two syringes and never, ever wear a skirt.

"Going down?" he asked.

I didn't trust myself to speak, so I just nodded. He reached over me and pressed the button to call the car up, brushing his bicep against my shoulder and pressing his chest against mine. My ass hit the wall before I realized I was backing away. My head screamed at the invasion of space, and I held my breath to contain it.

He extended his hand. "Christopher Desollador. A pleasure meeting you, Miss…?"

I never took my eyes off his. They were the color of aged Merlot. *Damn.* "Stacy," I said.

The elevator doors opened. He leaned inside, punched the Lobby button for me, then held the door until I entered. I resisted the urge to press my back into the corner farthest from him. His mouth curled with mild humor. "Next time, you'll have to tell me your real name."

I hoped there would never be a next time. Barring that, I hoped if there was a next time, I would have another syringe between my breasts and a much bigger knife.

It would be so convenient if vampires turned to dust when they die like they do in the movies. My world would be a lot simpler if the legends were true. In reality, vampires die messy deaths, leaving bodies shriveled like leeches and lots and lots of blood behind.

After I picked up my boots and jeans from the next-door boutique—where I was pleased to learn the sales associate did not burn them after all—and bought another white button-up to replace the one I had thrown away, I parked myself in a café across the street from Harlin's office to see who showed to clean up my mess. Fifteen minutes after the waitress took my order and five minutes before my coffee arrived, a black Monte Carlo pulled up to the loading zone in front of the building. A young man got out of the passenger side, pulled an oversized black garment bag from the trunk and carried it into the building. Five minutes later, he exited with the same bag slung over his shoulder, weighted down this time with Harlin's body.

The Monte Carlo and its passenger struck a chord of familiarity that unsettled me, but before I could place them, Desollador emerged from the building. He squinted into the sunlight, then lowered his head and, even though every window looking into the café was mirrored, our eyes met. I touched the hilt of my knife to confirm it was clear in its holster and evaluated my exits.

While I was fishing a bill out of my pocket to cover the coffee, Desollador appeared at my table. "Is this seat taken?"

I took a sip to hide my gasp. "It is if you plan on sitting in it."

"I'd like to join you."

"Absolutely not."

He sat anyway and began to peruse my menu. "Have you eaten yet?"

"I was just leaving."

"We both know if you do that I'm going to follow you. We can have this little chat here or it can wait until we're alone. Let me buy you some juice and a plate of eggs to go with that coffee. They serve brunch here, I believe."

I reached under my shirt for the dagger. He shook his head. "There's no need for that."

I didn't draw, but I didn't take my hand off it either. "I think you should leave."

"I bet you do." He flagged the waitress. "But that's not going to happen."

"I am so sorry," she said by way of greeting, splaying fingernails painted the color of pink gumballs. "You must think I am so rude. I had no idea this was going to be a party of two. I'm Carrie. What can I get you, darlin'?" I couldn't recall her even telling me her name.

Desollador gave her a wide, humoring smile. "If I could get the special, medium rare, and a glass of water, that'd be great. A tall glass of orange juice, two eggs over medium, and a side of toast for my friend."

I was too busy wondering how he knew how I liked my eggs to

object to him ordering for me. "I don't like juice."

"So no juice?" Carrie asked without looking at me.

"Go ahead and bring it. It won't go to waste."

When she was gone, he leaned back in his chair, crossing an ankle over one knee. "I hate these places," he said with a sigh.

"You could still go."

"And miss the chance to enjoy your company? No, I'll manage. It's just that I would much prefer we were dining alone."

"Not going to happen."

He barked a laugh. "You take playing hard-to-get to a whole new level." His gaze locked on to my throat where I wore a three-inch leather collar that tied in the back like a corset. "That contraption is an offense to good taste."

"Function over form. It's not a decoration."

"Really?"

"No, it serves a very specific purpose."

"You think so?" I didn't answer, but I did meet his gaze in a way that dared him to deny it. Instead he ordered, "Take it off."

I felt an intense pressure at his command, accompanied by a faint sound like television static in my head. I winced and tried to shake off the feeling.

"It's a compulsion," he said. "The longer you deny it, the worse it's going to hurt."

I curled my fingers and fought it anyway. "Get the hell out of my head, vampire."

"Make me."

I started to stand, but the static surged, the cumulative sounds in the room becoming an over-modulated cacophony. I plugged my ears, but it didn't help.

"I just want to talk, Diane."

So he knew my name after all. "So talk."

"Let's try this another way." The sound died down, and the pressure in my head abated. His eyes flooded with color. "Take it off."

I felt like I'd just popped a couple of Vicodin and chased them with a double whiskey. I bared my neck to him even as I shook my head to deny it. "Son of a bitch."

"Interesting. An all-out compulsion you resist, but you succumb to swoon like a lover." He leaned forward and put his lips to my ear, his breath a surprising warmth against my skin. "Tell me, what purpose does your decoration serve now?"

How had I been doing this for three years and never managed to get myself into this predicament? I jerked my head away from his mouth, touched my fingers to my throat and checked the tips of them for blood. "Screw you."

"I want to know why you killed Harlin."

"I kill vampires."

"I see. And you hang around until the body is gone…why? Does it excite you to see the aftermath of your handiwork?"

"I hang around to make sure the job is done. Saving innocent lives excites me."

"That's where I'm confused. See, Harlin Barnes never killed anybody. He was a womanizer, probably a crook—he was an investment banker—but not a murderer."

"He had to be a murderer." Else that would make me a murderer.

"No, he wasn't. Nor was my tax attorney or my estate manager. The others you've killed, yes, flesh peddlers and thugs. But this is where I live. My connections here are businessmen and generally squeamish about leaving a trail of bodies in their wake. A compunction which you apparently don't share. So I want to know why you are targeting them."

That made two of us. "Wait, are you telling me you knew all of these men?"

"No, I am telling you I sired them."

Our meals arrived. I cut into my eggs without much thought, but regretted it once the yolk started to run. I felt a weakness in my stomach that tickled the back of my throat. "All of them?"

Desollador lifted a triangle-shaped piece of steak to his lips. "Every single one."

What the hell? "It must be a coincidence."

"Some coincidence."

No kidding.

"You're not drinking your juice."

"I told you I don't like juice."

"Vitamin C helps your body absorb iron. Egg yolks, by the way, are a good source of that. Eat up."

"I'm not hungry, and I'm still not drinking the juice."

He took another bite of steak. "I assume you know why I'm suggesting measures to beef up your iron levels. I don't need to spell it out for you, do I?"

"Screw you," I repeated.

"We'll get to that."

"Wasn't an invitation." I tried to stand again.

"Sit down and eat your brunch." This time there was no manhandling of my will, just smooth and absolute control.

My face was on fire. "I've killed a lot of vampires in the last three years. I think you might be the first I am actually looking forward to ending."

"You've killed a lot of fledglings."

"I'm still looking forward to killing you."

He waved my claim away. "You don't need to do that. I didn't come here to exchange threats. I just wanted to meet you."

"Well, now we've met."

"Not really. I want to know you. I hoped we could enjoy a polite conversation, small talk, before getting down to the dirty business."

"I'm not interested."

"Have you ever been bitten?"

"I've donated blood. Does that count?"

He smirked into his glass of water. "No, I think you'll find it most definitely does not count."

"I'll pass."

"I believe you know you won't." He folded my choker and stuffed it in his lapel pocket like a handkerchief. "I actually like you. I imagined it was a man killing my progeny, some hothead Van Helsing wannabe with more balls than brains, but then I find this beautiful girl with ballerina slippers and dainty collar bones. "You are fortunate that I am more intrigued than angry."

"Yeah, I feel fortunate." I wished the waitress would return. My coffee was cold, and I was determined not to drink the damn orange juice.

"Tell me, how did you decide to become a vampire hunter?"

"When I was seventeen, a vampire killed my family," I said through clenched teeth. "I guess it was my calling. How did you become an abomination?"

"A prince thought I would make a better warrior dead than alive. Rather backfired on him, I think."

"How long ago was that?"

"A millennium or so. You are not the first hunter who's caught my attention, though you just might be the prettiest."

"What happened to the others?" I knew by the way he brought it up that he had killed them, but I wondered if they tried to kill him first and, more importantly, why they failed.

"They failed because they had no weapons against me. They discovered it rather violently, I'm afraid. I think your education might be more pleasant."

"Doubt it," I said. I had the weapons. OK, I didn't have them with me, but I would never let myself be caught off-guard again. I would worry later about why I had been caught off-guard in the first place. There was only supposed to be one vampire in that office building. "I plan to show you what an assassin actually does to vampires."

"Confident little thing, aren't you?" He leaned over the table and cupped the back of my neck in his hand. "This is what is going to happen. You will stop hunting in my city. You will burn every disgusting leather dog collar you own and possibly buy yourself another skirt or two. And you will drink your orange juice." When I didn't move, he added, "Now."

Even as I brought the glass to my lips, I said with all the venom I could muster, "Enjoy it while you can, vamp."

"I haven't started enjoying myself, Pet. You'll know it when I do. In the meantime, if I can give you a piece of advice—"

"I'd rather you didn't."

"You need to take better care of yourself. I'd lay a compulsion on you to finish that juice after I leave if it worked on you, but since you seem to be largely immune, I will just suggest it strongly." He threw a hundred-dollar bill on the table. "I'll see you again soon, Diane. It has been a real pleasure meeting you."

Though moving my arms against his will felt like lifting a small car, I somehow managed to toss the remaining contents of my glass in his face. "Same here."

He soaked up what he could with his napkin. Carrie, conveniently absent when I needed hot coffee, swooped in then. "Oh gosh, are you OK? Let me get you a damp towel." She gave me the stink eye and scurried off again.

Desollador's face was devoid of any discernible emotion, though his eyes morphed from burgundy to black. "Take off your blouse."

"No."

"Take it off, or I will take it off for you."

I had no idea what the distinction was between compulsion and swoon, but I had no power to resist whichever he was using on me. I unbuttoned my blouse and slid it off, grateful I was still wearing my camisole. He snatched it out of my hands, dipped a sleeve into his water glass, and used it to wipe the rest of my orange juice off his face.

Carrie showed up with a damp towel which he declined. "I believe I am all set, but my friend needs another glass of juice."

I felt nude in the worst way when she looked at me and asked, "Are you sure?"

"Carrie, bring my friend another glass of juice please."

"Yes, sir."

"And Carrie?"

"Yes?"

"Be quick about it."

We sat in silence until she placed the new glass, filled to the very brim, in front of me. I felt like everyone in the restaurant was watching when he said, "Drink."

I did.

"Have you ever heard the term 'blood toy'?"

"No."

"A blood toy is a human, usually a girl and sometimes willing, used for blood and sex."

"Sounds fun."

"To put it bluntly, Diane, you are going to get the chance to find out."

I wanted to tell him he had another thing coming, but decided I had pushed hard enough without another syringe in my bra handy to shove up his —

"Still think you have a chance, even after all this, don't you?"

I wanted to stab him, but there were too many witnesses. Later, I thought.

"Fine then, later." My blouse still clenched in his fist, he circled the table to stand behind my chair and kissed my throat. "If you don't finish that glass after I leave, I am going to follow our lovely Carrie home tonight. I can drain her to death in three minutes. I trust you will be here a while."

I nodded. He left, or he didn't. I didn't look up from my glass for a long while, until the sounds of conversation resumed around me, even until some of the patrons that witnessed my humiliation paid their bills and moved on. Carrie, though, was a constant reminder, fluttering by every few minutes to ask if I needed more napkins or a refill of my coffee, another glass of juice maybe. I considered for the briefest moments letting Desollador kill her then, but just asked her for a straw and the check instead. I stuffed Desollador's hundred-dollar bill underneath my empty glass and left through the closest exit — which happened to be marked 'emergency' — feeling a perverse glee when the alarm went off behind me.

Street food reminds me of the traveling carnivals that used to set up once a year in the fairground outside of Benevolence.

The Tilt-a-Whirl, rusted through in places, that screeched relentlessly once it got going, and the carnies who told dirty jokes when we were still too young to understand them. You could get just about anything there deep-fried on a stick. Cheese, Twinkies, Snickers, even hamburgers. Those carnivals had been the best part of every summer until the one when my childhood died.

A week passed uneventfully after I killed Harlin and met Desollador. The following day I replaced my leather collar with a multi-strand choker of amethyst beads. I became such a regular in Café Diem that Carrie started refilling my coffee before it got cold and remembering how I liked my eggs.

I would have given anything for just one ride on the Tilt-a-Whirl to get my mind off vampires for three and a half minutes. In the end, I settled for something deep-fried on a stick.

"Hey, long time no see." Frank took my dollar and passed me a corn dog and a napkin.

"How's business?"

"Any better, there'd be a law against it. You rich and famous yet?"

"Almost."

"You better hurry up and get to it. I wanna retire while I'm still sexy." He rapped his knuckles on a 9 x 11 sketch framed under a sheet of plexi. It portrayed him, a big, toothy grin on his weathered face, passing a kid a wand of cotton candy so big it barely fit through the window. He had talked about selling it for riches since the day I forgot my wallet and bartered my services to him in exchange for lunch.

I lifted my sketchpad and pointed my corn dog up the hill. "I'm about to work on that right now."

"Go on then. Make us a masterpiece."

I spread a blanket out below my favorite dogwood and spent some time just people watching. Off-duty executives and arm-piece girlfriends jogged by me, flashing professionally whitened teeth in conversation. Several children ran alongside a merry-go-round. A charcoal-colored man with matching beard slept in the shade, a hound dog tethered to his bare foot, chewing on the shoe I presumed belonged on it.

The man's head rested on a twenty-pound bag of dog food.

I could imagine that dog and that bag of Ol' Roy were the only two things of value the man had left in the world. I wondered what I would give up for a connection like that. I recognized the moment as an occasion of profound intimacy and needed to capture it before it faded. The act of recreating a moment or a character on paper usually helped me slow down, shift my perspective. Right about then, I needed a change of perspective.

The vampire had wrecked my world, and I had no idea what to do about it. I couldn't take credit for knowing that Harlin was a vampire or that he had a shoe fetish or even that he worked across the street from Café Diem. I killed Harlin because a voice in my dreams told me to do it.

The first time it—she—spoke to me was on the night my parents were killed, with three cryptic sentences that changed my life forever: *Amethyst to bind him. Salt in his veins to kill him. Wake up.*

The thing is, I did wake up. I even remembered her words, vague as they were, before I fluffed my pillow and went back to sleep. In the morning with the sun, I found their bodies. I hadn't noticed how loud the whick-whick-wicking noise of the fan was until that morning. It was the right rhythm though for chest compressions. I couldn't do those on the bed—too bouncy—so I dragged my mother onto the floor. Her back was already bruised purple, her face nearly gray, and her neck was stiff like a doll's.

I don't know why I went through the motions of trying to bring her back to life. I could see she had been gone too long, but I kept pushing until I heard her ribs crack, remembered from CPR class that was supposed to be OK. *A cracked rib is better than dead.* Somebody called 9-1-1; the paramedics found me still trying to save her, choking on snot and tears, yelling "Momma" over and over.

My parents died because I ignored the voice in my dreams. By the time she returned to send me on my first mission, I had buried them and finished high school. It takes a great leap of faith, an iron conviction, or a whole lot of crazy to kill a man because the disembodied voice in my dream told me to do it. I had killed two dozen vampires, give or take, since then.

After my conversation with Desollador, I spent a lot of time wondering if all of them deserved to die. I also found myself wondering why she hadn't warned me he was coming. I wished for the one thousand two hundred and seventy-second time I could summon the bitch at will.

I had been drawing for a couple of hours when I heard a familiar voice say, "Hey you."

I cracked the first genuine smile of the week, put my charcoals down and got to my feet to give him a hug. I had to rise up on my tiptoes just a bit. Hugs weren't really my thing, but they were Roger's, and I hated to hurt his feelings. He was the closest thing to a friend I had in the city. "Hi yourself."

"Whatcha working on?"

I gestured to the sleeping man, though Roger was only making small talk. I was almost done with the piece. I wondered what he'd think if he knew I would set fire to it later.

"I think I'll call it Protector," I said.

"Who's protecting who?"

"I'd like to think it's mutual."

Roger stuffed his hands in his pocket. "It's sad."

"You don't know that. Things could be a lot worse."

"Easy to say when you're not homeless or hungry."

"Not true. It's been hours since I had a corn dog. I'm starving."

He tried to suppress a grin. "You get my meaning."

Yeah, I did. I hoped he'd never get mine. "How about you? You doing your dog whisperer thing?"

He picked up the whistle around his neck and let it drop. "Slow day. Only the regulars are out, and I can't think of any new tricks to teach them."

"I guess no one wanted to brave the rain." The weather had been suspect all day, but so far the skies were only overcast and grumbly. "You could always give a pro-bono lesson to Hobo over there."

"Hmm, what would be useful talent for a homeless dog? How to look even more pathetic?" The dog looked up from his shoe and whined.

"Oh fine, you look pathetic enough. Why don't you just go curl up with your buddy there and keep him warm?" That's exactly what he did, carrying the shoe in his mouth like a kid with a teddy bear and settling himself down next to the charcoal-colored man with a heavy sigh, an old dog sigh.

"I'll never figure out how you do that."

He slicked back his surfer-blond hair and winked. "It's just my charm."

"Ah, is that it?"

"Hey, you doing anything tonight?"

Ugh, this part. "Yeah, I got some things to finish."

After a pause that made me feel like hiding behind my sketchpad until he was gone, he said, "That's cool. We'll have to get together one of these days. You got my number. You should call sometime."

"Don't feel bad. I really don't call anybody." *Don't have anybody to call.* "I just hate talking on the phone." *And in person. And over email.*

His blue eyes closed, and I held my breath. I wasn't ready for this to be over, even if this would never be anything more than a casual acquaintance. After a pause that was just a moment shy from being awkward, he said, "Yeah, yeah. Whatever."

Behind us, someone called, "Hey, are you the dog man?"

He gave me a quick, spontaneous hug. One was usually my limit, but I tried not to flinch. "That's my cue. See ya later, Di."

I patted him on the back like he was an old woman, like I might break him. "OK, good seeing you."

Roger left a lightness in his wake that I wanted to follow. Things with him were simple, normal. Truth is, I kept coming back to the park mostly just for these little chats. I felt a pang of regret knowing he hoped for something more. Had I led him on? I had no experience with these things, but I didn't think so. We met at the food truck a few months back. He struck up a conversation about hot dogs and beer, and I caved at the chance for company. It had never been about anything more. For me.

When he left, it took no time at all for the semblance of normalcy to fade. My drawing finished, I decided Roger was right. It was sad, a reminder of just one of the things I could never have.

I spent about two hours capturing the image of the homeless man and his dog, those watchful eyes meeting mine over the shoe. I spent another two hours back in my rental scrubbing at the shadows until my fingertips were black with charcoal, until I had nothing left to do but burn it.

After my parents died, I lived with a distant great aunt once-or twice-removed in Denver. I had no other family left, but we were miserable together. So I drew. Old men and babies, trees that looked like monsters, creatures that never existed except in my head.

Then one night I heard the voice again. *He's coming here next. No one of yours is safe. Salt in his veins to kill...* I stormed into Aunt Sandra's bedroom with a baseball bat in one hand and turkey baster full of saltwater in the other. No vampire there, but I scared the living hell out of her and came a gnat's ass away from spending the rest of my senior year in a residential facility.

The voice came back again the next night and the next, and my life, already once wrecked, was irrevocably changed. No matter how real and tangible my world had been, it was just gone. Never coming back.

The night I accepted that—just weeks after graduation, while my peers were planning summer road trips and getting excited about college—I took a match to one of my favorite old man portraits, watched the fire blacken and disfigure it. The flame ate up one of his eyes, leaving behind a charred patch that made his smiling face look sulky and disapproving. I burned little bits of all my art that night, then I put them back in their frames to serve as reminders never to love anything I couldn't bear to see so damaged.

It's strange how our minds interpret what our eyes see. I eventually learned to block out the burned parts of my portraits until I could make a whole image from what remained. Although not always, not even usually, the image became what it had been before.

After I killed my first vampire I knew I would never need a reminder again, so I auctioned them online. Charred art, I called it. I made enough money to pay my rent for six months.

After that, I hired a graphic designer to set up an e-Gallery for me and gave him a hefty commission to handle the orders. I mailed it to him one piece at a time and collected my cut when it sold.

When I finished with Protector, a hole gaped where the dog's sneaker had been, so his eyes looked more heartsick than watchful. The dog food bag and most of the homeless man's torso, all evidence of his hunger, was burned away too. I wondered which one of the pair would have garnered Roger's sympathy if he saw this version of my drawing. I shuddered and hoped they both slept fat and happy somewhere tonight. I'd send it off to McClain Designs first thing in the morning.

The ritual of drawing and burning helped me to gain perspective. Maybe Desollador told me the truth. Maybe Harlin wasn't a murderer, but not killing him when I got the Call would have amounted to going back to sleep. Better to destroy ten vampires that never killed a soul than let one innocent die due to my inaction. As for Desollador, he proved himself the strongest vampire I had ever faced, but he was still only a vampire, and I was a vampire killer.

I wondered what he was waiting for. To see if I'd hunt him? Believe me, I tried. Every night. But my dreams were stubborn.

Until they weren't.

Hurry, a familiar voice said in my ear. She roused me from sleep, only my body did not follow.

About time!

There is no time.

Did you send me to kill an innocent vampire?

There are no innocent vampires.

Who is Desollador?

Hurry, and see.

I wanted to know more. I wanted to tell her that her answer was no answer at all, and I deserved to know. I was the one with dirty hands. My dream self had difficulty holding on to such petty notions.

The Dreamer succumbed to the urgency in her message and

plunged into the deep, black waters, letting them sweep us along to our destination.

We found him in a seedy dive bar, exactly the type of place I would expect to find a vampire, but oddly enough not where I expected to find him. I watched him stroke the lip of an untouched glass of amber liquid, while whispering into the ear of a petite blonde whose name I'd later learn was Trina. She crossed her legs inside his thighs and tossed her hair over her shoulder to reveal her throat. Porcelain white and adorned with a miniature gold cross, it glowed with vulnerability.

He cupped the back of her head in his hand and ran his thumb up the length of her jugular. An odd sort of anger twisted in my gut as I saw I wasn't his only intended victim in this town, apparently not even his most important. She touched his wrist, petted his shoulder, gave up her affections like idle chit chat. I drifted closer, a fascinated voyeur. She whispered something in his ear, her neck stretching across his lips, and I winced with pity. Poor, doomed girl.

Over her shoulder, the vampire's eyes shifted. His head tilted as if trying to pinpoint the source of a faraway sound, before swinging his gaze in my direction.

What the fuck? How could he see me if I was just a dream? I rationalized the stare—surely the direction of his gaze was coincidental—while he turned his attention back to Trina. She was, after all, the one with flesh and blood. One hand, fingernails painted cotton candy pink, rested on his hip; the other fluttered at her breast like an erratic moth at a flame.

He placed his hand on the small of her back, bent his lips into the crook of her neck and whispered, "Let's get out of here."

She nodded, drunk with him, and he smiled, a broad-toothed expression of anticipation. Then the vampire looked at me again, right into whatever serves as eyes for a ghost, and winked. He gave Trina a push toward the door.

I followed them to the top of a parking deck with a dazzling view of the city, not that she could see it. I told myself to look away or, better yet, wake up. In the end, I looked.

He had her pinned beneath him in the rear seat of the Monte

Carlo, his mouth against her throat, drinking in long pulls that lifted her from the seat.

"You're hurting me." She made a gasping, rattling noise. "Get off me. Somebody—" Her spirit shimmered through her skin.

My dream self reached out to it with a morbid empathy. Reached into the twinkly, panting essence of her.

"Somebody help me."

I felt a tug within her words, as strong as Desollador's compulsion, maybe stronger for the lack of static.

"Help!"

Her cries drowned out every voice of reason and sanity I possessed, seizing my dreamer's soul with the rigor grip of the dying. She called me to her, or more precisely—and I don't know how to explain this except to swear that it happened—into her.

With a start, I awoke in the sticky leather backseat of Desollador's Monte Carlo, feeling like the vampire was sucking me inside out. I don't mean to say that I dreamt I woke in that awful position. I was *awake*. I had flesh and blood, Trina's flesh and blood. Somehow she invited me in, and I possessed her. The tenor of my cries must have been different, more panicked than hers if that's even possible, because he chuckled.

He spoke without extracting his teeth. "You just keep screaming, kitten."

With this, he ground his hips into mine/Trina's. I heard my voice as hers cry out, felt her intimate pain as my own. I cried out again as much in shock this time as pain. Seems to me, it's just bad manners to screw a girl while you feed on her. But then, I'm human.

Besides that, I wore Trina's flesh now, and I despised his actions on myriad levels. "Stop! Get off me, vampire. I am not this girl."

Desollador stilled inside me, lifted his head and gave me a measuring stare. "Hmmm, interesting."

I pushed against his chest, but my new body weighed a buck-ten at best, had never been conditioned beyond an occasional spin class and had already lost more than a pint of blood.

"And what girl are you?"

"You know damn…damn well, vampire. One that's going to…end you."

"Really."

"Like all…like all the ones you sired."

His expression sharpened. "Is that you, Pet?"

"I am not your pet, vampire." I said it with more conviction than I felt. Truth is, I didn't know what I was at that moment.

"Quite a predicament you've got yourself in." The vampire forced my wrists over my head, buried his face in my throat and started *moving* again.

My heels slid on the upholstery. My chest ached with the struggle to breathe against the weight of his body. My heartbeat, which had been keeping time with the smack of his flesh against mine, stuttered. *This can't be happening. I can't die like this.*

No, Pet. This little slut is dying. You are only riding her death.

The fuck I am!

I would not let it happen. I would get myself out of that damned Monte Carlo. At that moment, my wrists were cuffed in the vampire's hands, my legs were spread over his thighs, and that would just, damn it, not do. Taking advantage of the slippery layer of sweat that coated the leather seat and my bare torso, I wiggled out from under him and onto the cramped floor board. He still held my wrists, but I managed to dislodge his fangs and other penetrating extremities.

When he attempted to jerk me out of my cubbyhole, I head-butted him. His nose exploded in a smear of blood and bone. It started to heal before the spots faded from my eyes, but that was time enough for me to get the door open.

He let me run, down the stairway and out of the parking deck into a manicured wilderness sprawled out behind some office building. The open air felt like freedom. I saved one! After so many bad dreams, so many prophecies, I managed this time to intervene before the damage was fatal. I started to wonder how I would return Trina's body to her when I ran headlong into the vampire.

I would have fallen, but he steadied me with a hand. I stepped back—he allowed that much—but when I tensed to run, he locked his thumb and forefinger around my wrist and shook his head.

"I told you I would come for you. Did you get impatient?"

A wall of vertigo hit me, and I clung to him for support, though I hated myself for doing it. "Son of a bitch."

"Just indulging in some of my, ah, more human urges. So I don't get too carried away with you on our first date."

"Human? That was…obscene."

"Your version of obscene and mine differ greatly."

"I will end you."

"Maybe one night, Pet. But not this one. Tonight I'm going to show you what it feels like to die."

"You," I raged. "You put me in this body!"

He held me at arm's length, his brows crinkled. "You think so?"

The night was madness, impossible, but I should have known by then that nothing was actually impossible. The vampire held me against him with one arm and lifted my legs out from under me with the other. He lowered me to the ground, freshly sodded. I wondered if he intended to rape me.

"No, I'm not." The vampire put his lips to my ear. "I want you in your own body when I take you." His laughter reverberated like thunder through my chest. His bite took me by such surprise, I didn't even fight him. Though I could not suffer injury in this borrowed body, Trina would suffer and die for my inaction.

More than madness, the night was wrong, unfair, and just plain cowardly of him. I must have been thinking something along those lines to make the vampire stop to ask, "Would you rather feel the brunt of her pain? Would you rather be brutalized? Rather I ravage you until you exhaust yourself and beg me to kill her? Is that what you want?"

"Yes," I gasped, "I would rather fight."

"Good. I like it when they squirm." The vampire laughed. It may have been with Trina's ears that I heard it and down her back that the subsequent shiver raced, but his laughter was pointed at *me*.

Damnsonofabitchingnogoodmotherfuckingvampire!

Driving his knee into my kidney, he said, "I warned you." He chopped the heel of his hand into my collarbone so hard it shattered. "This is a bad idea, Pet, but better you learn in this disposable body than your own. So tonight you're going to learn well."

The vampire changed, acquiring the substance of shadow, and became the Dog. Where the vampire had been, now stood something that looked like a wiry-coated Doberman. He had the height and bulk of a mastiff, but with the vampire's wine-colored eyes. I knew a brief moment of relief. I must be dreaming, I thought, really dreaming, because vampires don't shape-shift.

Then his voice thrummed in my head. *None you've killed were old enough to do it.*

I remembered my nudity when claws raked over my exposed breast. Snout and fangs clamped onto my shoulder, and he lifted me in his mouth and shook his head side to side. My dad had a dachshund once that did that with his squeaky toys. No wonder we found chunks of plastic missing from it every few days. This time I felt flesh tear and veins pop. My voice felt raw, but I wailed against the pain anyway. He dropped me with as much force as he picked me up, curled his lips back over canines stained with my blood, and growled. I shook my head, struggling to come to grips with the assault. A vampire and a dog. Neither had ever attacked me until that night.

As much as I feared breaking eye contact, I rolled onto my stomach, knowing if I didn't get away before he/it struck again, I wouldn't get away at all. I army-crawled ten or twelve feet and tried to pull myself up on a park bench. I thought if I could get my feet under me again, I might stand some chance. The Dog clamped down on my thigh and dragged me toward him. My forehead hit the concrete with a sickening crunch. The ability to fight back felt like a shitty consolation prize for my conscience. Trina was going to die.

All this pain for nothing. If agony were pleasure, mine would have been an orgasm. Desollador tore and clawed and pierced every part of my body.

I must have passed out from blood loss or concussion or both, but I awoke, still in my borrowed and broken body, to find Desollador, man again, leaning against the bench.

There might have been a bone or muscle in that body that would have borne my weight, but I doubt there was more than that. If Desollador didn't kill me, Trina would die from her injuries. I just wanted him to put me out of my misery.

When I whimpered, Desollador turned his attention back to me. I envied the ease with which he moved. For what seemed like forever, he just stood above me watching my face. He studied me without smiling, without mocking, and for that, I almost loved him.

Stupid girl, I told myself. *Learn to pick fights you can win.*

Desollador knelt beside me. "When I attack again, the adrenaline will help you fight back."

I closed my eyes, wet with tears. "I don't want to fight."

His eyes turned into heaven, red as the six o'clock dawn. He scooped up my broken remains, curled me in his lap and peeled the clotted mass of golden hair off my neck—a lover's gesture.

I shuddered with pleasure when his fangs claimed me this time.

His voice resonated in my blood. *I hope you learned your lesson.*
What lesson?
It doesn't have to hurt, Diane. But it can.

With that counsel lulling me to sleep, Trina died. I became the Dreamer again, swirling as a ghost above Desollador and the girl who had been Trina, then me, and now just a body. The vampire looked from the dead girl to me and smiled.

Now he gloated. "I hate it's over so soon." He threw off the dead thing in his arms and, in between one moment and the next, appeared so close we could have touched if I had flesh. "It will, though, be more fun to take you in your own body."

I shivered. *Bastard.*

I'm sure he heard, but the vampire ignored me. "I'll take my time with you then…over and over again."

Teeth chattering, I awoke.

That was how it started. Not when a vampire I could not name killed my parents, not on any night when I stalked and killed countless others just like him. When I died in a stranger's body, I started to fear.

CHAPTER 2

The mirrors annoyed him. Salvion could feel their pull, the ones inside watching him, shadowing his movements. Seemed like the nicer the bathroom, the more mirrors were in it. This was a really nice bathroom.

He avoided his reflection as he washed his hands. The automatic faucet cut off three times before he finished, as if to say, "Surely you are clean enough already."

After a flush, another man approached the counter. Well-dressed, with a dark swath of hair groomed into a stiff, shiny side part, he was handsome in an All-American sort of way. Side Part nodded "hello" and then did a covert double take.

Salvion could feel the other's scrutiny, even in their reflection. He was handsome too, but most definitely not in any usual way. His hair, held in a tight ponytail against the base of his neck, could pass for silver or white, which gave the first impression of an old man. His skin though — nearly the same color as his hair — was tight and supple over a chiseled jaw. A younger man's jaw.

Side Part either forgot to wash his hands or never intended to in the first place and instead pulled a toothpick from his pants pocket. It was the plastic kind, pointy on one end with a small length of floss on the other. Salvion suppressed a gag.

Side Part bared his teeth to reveal a glob of green — spinach or arugula — wedged between his bottom incisor and canine. Salvion couldn't help but stare and wasn't covert about it. The man didn't notice, too consumed by the task of working the thin filament deep into his gums. When he popped it out again, three dots of pink saliva splattered the mirror. The floss, with its green glob, he tossed in the trash on his way out.

Salvion watched him go. He stood for a good ten seconds clenching and unclenching his fists, gaze transfixed on the mess, before snatching up a paper towel. After he scoured the mirror free of the other man's spit, he looked at his reflection and said, "You're welcome."

He returned to the restaurant and joined his companion at the table, eyes still on Side Part now seated across the table from a pretty blonde woman in a slim belted sheath dress and patent leather pumps.

Salvion's companion either didn't notice or didn't care that his attention was elsewhere. "I think I'll head out to Vegas next."

He never took his eyes off his prey. "Sin City?"

"There's a speedway there, thirteen exotics—Ferrari 430 Scuderia, Aston Martin Vantage, Lamborghini Aventador."

"Scuddledy what?"

"Scuderia. Four point three liter V8, 508 horsepower. Will take you from zero to sixty in about three seconds. It's got no radio, no floor mats. Damn thing is a carbon fiber bullet."

Now he did look at his companion, this hulk of a man, modeled after a Spartan warrior, talking about sports cars. "Really, Eddie, you and your…machines."

A fist came down on the table with enough force to upend a glass of water and get the attention of every yuppie in the restaurant, including Side Part. "It's Edward," his companion said. "And machines are the only interesting thing that's happened in the last two hundred years!"

Their waitress did her best to become invisible as she cleaned up the spill and started to refill the glass. Salvion stopped her. "Too lazy to bring another?"

"But," she said, "it was only tipped on its side."

"Oh then we don't need plates either. The table is clean. We'll just eat off that."

"No, no. Sorry. I'll get another glass."

"Mmm-hmmm. Good idea."

Edward watched her go. "She'll probably spit in it now."

Speaking of spit, Side Part had launched into an animated

conversation with the woman. Well, more like he gave a speech with his hands, and she nodded her way through it. She wore an engagement ring, but the way she crossed her legs away from him and held her arms in her lap except to spear a bite of salad or tip her wine glass said he was not the unlucky son of a bitch who would be waiting for her at the altar.

He touched his cufflinks once or twice every minute and continued to talk, a forced smile stuck to his teeth where the spinach had been.

"I'll bet he's selling something."

"Who?"

Salvion pointed. "Whatever it is, she's not buying."

"Hmmm." Edward did not glance their direction. "All the advancements they've made creating their incredible machines. They remade the world while we slept."

"Yeah, got it. Machines are awesome."

"Yet for all the progress, the snake oil salesmen are still the same old snake oil salesmen."

"He knows he's lost her. He's fidgeting." Salvion touched his own cufflinks as if to demonstrate.

"The oldest profession hasn't changed at all."

"Isn't whoring the oldest profession?"

"It is."

Salvion chuckled. "You cryptic fuck."

Edward didn't crack a smile. "It's time, Salli."

"What do you think I'm doing?"

"What you always do. You fixate, you rush, and then you waste." He passed his hand idly over the votive candle burning between them. The flame rushed up to meet him.

"I wouldn't know. I don't exactly get the same benefits from it as you, do I?"

"Slowly this time. That's all I'm saying."

Another laugh. "That's rich coming from Mr. Zero to Sixty in Three Seconds."

Edward pulled his hand away. The flame blazed like a miniature campfire in its glass dish. He lifted his spoon, turning it into the light until he just could make out a tarnished reflection. "Any one of them would trade places with you."

The waitress brought a new glass of water, but Side Part finished his sales pitch just then, so Salvion excused himself before he could bully her about the delay. He also let Edward's comment slide, which was probably for the best.

He followed Side Part to an office building, one of those high rises with silvered glass for bricks, marble floors polished to a high gloss, and long rows of elevators with mirrored doors. Salvion wouldn't step one foot in the place, so he waited. They didn't leave until the sun set, and Side Part drove, which was stupid. No one had to drive these days, except those who got paid to do it. Salvion hailed a cab and told the driver to follow.

"You in town for business?"

He pressed a twenty-dollar bill up to the glass. "Tip meter starts now. I take a buck off for every word."

Side Part lived in a three-story brownstone in the nice part of town. *He must be good at selling something to someone.* Salvion slipped inside the house behind him as he checked his mail, postmarked to George Roberts. Side Part had a name.

He dumped his mail in the foyer along with car keys and a TAG Heuer wristwatch, poured himself a glass of wine and opened his laptop. Salvion waited. When George headed upstairs to shower, Salvion started digging. Filed away in an untitled folder nestled between 'Vacation' and 'Taxes', he found pictures of George and a mousy woman in front of a waterfall, smiling on a beach, ice skating. All were dated a year ago and earlier, nothing but photos of skyscrapers since. And bird's-eye views of the ground below.

The brownstone was all bachelor, no Better Homes and Gardens. Stainless steel everything, high ceilings and a wall-sized TV facing a quartet of leather cinema chairs, each with its own armrest and cup holder. Salvion opened the fridge and swiped a beer, noting that's about all the man kept in it.

He returned to the computer to continue digging. George had his bank accounts and credit cards programmed into his bookmarks menu. His savings account was flush with cash, and all his credit cards had zero balances.

Digging a little deeper, Salvion saw George had them paid down just a few months ago. About the same time he became obsessed with skyscrapers.

Next, he examined the documents folder. Aside from a will leaving all his assets to his little brother, this proved to be a treasure trove of love letters. *Jeanie, please come back. Jeanie, he'll never love you like I do. Jeanie, we were so good together. Jeanie, you are my soul. Jeanie, I live for you. Jeanie, I can't live without you.* And then the one Salvion had been looking for. *Jeanie, I can't bear to be alone one more night. I have decided to end it. I want you to know that—*

Salvion couldn't guess what George wanted Jeanie to know, because the letter stopped there and had been left hanging like that for months. Apparently George lost his nerve.

Upstairs, Salvion found him standing in front of the bathroom mirror, naked, flexing his pecs. Then he picked up the damned toothbrush. Salvion punched a hole in the bedroom closet.

George rushed towards the noise to investigate…and stepped into thin air. Below him, concrete ropes of freeway stretched out into a thick fog that pooled around the tops of buildings and swallowed cars the size of gnats. He leapt back, tried to push himself up against the side of the building that appeared behind him, and fell right through it.

He landed in the bathroom again, breathing so hard Salvion wondered if he might pass out. Slow down, he told himself, remembering Edward's warning.

George said, "Fuck, I'm pouring that wine down the drain. Gotta get my blood pressure checked. Man…"

Salvion waited until George stood in the middle of the bedroom before reaching out again. He took the floor first; it dissolved into checker-sided skyscrapers floating in a lake of pavement. George hit his knees, pressing his hands into a floor he couldn't see. "Not real!" He squeezed his eyes shut, but this wasn't the kind of vision you see with your eyes. "Man,

I didn't do this!"

Salvion lowered his voice for effect. "Didn't you?"

George scrambled away from the sound, and Salvion dropped the illusion again.

Back in his bedroom, George's laptop sat open on the bed, opened to a particular word file. The light from the screen, vivid white, glowed bright against the darkness. George edged toward it, his face contorting. "No, no, I never finished this."

But someone had.

Jeanie,

I can't bear to be alone one more night. I have decided to end it. I want you to know my last thought will be of you. Only one way I will ever fall as hard again as I fell for you.

George.

"No, that's not the way it happened."

Salvion turned it on again, and this time George wasn't walking on air, he plummeted through it. He flattened himself on a floor he couldn't see, covered his head with his hands and squeezed his eyes shut. He cried "No, no, no," until the final moment before impact when Salvion punched the closet again. Boom!

The world stopped moving. Alone on an empty blacktop, George got to his feet. A single traffic light blinked red, then black, then red again. High-rises surrounded him, curving and crowding over him as if he were looking at them through a fish-eye lens. At his feet lay a broken body, still dressed in the suit and TAG Heuer wristwatch he'd worn to the office that day.

Salvion could almost hear his psyche snap.

"I didn't mean to do it. I wasn't really going to do it. I just...I just wanted her to hurt like I hurt." He tried to touch the body, as if he might put it together again, but his hand passed right through it. "I'm sorry. Oh Jeanie, I'm so sorry."

A light of unimaginable brightness cut through the space between buildings, spread to blot them out entirely.

"I don't want to go. I don't...surely I didn't."

Another reverberating boom and the light started to flash.

"This must be a dream."

Boom.

"It can't..."

Boom, and the light started to recede.

He chased it. "Don't leave me. I'm sorry, I'm coming!"

Up in the air now, it flashed again.

"Please, what do I do?"

Boom.

He jumped, a daring leap to catch the light, crashed through the banister of his third-floor staircase, and started to fall in earnest this time.

Salvion wore George's brother's face when the paramedics arrived. He made George see blue-winged angels pushing the gurney, or demons alternately. As George sobbed his apologies to Jeanie, Salvion signed papers committing him for attempted suicide. He'd have to be admitted anyway for the broken hip and arm of course, but yes, it was a miracle he survived at all. It was hard to believe he meant to take his own life, but the letter to Jeanie proved it. Poor guy was not in his right mind. His repeated appeals for the light to come back for him and for the demons to spare him were proof enough of that.

Salvion kept the illusion up until the EMTs loaded George into the ambulance, then planted the idea in his mind that he'd ended up in Purgatory for missing the light, and no matter how real it seemed, Purgatory only looked like life. They hooked him up on enough IV diazepam that Salvion figured the hallucinations would continue unaided for some time.

Edward showed up not long after the ambulance left. He whistled through his teeth. "Very good, Salli."

"Thanks. Guy's got some cash tucked away, so we're set for a while."

"What did you do to him, anyway? It's still coming." Edward had the flushed look of a guy who had just gotten laid. That's what feeding did to him. If Salvion was bitter about being his supplier, he held it in check.

One reminder was enough.

"You did say to take it slow, make it last, something like that."

"I did. So..." He smiled. "What kind of car does he drive?"

No matter how much I rubbed my wrists, I still felt the pressure of Desollador's thumbs. I curled my knees against my chest and squeezed my legs together, trying to forget the feel of him between them. Not my body, I reminded myself. But it had been, for those critical moments.

I ran the shower as hot as I could stand it and knelt under the spray, head down so the water ran off my nose. I didn't feel like such a wimp crying when the spray washed my tears away as quickly as they fell. I stayed in until my skin turned pink and wrinkly.

As soon as I stepped out, I saw the writing on the mirror, shrouded in steam.

Couldn't wait to see you again. —Desollador

Swiping my robe off its hook and wrapping it around me, I locked the bathroom door and put my back against it. *Too soon.* I was still reeling from Trina's death and the struggle to extract my memories of being torn apart from the reality of unbroken flesh. I wasn't ready to fight again, but I was prepared. I dropped a pair of syringes from the medicine cabinet into the pocket of my robe and grabbed the cut-down, twelve-gauge duct taped under my sink. With it leading my steps, I slipped into the hallway and started clearing rooms.

I found him on the balcony, his back to me. I started to squeeze the trigger, but before I felt it break, he turned to me and shook his head. Just that subtle command defeated me. I relaxed my hands, relinquished my grip on the weapon, as the vampire clucked his disapproval. "You would shoot me in the back?"

"If it would kill you."

"No opportunity to defend myself?"

"Did I miss something? You came to kill me, right?"

"I told you what I plan to do to you. Killing is a long way off."

He took a step toward me; I took two away. This dance of advance and retreat continued until I backed myself into a corner between the dresser and the bed. I drew a syringe from my pocket. This time I felt no gentle swoon to win my resolve. A spasm racked my spine and I depressed the plunger, forcing the barrel's contents into empty air.

Desollador plucked it out of my hand. "Are you beginning to understand how fucked you are, Pet?"

"What do you want?" I asked, poking at the answer like a bruise.

"Stop asking stupid questions." Desollador wrapped his fingers in my hair, wrenched my head back until I could only see the ceiling, bent his lips to that smooth crevice between my clavicles, and breathed. Heat filled the hollow, spilled down my breasts, slid across my abdomen and along the ridge of bone at the root of my thighs.

I gasped, remembering the inch-wide path of flesh from throat to feet that my robe exposed. I fumbled with the belt.

Desollador released my hair, shoved my hands away. "Leave it open."

"No," I told him, but I couldn't make good on it, because Desollador still held my will with his eyes. I could no more move my arms again than move a mountain.

"No? Then I'll have to relieve you of temptation." He slipped the offending garment off my shoulders where it fell unhindered to the floor, leaving me clad in nothing but my amethyst choker. To his credit, he maintained eye contact for at least three seconds.

"So now that you are back in your own body, do you care what I do with it?"

"Get the hell out of my apartment."

"Because I am going to break it. Absolutely desecrate it." Now his gaze roamed lower.

The temperature, I would swear, dropped ten degrees in that very second. The vampire's lips widened, flashing the tips of his canines in an obscene leer. "I have a sneaking suspicion that you might want a breaking."

"Fuck you."

"OK," he said and shoved me on the bed. "This would be a good time to tell me how you like it." He climbed on top of me, tearing the choker from my neck, scattering beads across the covers like flower petals.

"Get off of me," I growled.

Holding my wrists over my head with one hand, he unbuckled his belt with the other. "I told you how a blood toy gets used, didn't I?"

"You're nothing but a rapist with fangs."

He backhanded me so fast I never saw him move. "Think carefully before you insult me again, Pet."

It took a couple of seconds for the bloom of pain to catch up to his warning. Along with it, I could still feel the echoes of Trina's wounds, the thrust of his member inside her. *Too soon.* With that defeat fresh in my mind, I knew things were going to go from bad to awful if I didn't figure out a different strategy.

"I'm sorry," I whispered.

"So you don't think I'm a just rapist with fangs?"

"I'm sorry for killing Harlin."

"I was coming for you long before you got to Harlin. You've worked awfully hard in the last few years to get my attention. Well, now you have it."

"I give."

"You what?"

"I learned my lesson. You said it doesn't have to hurt. Right?" I forced by body to relax under him.

He caressed my face. "Your eyes are the prettiest blue when you cry."

I felt him shift above me. Not much, but enough. When the pressure on my hips relented, I shimmied out from under him, slammed my foot blindly into his nose, and rolled onto the floor. I opened my eyes in time to see him crack bones back into place. His expression read: *We'll do it the hard way.*

One moment he knelt on the bed; the next he stood behind me. I felt his hand on my waist, another on the back of my neck, shoving me on the bed again. He pinned one wrist, then another, against my back. When he kicked my legs apart, I started to beg. I'd do anything to make him stop, really this time. Then he shoved my face into a pillow, his palm on the back of my head so I couldn't talk, couldn't beg, could barely breathe.

Stop. Wait. Don't. Please. No!

Desollador's voice threaded in between my pleas. *Why?*

I can't think.

For this, you don't have to think. You only have to lie there, though it's more fun if you squirm. Maybe I'll let you.

Fuck.

Getting to it, Pet.

I cried "No" when I heard his zipper. *This can't be happening. Not like this.*

He took his hand off my head. His belt buckle jangled, scraped against my thighs.

"Don't do this."

"*This* is what I came here to do." He pushed my head back into the pillow.

"I'm a virgin!" I screamed into it.

He let go of my head. "What was that?"

"You heard me."

"Say it again."

Son of a bitch. "Fuck you."

He wound his hand up in my hair and bent over my back. "How hard?"

I struggled under him with all my might, but he allowed me no leverage. "OK,OK,OK. But don't make me eat a pillow while you do this. Please?"

He let go of my wrists. I held my breath. "On your back," he said.

It was in the moment of resignation that I remembered I had a chance. My .410 Judge—loaded with rock salt and amethyst—was under my pillow. I rolled onto my back. For that moment, he left me open.

He got as far as "Don't you dare—" before my fingers closed on the ribbed grips. I drew my elbow into my side, the business end of the revolver level with Desollador's torso.

He charged. I fired. Once, twice, three times before the vampire disarmed me and brought the side of the gun down against my temple.

Blood seeped through his shirt in a basketball-sized smattering of holes. I loaded every one of those rounds myself. Rock salt, amethyst, shot, powder. They should have been lethal. Any minute, he should start to die. Only he didn't.

He set his nose again and wiped the blood against my quilt in a bright red smear. Picked me up by my throat and heaved me across the room.

I hit the ground limping, unaware now of my nakedness. I made it a few feet when he lunged for me. I managed to drag him outside to the balcony, ignoring the pain as I scraped my bare belly across the concrete. My hands were strong and sure when I retrieved my shotgun, rolled over and buried the muzzle of it in Desollador's groin.

With my finger on the trigger and pulling, he seized my will and hissed, "I warned you," as he drove a fist at my abdomen.

I clutched my stomach, releasing the gun again, which he launched into my bedroom wall hard enough to crack the sheetrock. He drew back his fist again, this time over my head, and I covered my face. Through my elbows I watched his methodical assault on my balcony floor. He punched the concrete in a horseshoe shape around my head, chips of it pelting me with every blow. I squeezed my eyes shut and waited for one to land on me.

"You're asking for it, Pet, but I'm not going to break you just yet." He forced my cheek against my shoulder and pressed his lips hard against my throat. I felt a brief stab of panic, then the tips of his fangs. How often had I feared and wondered about this moment. *Will it hurt? Will I survive it? Will it change me? Will it feel different when it's my blood, my body?*

"I'll show you," he whispered.

Nonono!

I think I screamed when his fangs broke skin, a burning pressure radiating from the twin punctures like molten lava squeezed through veins too narrow to channel it. It spread down my arms, my spine, my legs and, for a brief moment, my body felt like it would separate from my head, and I was sure I would never recover.

Then he began to suck. The burning at once mellowed into a comfortable flush. The pressure, an intensity that had forced me to the brink of unconsciousness, lifted so much I felt weightless in comparison and seized Desollador's shoulders to keep from falling.

When his fingers threaded through mine and pressed my wrists back into the concrete, I remembered we were already on the ground. My hands convulsed in his. His dead heart started beating in tandem with mine. I felt no distinction between the place I stopped and he began.

A wall inside me broke, and emotions I knew no words for yet—Intimacy! Connection!—flooded me. Tears squeezed between my eyelids as I sighed, "Oh."

I believe you are enjoying this, Pet.

I didn't know.

When I began to lose consciousness, the vampire released me. The world swirled into focus, his head foremost in it. "I'll be damned. You liked it."

I shook my head, but couldn't say the words to deny it. "I hate you."

"Maybe, but that does not change the fact that you didn't want me to stop."

"Why aren't you dead?" I loaded those bullets myself, and I knew I hadn't missed. His shirt hadn't fared as well as the fully healed six-pack that it revealed.

"I wanted to keep going too, but somebody hasn't been drinking her orange juice."

"I shot you three times. You should be dead."

"If you don't start taking care of yourself, you're not going to survive me long."

"What are you?"

Desollador held my face in his hands and kissed me. I tasted my blood on his tongue. "I am your Master." He kissed my throat where he bit me. "Have you been listening to me? I'm going to be back soon." Another kiss. "I'm going to keep coming back over and over. You need to prepare yourself."

"I would rather die."

The vampire stiffened. "And eventually you will."

I hugged my knees. "Go away."

I intended to go to sleep very soon on the concrete. Instead, the vampire carried me to my bed. I didn't even pull away when he caressed my thigh. If he decided to take me now, I could almost pretend it was just a dream.

"I can wait," he said.

I shrugged and rolled away from him. "Your loss."

I felt his weight settle on the bed behind me. "Is it true you are untried or was that a lie too?"

I didn't answer, just willed him to leave it alone.

"There is an easy way to find out." He spread his palm over my belly.

When it slid down past my navel, I covered it with my own. "I wasn't lying."

"How? You're, what, twenty-one?"

"I don't get close to people." My hand still resting on his, I felt a strong urge to slide my fingers between his knuckles. *Christ, what I am I doing?* I shook my wrist like it burned and clutched a pillow to avoid further temptation.

"You know I am going to take your virtue."

I drew a breath to deny it, but his hand moved again, and only managed a strangled gasp.

"It doesn't have to hurt." He stood, and I let out a breath I didn't know I was holding. "But it will."

I cried myself to sleep on a bed stained with his blood.

Edward wished George owned an exotic, but the Saab 9-3 Turbo impressed him anyway. It hugged the switchbacks at highway speeds without barking a tire and hit triple digits on the straightaways with a sexy MagnaFlow growl. Damn fine machine.

The speedo read ninety when it hit him, like lightning drilled straight into his marrow. Or, if you're human, adrenaline into his heart with instantaneous effect.

He could make out minute details of the road, even ripples in the asphalt, as far as the horizon. Calculate the trajectory of every vehicle in his path. He accelerated to a buck twenty while the world around him slowed to a jog.

It lasted for miles, minutes. Even after the initial rush wore off, Edward felt as sated as the day he took his first soul, the day the bitch created him. There were only three possibilities. Not likely to be Salvion, given how recently he'd rolled George. Kayin was, well, Kayin. So that left Desollador.

The vampire picked up on the third ring. "Christopher," he said. "Tell me you didn't kill her."

"Depends. Which one?"

"The one that wasn't easy."

"Then no, I didn't kill her."

Edward didn't know what elation felt like, but felt pretty sure it was appropriate for the occasion. "Do *not* kill her."

A pause on the other end of the line. "That's an unusual request."

"It's not a request. I will sever our bond if she dies."

"Do not threaten me, old man. You need me more than I need you."

The conversation made the drive far less pleasant. He sought a change of tactic. "Why didn't you kill her tonight?"

"She's interesting."

"I'll bet she is. I felt something...different, incredible...when you fed tonight, Christopher. Do you think you might enjoy feeding from her again?"

"I want to break her."

Edward wrinkled his nose at the longing in Desollador's tone. "How long will that take?"

"Cut to the chase, old man. How long do you need it to take?"

Until he figured out how to harness—and sustain—her power, but to be on the safe side, he answered, "Forever."

"Yeah, I can make that happen."

"Oh, and Christopher, feed as often as she can survive it."

"I am so far ahead of you."

Edward hung up without filling Desollador in on the rest of his plan. The vampire wouldn't like to know he wouldn't be the only one playing with his new toy.

"What do you mean Desollador sired every vampire I've killed in the last three years?"

I dug through a pile of clothes stuffed in the laundry basket, peeled a dryer sheet off a slim-waisted white oxford and gave it a sharp snap. "Maybe that's a little fact worth mentioning at some point. 'By the way, Diane, better watch your back because the vamp that made all these others you've been hunting, he's probably going to take notice sooner or later and decide to make you his personal chew toy. Oh, and did I mention he's a shape-shifter?'"

No one replied. The object of my aggravation only talked to me when she felt like it, and ever since the dream that landed me in the body of a dead girl, she hadn't. "Speaking of dead girls, I'd really like to know just how in the hell I switched bodies last night."

I pulled on a pair of dark denim bootleg jeans, wincing as I buttoned them over the bruises on my abdomen. "What about this? 'Salt in his veins to kill, amethyst to bind.' Remember that little jewel of wisdom? Well, that vampire took a gut full of both last night, and it didn't even slow him down. I could really use some advice right now."

I braided my hair and dabbed some concealer on my black eye. "But your way is much better. I'll just wait here until he murders another girl or comes for me again. Then I'll figure something out. Or I'll die. Sounds like a plan."

"You know what, I have a better plan. How about I'm not here when he comes looking?"

I called my landlord, Barry, told him my abusive ex-boyfriend had trashed my place and I no longer felt safe here. I offered to pay to have the apartment cleaned and the wall and balcony repaired if he could put me in one of his other properties that day, within the hour if possible.

"What about your belongings?"

Except for weapons, they could fit into a backpack. "Packed."

"Well, I don't have another apartment available until the end of the month, but if you could swing the higher rent—"

"I need to leave here now. I will make it work."

I met him at a two-story craftsman-style bungalow with copper rain chains hanging from a low-pitched gabled roof. The interior displayed an impressive collection of handcrafted woodwork and stone. Not so impressive were the eighteen windows and two exterior doors at ground level and half that many on the second story, making it the least defensible lodging imaginable. I'd do better in a tent. At least it wouldn't be as conspicuous.

"I can't stay here."

"Why not?" He fixed kind, green eyes on me. "It's a gorgeous property, and I am giving it to you at a bargain."

"Look, Mr. Krise, I really appreciate your help, I mean, moving me on such short notice. But this place is too open. I couldn't sleep here with all those windows. I would just feel too exposed. Is there anywhere else?"

"You might be better off in a hotel for a few days."

Stuck in a twenty-by-twenty box, forced through a funnel of death every time I came or left. "I don't want to live like that. Please."

Barry studied my face, no doubt looking at the shiner Desollador had given me. "Alright, alright. I can show you one more place. Just promise me you'll get a restraining order against that man of yours."

I nodded. "I promise."

I followed him to a white stucco building with narrow, high windows and stained-glass accents that reminded me of a Spanish church. The floors creaked where I walked, and every door groaned upon opening. "It's a restoration," Barry said. "But you've got to admit it has charm."

The interior walls were as white as his hair and made of sheetrock. It wouldn't take much to get through them in a pinch. "I'll take it."

"Do you need any help moving your furniture? I bet most of it would fit into my pickup." Humans have such capacity for kindness. I regretted that I never had the opportunity to spend more time with them.

"No, it's all secondhand anyway, and I really don't want the reminder. Keep it, will you? You can sell it, donate it." The less traffic between my old apartment and my new place, the less likely Desollador would find me again.

"How about I leave it where it is until I find another renter, then we'll see how you feel?"

That'd be nice. If Desollador didn't kill me before then, I might like to have my stuff back. I nodded.

"What about tonight? You don't even have a bed."

I glanced down at my watch, remembered why I seldom spent much time with humans. Relationships were time consuming. "I've got a friend bringing a mattress," I lied.

"Well alright then. You got family in the area that can come check in on you?"

"Yeah, I'll be fine."

He looked skeptical. Neither of the emergency contacts on my rental application—my aunt and a childhood friend I'd last seen three years before—were local. "You'll let me know if you need anything."

"Thanks Barry. You're one hell of a landlord."

"I've got a daughter your age," he explained. "I'd want someone looking out after her if she got into trouble."

I felt my breath catch in my throat. Now I needed him to leave. "I'm gonna unpack. Thanks again." *Take the hint, take the hint, take the hint.*

After he left, I set my reloading equipment up on the butcher block in the kitchen and spent the rest of the dwindling day making bullets. The next time I shot him, there would be no doubt my loads were vampire killers. I emptied every syringe in my arsenal and refilled it with fresh saltwater, about three times as strong as I usually used. Since I had never killed a vampire as old as Desollador, I figured he may just have a stronger constitution. I *had* to believe that.

I didn't sleep that night. I put my back in a corner and hunkered down with twelve gauge in hand waiting for the shadows to move wrong.

When morning came, I went into town to rent a new sofa and a bed.

The sales agent introduced himself as Tom, though his nametag said Thomas. He insisted I would get a better deal renting the living room group instead of the sofa by itself. I agreed just to speed things up, then tried to pick out a mattress and boxspring and ended up with a whole bedroom set. We drew up the paperwork before he could sell me anything else, even as he told me about a flat-screen TV that could be bundled for another five dollars a week. For personal references, I used Barry and Roger. I tried not to dwell on the sad fact that they were the only locals I knew besides Frank.

The rental center delivered my new furniture just before dinner, which I skipped in favor of sleep. As much as I feared leaving myself open to threat, I needed to talk to the prophet...on my terms.

In preparation, I duct-taped closed my windows and doors, both interior and exterior. In the laundry room, I found a broom and propped it up against my bedroom door so it would fall with a clatter if the door opened. Handfuls of screws in the window frames would prevent them from being opened more than a hand's width. A dog would have been a good idea, but the idea of committing to the safekeeping of another life made me feel like vomiting, so that wasn't going to happen.

I dozed off with my twelve gauge under my pillow.

CHAPTER 3

Edward followed Highway One up the Pacific Coast from California to Washington, mile after mile of green fields on one side, sheer rock cliffs dropping into ocean on the other. The route twisted so tight on itself he felt like it might launch him right off the edge of the earth at times. He made it through the Canada border without having to kill anyone and hired a private pilot to fly him into the Alaskan wildness.

Looking down on the snow-striated mountains from that bird's-eye view, he decided on the spot he'd learn to pilot a plane when this was all done.

"How much does one of these cost?" he called up to the pilot whose name he hadn't bothered to remember.

"This is a G-21 Super Goose. She'll take off in weeds and land in three feet of water as easy as pavement. Three million all day long."

Money didn't go as far as it used to. After his learning was sufficient, he would just kill his instructor and take his plane. Maybe this one.

"Do you own it?"

The pilot shook his head. "Not yet. About twenty thousand more jobs like this, and she's mine."

So, not this one.

Edward settled back in his seat and sipped on a single malt scotch the pilot promised was the "good stuff".

Snow ate up more and more of the landscape beneath them until he couldn't distinguish mountains from lakes of low-lying clouds. Trees looked like sticks from this height, barren. Kayin favored dead places.

They landed on the water in the middle of nowhere, not even a lean-to in sight.

"I gotta tell you," the pilot said. "I don't feel right about just taking you out here and leaving you. This is grizzly country."

"You will be back tomorrow."

"Right. I'm a good man, Mr. Lines. Lord willing, I will be back tomorrow, same time, same place. Mind your watch. Time gets away from you with so much daylight, near twenty hours of it you know."

Edward was busy pulling on gloves and buttoning up his wool duster, which the pilot insisted was not 'practical' for the bush. "Tomorrow then."

"Are you sure I can't talk you into hiring a guide?" He parked the plane close against a dock that was more rot than wood.

"I told you. I am meeting my guide here."

With multiple assurances that he would survive to meet the man the next day, Edward was alone. The air was cold, but clear, the snow packed hard beneath his feet. The pilot was right. Edward would freeze to death by this time tomorrow if he was susceptible to such a thing. And the duster *was* impractical. He was in shirtsleeves rolled to his elbows by the time he found Kayin, who was reclining on a man-sized rock overlooking the lake.

Kayin's red hair was rimmed with frost, his beard grown so long it touched his collar bones. He wore a thick green scarf tied like a turban on his head and nothing else. Kayin's form made clothing an inconvenience, one with which he seldom bothered.

"Why are you here?" Kayin asked.

"Desollador found something."

"My brother doesn't care for things. Do you mean some*one*?"

"I believe she is key to getting my power back."

"She has the Athame?"

"No, but I believe if I can take her soul, I won't need it anymore."

Edward stepped back as Kayin stood, giving him a wide berth and room to stretch his wings. "You have not said why you are here."

"I need your help to get it."

"The Athame."

"Her soul."

Kayin leapt from the rock, hooves landing with a heavy crunch. "And if I die before I wake, I pray the Lord my soul to take."

Edward waited.

"I cannot remember if I prayed. I don't think I did." He squinted at the sky and then at Edward. "Would that you and I could have made each other whole. Wouldn't that have been something?"

Still, Edward waited.

"I forget. Why are you here?"

"Desollador found someone. I need your help to take her soul so I can be whole."

"You were never whole."

Edward fished from under his shirt a juju box suspended on a leather thong, opened it up to reveal a piece of bone. "But you were."

Kayin raised his hand to touch one spiral horn missing an inch of its tip. "Was I? That's right. I was whole, and then I was dust. But *you* were flesh. I could have been content with your flesh."

His eyes showed such longing that Edward itched to take another step back, but it would be a danger to show such weakness when Kayin was in one of his moods. He had been in these woods too long; it would take time for him to come back when he was so far deep in his head. "You got a lot more than flesh in our bargain."

The wind rattled snow from the branches of faraway trees and funneled it past them in a silvery gale. "It is a strange element to wield. Now, if you could have given me earth…"

"I did."

"That's right. I don't deserve that gift. I think I never did."

Edward tamped down the aggravation. One gift wasted, the other bartered. He'd had to sacrifice two elements—half of Edward's birthright—and steal that little extra insurance he kept tucked away in the juju box to convince Kayin to give up this idea of completing each other the first time around.

"Will you help me?"

"I can't go anywhere like this," Kayin said, sweeping his hand down the length of one snuff-colored wing.

"I can have a body for you tomorrow. The pilot who brought me here—"

"No. I will choose."

Edward spread his arms wide. "Where? You have sequestered yourself in no man's land."

"We are not so far from the bay. The walrus are migrating."

"You want me to secure you a walrus's body?"

"No," said Kayin, hopping back on his rock again. "A poacher's."

What a strange sight they must have made as they headed out later to where the walrus were mating, Edward with his shirtsleeves rolled and his fine wool duster folded over his arm like a waiter's napkin, and Kayin looking like a demon from the worst parts of the New Testament. The headless bodies scattered on the ice pack were not an easy sight, even for Edward. Not that he felt pity for the creatures slaughtered for ivory. It was just so much ugliness. People should clean up after themselves. Not only were there five dead walrus, but at least five more injured by the poacher's bullets.

They found the hunter sawing through the spinal cord of his last kill, using the tusk for leverage, covered to his elbows in blood and dirty ice. When he saw them, he dropped the nearly decapitated head and thrust his blade out in front of him. Backing away, he tripped over the carcass and landed in a dark red smear.

With the hand not holding the knife, he crossed himself. "Saint Michael, defend us. Be our protection against the wickedness and snares of the devil. Cast him to hell, Satan and all the evil spirits."

"If you choose to beseech the Archangel, it is imperative to get the words right," Kayin said. "May Adonai rebuke him, we humbly pray; and do Thou, O Prince of the Heavenly Host, by the Divine Power of Adonai, cast into hell—"

"Have mercy. Please have mercy."

Edward stepped over the narrow sinew connecting the walrus's head to its body like it was a dirty towel. Passing his coat to Kayin, he asked, "Are you sure this is the one you want?"

"Do it."

The man screamed when Edward wrenched the knife away, but when he dragged the blade across the thick meat of his shoulder, the man cried in great hiccups.

Something peeked out of the cut, something ephemeral and shadowy. Edward plucked at it with the knife tip and pulled it out, like plucking a lobster from its shell. The hunter's cries became a shrill howl as his soul came free of its flesh.

In that moment, Kayin's body disintegrated, into so much dust, scattered by the wind to every corner of the earth, and his ghost climbed through the cut to occupy the hunter's flesh.

The disembodied spirit twisted on the end of the blade. "Since I can't consume you, and we have taken your body, we should give you another." Edward slammed the blade into the dead sow's carcass, and the human soul — with no place else to go — bled right into it.

"He will return to the Source," Kayin said in the hunter's voice.

Edward smiled and made a gesture with his hand like asking a chorus to rise. The waters obeyed, the weight of a shallow wave rolling over the body, lapping away at its blood. "But maybe the sharks will get here before the Light."

I stood in the elevator again in Harlin's office building. Cindy smiled at me, though she was heads taller than I remembered. "Are those Louboutins?"

I looked down at my feet, which were stuffed into black galoshes decorated with blue and purple flowers. I was eight years old the last time those boots fit me. I looked back up at Cindy. "What are Louboutins?"

"I've always wanted a pair," she said.

I crossed one foot over the other and rocked forward on my heels. "Well these are mine."

"They're very pretty. Anyway, what are you supposed to be?"

Along with my galoshes, I wore a toy gun and sword on opposite hips and a glittery staff strapped across my back with one of Dad's belts. Dad had taken me shopping for Halloween, I remembered, since Mom had to stay with Grandma after she got sick.

I wanted to be a princess, but the store sold out of all the best costumes by the time we got there, leaving only a few tubes of grease makeup that matched my boots and the bottom half of a pirate girl costume—purple pantaloons with a jagged hem that tickled my calves. I wanted a scepter and crown, but we only found a cap gun, a foam pirate sword, and a wizard's staff. Mom could have pulled together a princess costume with little more than a nightgown, some satin ribbon and the glitter staff, but not Dad.

"I'm a warrior princess," I answered. I wore my bathing suit under the pantaloons because it sparkled like the staff.

"Well, you are very pretty," Cindy said.

"Can I have some candy?" I held out my pumpkin bucket.

"What do you say?"

"Trick or treat."

She smiled and fished around in her purse for a treat, finally pulling out an orange. I almost pouted, but remembered my manners. I hated it when grown-ups gave out fruit instead of candy. But I took it anyway and tried to sound sincere when I thanked her. The elevator doors opened, and she got off. I started to put the orange in my bucket and noticed something special about it. It wasn't a real orange at all, but plastic, green-capped and filled with flavored sugar.

I squealed. My favorite.

Through the open door, I saw another orange resting on the low-pile green carpet, like fruit dropped from a tree into the grass. I darted from the elevator and snatched it up to stuff in my bucket. Noticed another and gathered it too. I followed a trail of plastic oranges so far I lost sight of the elevator. When the path ended, I found myself in the park in front of Frank's food truck.

A nonspecific collection of light and shadows surrounded the vehicle. Frank appeared to be the only solid image in the whole landscape. His hair looked sketched in light charcoal strokes, his beard a dark smudge. Though I knew it contained an intricate map of lines, only the ones essential to his character showed. When he smiled at me, two lines formed deep fishhooks on either side of his mouth.

He pushed through the tiny window a wand of cotton candy as big as his head and a syringe not one bit smaller. "You have to pick one."

I peered into my bucket at the mound of plastic oranges while I considered my choices. I stuck my bottom lip out, stomped my galoshes. I wouldn't make it. I wouldn't choose. Instead, I turned and fled up the hill.

Roger waited for me at the top.

"You never told me you were a warrior princess. You lied to me." His mouth made a hard line.

I ran a finger over the hilt of my sword. "I wanted you to like me."

"I did like you," he said. "Only you were never real."

"But…this is just a costume."

"What if this is real and the rest is the costume?"

I shook my head and started running again before he could ask any more questions, before the truth came out and I lost him. I ran up to the top of a mountain I hadn't seen in three years, up to the steps of a house that had stood there for more than two hundred.

Another eight-year-old girl waited for me on the steps, a furry tail pinned to her leggings and a headband with pointy pink ears peeking out from her pixie cut. I crushed her in a tight hug. "Renn, I missed you so much!"

"Where have you been?" she asked.

"Trick or treating," I told her.

"Why didn't you come get me? I would have gone with you."

I shook my head.

"Why not?"

"Because they're not just make believe anymore, Renn," I whispered.

"So?" She pointed at my costume. "Is that make believe?"

I rubbed my palms down the front of my swimsuit. "I'm supposed to be a warrior princess."

"And I'm supposed to be a kitty cat."

"But the bad guys," I said. "They have real fangs."

"I still would have gone with you." She grinned. "Did you get any candy?"

"A little. You know I would rather have stayed with you."

In a singsong voice, she said, "I know something you don't know." She pushed herself off the step and clutched my fingers in her palm. "Come on. I'll show you."

Then we were flying, out of the woods, above a road crowded with little plastic cars with rubber wheels and working doors, a toy town, abandoned now by some little girl who grew up and left all her playthings in a house she tried not to think about anymore. I felt sorry for her toys, the Barbie dolls reclining on their bandanna blankets and the teddies waiting for tea that would never come.

I clutched Renn's hand tighter. "What is it? What did you want to show me?"

She pointed to the road, to a tiny black Monte Carlo.

I let go of her hand. "I don't like it."

"But do you remember it?"

The question rippled up the toy town street, shattering paper houses, toppling the matchstick bridges, and melting Play-Doh men until the world was gone. Empty.

My pumpkin bucket started to fade, and I managed to grab a fistful of oranges before they were gone, too. Tears sprang to my eyes. Those little plastic memories, solid and whole in my fingers, proved I had been alive once, in a world without vampires and demons.

See! I am a real girl!

They felt like morning fog, bound to be burned off soon with the rising sun. I told myself not to let that happen. No matter what, hold on, hold on. Tight. Don't open a finger or they'll fall, and then they're gone forever. Memories like these were fleeting; little baubles get lost. But oh how I wanted to keep them...

"Diane!" Renn's voice sounded too sharp, and she was no longer a little girl, but seventeen years old, frozen in my last memory of her, wearing mauve-colored lipstick and a black dress of mourning that looked all wrong on her. "How could you forget? Just…how could you?"

"Forget what?"

She swiped up the Monte Carlo and pushed it in my hands.

"I don't understand," I said, and feared by the time I did, it would be too late.

She just shook her head and faded away like the rest of my childhood world.

I looked down at my hands, opened my fingers one by one, shook my head at the baubles. Just a dream. Rubber wheels and green plastic cap and my hands would be empty again when I woke. I cast off my warrior princess costume and resigned myself to my purpose. I had no business being a real girl anyway.

I flung my voice over the landscape of toys. *Who is Desollador?*

Her voice came from all around me. *He is the bait.*

Really, he's the bait? It feels like I'm the bait. Me!

Your calling is larger than you know, Diane.

Right now I don't give a damn about my calling. I want to know why you didn't warn me about Desollador.

There was no need to warn you. You were never in any danger of him.

Not in danger? I raged. *I apparently worked my ass off over the last three years to get his attention. Now that I have it, he plans to rape and torture me, and you think I am not in any danger?*

He wants you too much to kill you, so you are not in danger, especially if you bury him away again.

You'll understand if I think you're full of shit. But enlighten me, how do I do that?

There is a prison for him in Benevolence.

The word felt like a punch in the gut. *Benevolence? No. Why?*

Benevolence is where they were buried before and where they awoke. It's where you will bury them again.

Who? The vampire that killed my parents?

This is bigger than your parents, she said. *They are no longer important.*

They were my parents. They will always be important. I would spit my words in her eyes if she had any. *For three years I have done everything you told me to do, killed every vampire you told me to kill. In all that time, you have never showed your face to me. You've never even told me your name.*

It's Catherine. And it is difficult enough to make you hear me. You don't see me because you never cared to see me.

Bullshit! Show your face.

A wavering light appeared, reminding me of one of those crime drama TV shows, a dome lamp swinging over an empty interrogation room. Except the light came from candles, ugly coils of beeswax wrapped around thick white wicks. They cast long shadows over a circle of chalk on dirt floor. A woman knelt in the center of it, with dusky red hair braided to her knees, the barest slivers of silver at her temples, and a gown of fragile cheesecloth thin enough to reveal small breasts and narrow hips. Slender arms, the color of smooth bleached river stones, and bare feet were all of her the gown did not cover. Well, those and her face, round with wide green eyes and heart-shaped lips.

There. Now you know what I looked like, when I was alive. Are you finally ready to see how I died?

I wanted to tell her I didn't care, but it would have been a lie.

In the circle, Catherine started speaking in a cadence that reminded me of hipster poetry jams, though I couldn't understand a word of what she said. She cut her fingers with a dagger that I knew, in the way that dreamers do without being told, was called an Athame. She poured her blood onto the forehead of a man made of wax, a *life-sized* wax man, and it ran in intricate patterns down lines carved into his face, across his chest, down to his impressively sculpted male anatomy. When the blood reached his toes, Catherine lit the wick at the heart of the man and began to sing.

"I was trying to create for myself an Adam, someone to love, someone to love me. I was trying to create a life. A life! I breathed the four sacred elements and my very heart into it, but they were not enough."

As the wick burned, the offered blood dissolved into the man. "I created a life, but I could not create a soul for it. I was too young—though a spinster by anyone's standards — and so ignorant."

A darkness, like the opening of a mouth, fell around her. A moment later, the thing in the circle with her *moved.*

Born of fire, the creature called up a flame in its palm. His body looked like that of a man, though his head was bald and his eyes were a void that didn't even reflect the fire.

Catherine blinked, almost smiled, then noticed his eyes. "What have I done?" Hearing the prophet's voice come from her lips made me gasp, but neither of them heard me.

The thing shrugged. It must have known it was a mistake, but it was also a man, almost. "I am not complete. I am lacking."

"Lord, what have I done?" she repeated. The Athame flashed in her hands, bright as the decision in her eyes. She plunged the blade where his heart should have been. He frowned, looking down at it as she backed away. Then he plucked it from his own breast and, still frowning, sheathed it in hers. Catherine fell, one slender wrist obscuring the white chalk line, the circle broken. Her soul sputtered out of her flesh with her last breath.

"That is what I am lacking," the creature declared, pointing at her ghost. "Where may I find one of my own?"

"A soul? Oh Lord —"

"You repeat that strange word. Is that what I am? Lord?"

"No. He is the Creator."

"Then you are Lord?"

"No, I...I made a mistake. I sinned against Him. That is why you are incomplete, an abomination. Only the Lord creates. Only the Lord gives souls."

"I want to speak with this Lord. He must complete me. I should not suffer for your sin."

The ghost laughed. "That is the nature of His wrath."

"I think I do not like this Lord."

"You blaspheme, but you are right. You should not suffer. I must end you."

The creature regarded the ghost and shook his head. "I do not think so. I will just have to steal a soul if He will not give me one. I am hungry. I am empty."

"You cannot steal a soul."

The creature closed his eyes and curled his fingers, retreating into itself to take inventory of his power. He was a strong creation; Catherine had made him that much. He opened his eyes again and smiled at her. "Yes, I can."

A mistake, the fearful glance she cast at the closed door behind him. A small thing, but he saw it. The prophet feared for something in that room. Someone. A thing with a soul. She screamed with grief and terror as her creation opened the door. A girl child, not more than three, lay sleeping in a tiny, rope-bottomed crib on a thin down mattress with blue striped ticking. One perfect miniature foot peeked out beneath her quilt. The creature raised the dagger.

"No, please. She's innocent, just a child. Don't take her. You can have me. My soul, take it, take all of me. Just leave her, please."

The creature stopped to consider her offer. Then replied, "No. I believe taking your soul would destroy me. I will have the girl."

"She is my daughter. I beg you to leave her. She is the reason I made you. I just wanted someone to love her, someone who would not condemn her a bastard and me a whore for having her."

The thing laughed. "I don't have a soul. I cannot love. If you created me for her, then it is fitting she should be sacrificed. But if it is any consolation, I do not think you a whore. And she will be a bastard no more."

The Athame found flesh again. The child died in her sleep, her tiny confused spirit wandering up from the blood and blade toward a light too far away. The monster caught it in his hands as the valley between mountains catches fog. It writhed and rolled in his fingers, but could not escape.

Then he breathed her into him, and the light that shined for her faded into darkness. Catherine sobbed, but without the comfort of tears because ghosts have none.

The nightmare faded, and I sat cross-legged facing Catherine inside her white chalk circle. "My daughter sustained him for a long time, longer than any soul he took after, but eventually he craved another."

"Who is he? What is this?" I asked, gesturing to the circle, to her. "And what does he have to do with Desollador?"

"He calls himself Edward, and he is the reason Desollador is nearly immune to what kills other vampires."

"How is that possible?" I stood, throwing balled fists behind me in frustration. "Who are you?"

She didn't rise or even look concerned by my tantrum. "I told you, my name is Catherine. I am the witch that created the Soul Eater that calls himself Edward. And you are my weapon against him."

"Why does your Edward make Desollador invincible?"

"Desollador crossed paths with my Edward and tried to turn him."

"He's a vampire too?"

"No, Edward is what he is. He can never become anything else. But the exchange of blood forged a link between them."

"A link," I repeated, thinking. "You have been sending me after Desollador's line?"

She nodded.

"And only his line."

Another nod.

"Deliberately putting me in Desollador's crosshairs, ultimately to bait Edward."

Her hazel eyes met mine without a trace of emotion, not even shame. "You are my weapon against them."

"I am a girl, not a weapon."

"You are so much more than a girl, Diane. You are my Assassin, my warrior princess. And here, in the sleeping world, you are the Dreamer."

"Whatever that means."

"There are others," she said.

"Others what?"

"Linked to Edward."

"How many?" As if I needed more invincible vampires gunning

for me.

"Not vampires. Something else."

From the other side of the dream, where the waking world spun on toward midnight, I heard duct tape shredding. "How do I stop them?"

Catherine began to fade into blackness. Her voice swelled from the shadows. "Benevolence. In the house on the summit of the Serpent, you will find—" I felt, but could not see, her push something into my hands as the broomstick fell and I awoke.

When I opened my fingers to retrieve the shotgun under my pillow, what fell from them made me gasp, almost cry. On the floor where they landed, lay my tiny plastic oranges, green-capped and filled with sugar, a little toy car with rubber wheels and working doors, and a note from my prophet.

No matter what, hold on.
— Catherine

Easy for her to say. She wasn't the one with an invincible vampire standing in her doorway.

In the way of old houses, there were more rooms in my new place than I would assign purposes for, all interconnected, with multiple doors coming and going. During renovation, Barry had walled off the door connecting my bedroom to the one next to it with quarter-inch sheetrock and framed out a closet on both sides.

The day I moved in, I took a utility knife and crowbar to the drywall, and removed the closet door on my side of the connecting passage, leaving me with a back exit from my bedroom to the next. I positioned my bed in front of it.

When Desollador came through the door, I pulled the shotgun from under my pillow, aimed and fired. I heard the doorway explode into splinters, but I didn't wait to see if I hit him. I tossed the gun into the closet space, gripped the two cables threaded through the bottom of my rented mattress — *so* not getting that deposit back! — and pulled it up flush against the opening like a Tempur-Pedic drawbridge. As I searched for the tie-off point in the floor to hold the mattress in place, I wished I'd had the forethought to install a light.

My barricade wouldn't hold him off long, but it didn't need to. Ten seconds had passed since I got the shot off. I just needed ten more. I hoped the ringing in my ears would stop by then.

I'd left the connecting room barren except for three chairs, one wedged under the door, another waiting beside the closet to be used for the same purpose, and one under the window, the only one not taped up. Twenty seconds after Desollador broke through my bedroom door, I lowered myself into the driver's seat of the Jeep parked below the window like a warrior's steed. Twenty seconds is not a long time, just long enough to sing the alphabet song, but it felt like forever.

I released the parking brake and the Jeep started to roll. At the end of the driveway, I shifted into second and popped the clutch. Deep in a residential neighborhood, with no straightaways to put distance between us, I saw the Dog in my side view mirror in no time. He would have looked like nothing more extraordinary than a big-ass mutt chasing a car if he was barking, but he ran me down like silent death.

I made a hard right, curbing a tire and taking out a trash can in my wake. The Dog vaulted over it and kept on coming. When he got even with my door, I turned into him, hoping to run him over.

Big mistake. He leapt up in my backseat. As I reached for the gun, his jaws closed on my wrist, piercing clean to the bone in four places. My vision went black around the edges, but adrenaline kept me conscious. I pushed myself back against the seat and hammered the brakes. The Dog disappeared, a shadow closed in around me, and I was pretty sure I was going to pass out after all.

Then the shadow reformed. Desollador hoisted me out of the driver's seat, crammed me into the passenger floorboard — in which I didn't really fit — and took the wheel.

He looked only a little winded. "Love the new place."

I put pressure on my bleeding wrist. "How did you find me?"

"I can always find you."

"How?"

He gave me a look like I'd give a doctor asking 'how's your day?' when I show up bleeding in his ER (been there). "My other form is a dog. How do you think I find you?"

I eyed the shotgun, weighing my chances of getting control of it while his attention was on the road. Maybe if I caused a distraction...

He snatched the weapon from the front seat and dumped it behind him, grabbed a fistful of my hair and hauled me out of the floorboard. I let loose a very undignified squeal that made him grin. "I wonder what else I can do to inspire you to make that noise."

The way he said it made me regret I was only wearing my PJs, a thin white camisole, and a pair of smiley boxers. No shoes.

"What am I going to do with you?" I got a feeling it was a rhetorical question.

The ground rushed by in a blur out the window. I wondered if I would survive a jump at these speeds. *Now that's something I've never done before.* He reached across me and pulled the seatbelt tight over my lap.

I kept a syringe in the glove box. *If I can just—*

"Diane, you do know I can read your mind, right? Your saltwater won't kill me, but it will piss me off. And you don't want to play with me when I'm pissed."

I don't want to play with you period.

"I thought we'd go someplace with a little privacy. Get to know each other."

"I know enough."

"OK, then how about this? I thought we'd go someplace where no one can hear you scream, because you are going to fucking scream."

I fought to steady my breath. "Where?"

"My place."

Oh good. *Knowing where he keeps his coffin might give me an edge if I manage to survive our little date.*

"I don't have a coffin."

"Figure of speech. Get out of my head."

"I can't do that. As you said, knowing where I live would give you an unfair advantage."

"I didn't say—"

He met my eyes and said one word, "Sleep."

And I did.

I woke up feeling drugged, groggy, my shoulders aching. My hands were stretched over my head, my feet asleep somewhere under me, and my body an agonizing weight between them. When I tried to lower my arms, I realized Desollador had restrained me. He'd also covered my eyes with a heavy material that stuck to my face from scalp to nose like a hood. I wondered how long I had been strung up like that.

"A few hours."

In that state of sensory deprivation, Desollador's voice sounded amplified, like water falling in a cave. I exhaled with a squawk. The fabric slipped into my mouth, pressed against my tongue. Air filtered in at a weak trickle no matter how hard or fast I breathed.

"Claustrophobic. Interesting." He pulled the hood up until it just covered my nose. "There, you're OK."

Leather—supple, but unforgiving against my skin—encased my arms from elbow to fingertip. I could feel no buckle or hook to work loose. He'd left my legs free, but I balanced on my tiptoes. My camisole rode up to uncover most of my torso, and my boxers rode low on my hips. I felt an intense warmth against my skin and heard the unmistakable sound of wood popping.

"Where are we?" I asked.

"My bedroom."

"Do much sleeping in here?"

"Vampires don't sleep."

"Sorry I asked."

A cool fingertip traced my spine from the hollow between my shoulder blades to my tailbone. I sucked in a breath through my nose, struggling through the fabric. Then his hands slid across my hips, into the waistband of my boxers, which he rolled down once, twice, until they sat as low on my body as decency allowed, maybe lower. I would not whimper. *I would not whimper.*

"Yes you will."

Something warm and wet slid down my stomach, washing over bruises that hurt when I breathed. His hands claimed me again, massaging it into me. It had the viscous feel of motor oil. His touch both eased and repulsed me, and, if I'm being honest, excited me more than I'm happy to admit.

"What are you doing?" I asked.

"Humans can only take so much damage. I am healing the worst of yours. Must take good care of my new toy." He chuckled at himself.

Christ. "Is that your *blood*?"

"It is."

OK, mostly repulsed. "Get your filthy hands off me."

Pain bloomed on my cheek, accompanied by a resounding crack. "That's no way to say thank you."

"No shit."

Another blow, harder this time. "I can heal a lot of damage, Diane. Just how much do you want to take tonight?"

When I didn't answer, I felt his breath on my throat, his hands pushing against my shorts, working his blood into my flesh…lower. My heart seized. "I don't. Don't."

"You weren't expecting me in Harlin's office, were you?"

My breath sounded louder than his voice, my heartbeat like horse hooves on pavement. I filled up my lungs with as much air as they could hold and tried to let it out slowly. I expelled no more than half before I gulped down another lungful.

"You've destroyed so many of mine I've had to start creating more, though I despise exchanging blood with a man."

My shoulders spasmed, my cheeks burned and sweat slid down my nose, none of that half as distracting as what he did to me with his fingers. What did he want me to say?

"Did you know that in thirteen centuries, I have never turned a female? Even when I've met one I'd like to keep indefinitely." He nipped my neck and I jumped, then winced. "What I create, I control, and I enjoy my women having the ability to surprise me, even to fight me. So feeding from a man is what you would call a necessary evil."

"Actually, I would just call it evil."

"The first one you killed, I turned on the ship to America. He was a mean drunk even before I made him a vampire and after, well he had a thing for junkies, liked to get high off his kills. You left him dead in an alley for the police to find. I killed three people to get his body out of the morgue. How does that fit into your plan to save the innocents?"

The burning in my cheeks turned to ice at the mention of the morgue. Those deaths made headlines on news channels across three states for thirty-six hours. William was my first kill after I got the calling. I counted them my second. "I made sure that never happened again."

"No, Pet, I made sure that never happened again."

He waited, maybe for me to deny it. I pushed the memory out of my mind and focused on my breathing.

"I turned three slave-traders when America was first born. Four hundred years later, they were still trading, and I was making a pretty penny selling sluts and whores on the black market. You decimated our operation. Oh, I bet you were proud of yourself."

They lived like frat boys, all together in a house that stank of dope and sex. I burned it to the ground after I killed them and dropped six girls — drugged out of their minds and fifty kinds of crazy — at the local ER on the way out of town.

"Hell yes I'm proud," I answered. "I saved six lives when I killed those men."

"There were sixty-two girls we never accounted for after the fire. Locked in a warehouse or a storage unit somewhere. I wasn't involved much with that end of the business. I wonder if they ran out of air first or if they eventually died of thirst."

My gut twisted. "You're lying."

"At the time, I wondered why you didn't kill the others. We had two border guards, half the police force, and a judge in our operation. One of the largest skin trades in the country, all of it run by vampires, yet you targeted just three men. Either you lied when you said your calling is saving innocents or you didn't know about the others because I didn't sire them. Which is it?"

I didn't answer. I didn't even think on an answer. I pointedly avoided thinking about it.

"You got in and out again so quickly, I couldn't track you. I didn't even know where to look. Until you came here. Started killing right in my backyard, not murderers, not criminals. Businessmen. You left your scent all over this town, like you were just begging me to molest you. So what I want to know is this: if you didn't know about me, why did you kill them?"

"I told you. I kill vampires."

"You don't kill vampires." He pressed his cheek against mine, though the hood still muffled his voice. "You kill *mine*. I want to know why."

That made two of us. I wanted to know why the prophet set me up.

"Who is the prophet, Pet?"

I pressed my lips closed and tried to think of nothing. I soon discovered nothing is really hard to picture so I resorted to playing Christmas carols in my head because they were the first non-threatening thing that came to mind.

"I asked, who is the prophet?"

When I didn't answer this time, he pressed his thumb into the crease of my hip, just above my groin, grinding flesh into bone until I screamed. "That would be a pressure point. Takes very little effort to cause crippling pain." He jabbed two fingers into my abdomen halfway between my navel and the junction of my thighs, quick and hard. I would have doubled over if my hands were free. Instead I pulled one knee into my belly and pivoted in my restraints. "This is not going to get any easier for you, Pet. Talk to me."

"I'll tell you about the prophet," I said. "If you tell me about

Edward."

"Now there is an interesting name, but off point." He paused, and I tensed for another hit. "Maybe I'm going about this the wrong way."

His feet made soft tapping sounds on the hardwood floor as he circled me. I heard a sigh, then the hood dropped down tight over my nose and my mouth as he dragged my head back. I sucked in air through the thick fabric, but felt like I was trying to breathe through a stir straw.

"Who is the prophet?" he repeated.

After ten seconds that felt like ten minutes, Desollador uncovered my mouth again to give me a chance to talk. This time I did. "She's my muse. She isn't even real." He started to pull the hood back down. "Damnit, I dream about the vampires. That's how I know where to hunt."

"You dream about the vampires? You mean you dream about *my* vampires. You'll have to do better than that."

"I don't know what to tell you. Maybe I'm carrying a grudge against you from a past life."

"Yet you never dreamed about me."

"I thought you could read my mind. Can't you find out for yourself if I'm telling you the truth?"

"Well, Pet, you seem to be getting better at keeping your thoughts to yourself, or I just don't want to endure all five verses of Jingle Bells to get to them."

I focused on my breathing again and willed him not to pull the hood back down.

"How do you know about Edward?" he asked.

"I dreamed about him too."

He snatched the hood off. "You dream about him, yet in three years you don't dream about me. Did I mention I am a jealous master?"

I backed up, but my restraints didn't allow me much leverage. He took up the slack, pushing his body so far into my space I had to wrap my legs around his waist because my feet would no longer touch the floor. Cradling my hips in his hands, he kissed me, scraping a fang down my tongue to taste my blood, then opening his own so I could taste his. That brief exchange left me feeling high and took the edge off the ache in my shoulders. I wanted more. Judging from his slow smile, he knew it.

"Bastard. Let me go."

"That's a silly thing to say, Diane. Something I would expect from a victim who didn't know any better. You know better."

Primal scream. Thrashing. *I am not supposed to be the victim!*

"This position is hard for you, unfamiliar. You need control," he said. "I understand that."

He dropped me, and the weight of my body dragged against my shoulders. Scrambling to get my feet under me, I asked, "What do you mean?"

He made a 'just wait' motion with his hand and turned to the hope chest at the bottom of his bed. I felt like I might throw up when he took the key out of his pocket, and I almost did when he opened the top. He pulled out a girl, pale with ice-blue eyes and mousey brown hair. She looked like me, only stripped and gagged.

"I don't think you've told me the truth, Pet."

"I—"

"See, I don't think you've told me the truth because there are two of my own vampires in this house. In the very next room. Why didn't your dreams tell you about them?"

"My dreams suck." And my muse is a bitch.

"You've killed innocent vampires."

"There are no innocent vampires," I parroted.

"So only humans can be innocent?"

"Let the girl go, Desollador."

"Oh, this little slut isn't innocent, are you?" He knuckled her chin and she started shaking her head. "She was going to fuck me three nights ago though she is a married woman. How many years have you been married?"

He pushed her gag down to her chin. She fought to catch her breath between the tears. "Please let me—"

He slapped her. "Married seven years. How many times have you cheated on your husband?" She shook her head. He torqued her wrist behind her back. "If I have to ask again, I will rip your arm off. How many times?"

"Three. Or four…except you and I didn't…you know…so three. Please, let me go." I heard her bone crack from across the room a split second before she started wailing, collapsing on her side with her arm splayed out at an odd angle to her body. He stomped on her, like smashing a spider, and told her to shut up.

"Do you still think she's worth saving, Pet?" he asked, as if daring me to say yes.

"Yes."

"Even at the expense of her husband? Her devoted husband who has never been unfaithful?"

"People cheat. People get cheated on. It sucks, but it doesn't kill them."

"Actually in this case, it does." He pulled a syringe from his back pocket and held it with two fingers in front of my face. "From your glove box." Without taking his eyes off mine, he placed it on the mantle. "You could try using that on me, but it would be a waste."

My arms were encased in mitten-style opera gloves laced from bicep to fingertip and affixed to a hook on the ceiling. Desollador unhooked them and unthreaded the laces with deft agility. I rubbed at my skin as blood rushed back to it and the air around me took on the sudden texture of thorns. Eyeing the syringe on the mantle, I wondered at my chances of grabbing it before Desollador stopped me and, assuming I succeeded in that feat, my chances of being able to hold the damned thing when I couldn't even feel my fingers.

The bedroom door opened. A man came through it, gray in the temples, wearing a short-sleeved button-up, light blue with tortoise buttons. He looked like someone who spent too much time in a cubicle where no one ever saw his shoes. They were ordinary brown oxfords that hadn't been polished since the day he bought them.

He also looked like he was tweaking.

"This is Tony, the unfortunate husband of our promiscuous friend here. Wrong place, wrong time. Tony followed his wife on her last little excursion in hopes of finding proof of her infidelity.

He found me instead. Right about now, he needs blood. This is his first time, so it's going to be messy."

"Don't do this."

"Remember, I control what I create, so he won't touch you. But her, he's going to rip apart. So you see, you have a choice to make." Desollador opened his bedroom door and stepped through the threshold. "He's the evil vampire. She's the innocent human, right? Should be an easy decision for you."

He closed the door behind him, locking the three of us in together. I swiped up the syringe and tried to fit it between fingers too numb and uncooperative to hold it. When I looked back at Tony, I almost hoped I wouldn't be able to hold the thing after all. He stared unblinking at his wife, tears streaming down his cheeks.

"What's your name?" I asked the girl.

"K-Karena."

Tony stopped crying when he heard her voice and started sawing his jaw side to side like he'd just done two lines of coke.

"Tony, keep it together, buddy. You cared enough about Karena to follow her here, to give a damn if she was faithful to you. You do not want to kill her."

"No. Not kill. Tear her apart..."

"That's what Desollador said you'd do," I thought aloud. "You're under a compulsion. Karena, get back in the box."

"I'm not going back in—"

"Get in the damn box until I can figure this out."

She didn't move. Tony was still doing the hula jaw, only now his hands were twitching too. "Box! Now!"

We all moved at once. Karena made a reluctant shuffle towards the box; Tony lunged after her and I tackled him. Or tried to tackle him. He performed an acrobatic sidestep that seemed out of character for a man who had spent his life hidden in a cubicle, and I flew past him.

He sidestepped again to avoid walking on me, and again when I scrambled after him. He wouldn't touch me. Avoided touching me at all costs.

We made it to the box at the same time. I stuffed Karena inside, slammed the lid shut on Tony's fingers, and flattened my body on top of it, laying my hand over his as I did. He snatched his hand away.

"Karena, do you love your husband?"

She sobbed again in reply.

"Karena, I need you to focus. Do you love him?"

"Yes!"

"Then why did you cheat?"

The vampire, eyes blazing orange, circled to the head of the box and drew his foot back to kick it in. I scooted down to that end and splayed my palms against it to ward him off.

"Answer me, damnit. Why?"

"Sex! Tony is just...vanilla. I wanted kink, fifty shades stuff, you know?"

The vampire roared and went airborne, landing between my feet with a splintering thwack. I rolled onto my back, scissoring my legs, which he jumped to avoid. "Yeah, well he's not so vanilla anymore. How much do you love him?"

She sobbed some more. "I don't want to die."

"Not what I asked. How much?"

Tony got a kick in before I could reposition my body again and the box cracked up the center. Lucky for Karena, Desollador's hope chest was as hard to kill as the vampire himself. Inside, Karena issued a ragged scream. "Tony, please don't do this. I'm so sorry. I never meant hurt you."

He backed away at the sound of her voice with a crazy expression equal parts rage and grief. Then he charged. I draped myself again on the chest, arms and legs sprawled to cover as much of it as possible, and closed my eyes, waiting for an impact that never came. When I opened them again, Tony crouched on Desollador's bed, those flame-colored eyes boring into mine. "Tony, you don't want to kill your wife. Fight this thing."

"Then what? I am a *monster*. You *need* to kill me."

I looked from Tony's desperate eyes to the box and back at him. The only innocent in the room was a damned vampire. "Here's what's going to happen, Karena. You both live, or you both die. He is going to kill you, then I am going to kill him…or you can be the wife to him now that you weren't when he was alive."

I tossed the syringe and opened the lid in the same movement. We both dove into the box after her. He wouldn't touch any part of her I touched, so I got more intimate with a naked woman than I had ever wanted to be. He ended up with her wrist, the one attached to the broken arm, which was fine with me as long as he didn't rip it off.

"Tony, you can tear her apart later. Just feed. You hear me? Just feed." I looked into Karena's wide eyes that were too much like the color of my own, and said, "Scream, you hear me? And beg. Whatever you do, don't stop begging."

When she nodded, I lifted my head and shoulders to maximize momentum and slammed my temple into the edge of the box.

I came to when Karena cried, "Tony, please. Tony, don't do this."

"*Not him. Beg me, you stupid bitch,*" I told her, but she couldn't hear it because I was passed-out cold on top of her. She was halfway to dead before her cries deteriorated to nameless pleas for salvation.

This time, instead of a Monte Carlo, I woke up in a cedar box with my own body on top of me, a position only a little less jarring because I expected to find myself in it, but still creepy as fuck. The vampire took a deep drag, and I followed the blood. *Tony.*

He dropped my/her hand. "I'm not supposed to touch you."

Yet here we are, mind to mind. Doesn't get much more touchy-feely than this.

I'm not supposed to touch you.

So I touched you. Now drink, but go easy. I didn't say it; I commanded it.

He picked up Karena's hand again. Kissed her wrist. *Ick.* Then bit. His execution—sloppy and ragged—made me appreciate Desollador's skill, damn him.

I followed the blood deeper, until I could see inside him. A blue-

77

black fog like oil on water, but beneath it, rippling so far beneath the surface it looked more like a fantasy than a memory, I saw the warbling image of Karena standing in front of a waterfall, sunshine tangled in her hair, shaking her head and smiling at some private joke, a couple's whimsy. I pulled the image up through the muck and went deeper. More light, candles reflected off pale skin and sky-blue eyes, then wisps of smoke and a wish. I could feel the heat from the candles even after they were blown out. It burned away the fog everywhere it touched.

Deeper still, I sought more radiance, more heat. Karena, all dressed in white with miniature roses woven in her hair and a sapphire at her neck, holding a tapered candle like it was a baby bird, reverent and careful. Tony held its twin and together they lit the wick of a third, a large hand-dipped intricately carved pillar candle, a symbol of their unity. I lifted up the memory, pushing it ahead of me everywhere the fog obscured, burning it off bit by bit until only a coal remained. The compulsion.

Before I lost my nerve, I plucked it up like the plastic orange and the toy car and cradled it to my breast, pulled it with me, back through her blood, through her body and finally back into my own.

The pain of the thing woke me. It hurt. Exactly like I had swallowed a hot coal. I grasped my stomach as if that's where the pain truly resided and half climbed, half fell out of the box. Karena was conscious and alive. Tony had progressed from devouring her to clinging to her while they both sobbed and apologized to each other, so I assumed they'd be OK while I puked my guts out.

Then Desollador came back into the room.

"I love when you wear your hair down," he said as he held it off my neck while I finished dry-retching. I made a note to myself to braid it from now on, even when I went to sleep.

He ran his thumb across my temple. "That bruise isn't very pretty."

"I didn't much enjoy getting it, either."

"You seem to have removed my compulsion on our friend here."

"You said I had a choice to make. I made it. Neither needs to die.

Congratulations, I just spared my first vampire."

He reached past me and retrieved the syringe where I had discarded it. "A shame."

"What's that?"

"Well, you recall me telling you that what I create, I control?"

"Yeah..."

It all happened so fast. I careened after him, a fireplace poker in my hands, words of denial half-formed on my lips. Karena flew through the air and landed in an even more broken heap on Desollador's floor, and Tony started to puke up blood, my syringe protruding from his jugular.

"If I can't control it, I kill it. Looks like you chose the little slut after all."

Karena crawled toward her husband. Her one good hand flitted between her mouth and his, and I knew the tears she cried had nothing to do with her physical pain. She picked up the wrist of her broken arm and held it to his lips, begging him to save himself. Newly turned, he died quick.

We watched her try to make him rise from the mess for a long time. I looked away first. "Let her go now, Desollador."

"How about this? I'll give you another choice. No loopholes this time. You will give yourself to me, or I will kill her while you watch."

"Is this some game to you?"

"Yes, in fact. Now answer me."

"What do you mean give myself to you?" I asked, twisting the poker in my hands.

"Don't be an idiot; you know what I mean. One-shot offer, Diane. How much do you want to see her live?"

All this could not be for nothing. "Let her go first."

"If you back out, I will hunt her down and her husband's death will seem a mercy."

I nodded.

He pulled Karena, covered in her husband's sticky red ichor, off the husk that used to be Tony.

She never stopped reaching for his body, even as Desollador

dragged her across the room by her hair. At one point she begged him to kill her too. He ignored her, pushed her through the door, and said something in a low voice to someone in the next room. Then we were alone.

"How do I know you will let her go?"

"I give you my word."

"The word of a vampire. That's rich."

"I am many things, Diane, but always a man of my word."

Interesting. I believed him.

He closed the distance between us, tore the poker from my hands and threw it into the fire. "Take off your shirt." His jaw set in a hard grimace that made me feel anything but sexy.

I forced myself to look him in the eyes as I pulled the tank top over my head. I would not be ashamed, though I did cross my arms over my breasts.

He pointed to a door on the far corner of the room. "Move."

The door opened into a bathroom with a clawfoot tub. *Shit.*

"You're covered in blood, Diane. And not just mine. It's driving me nuts. Turn on the water. Set the temperature however you like it."

"You aren't going to make me take a bath?"

"Turn on the water. If I have to tell you again, it's going to be uncomfortable for you."

"With you watching?"

"I'll be doing more than watching." He held my blue scarf in front of him. I didn't remember when he'd taken it from me. "Turn around."

"Wait, let me…" I tried to affect nonchalance when I walked past him, but he caressed my breast when I passed and made me shudder under his touch. I bent sideways, twisting my body in a ridiculously awkward position to avoid giving Desollador my backside when I started the water. He noticed and caressed that too.

I stood. He turned me around so my backside was facing him after all, trapped my legs between the tub and his body, and fastened the scarf over my eyes.

I didn't move, tried not to breathe, even when his hand skimmed my side from armpit to waistband. He swept my hair off my neck with his other hand and kissed my nape as he pushed them down to my thighs. I didn't know what to do with my hands. I couldn't help it. I reached for my boxers to hold them in place.

His fingers covered mine. "Take them off, Pet."

My breath was so damn loud even over the sound of the water. "I don't...don't make me?"

He didn't take his hands off mine until my shorts were all the way down around my ankles. More than I hated being naked — I guess he had seen me that way before — I hated not being able to see his face while I was naked.

He stood me up again, flattened my back against his front, close enough I could feel the buttons on his shirt and the metal of his belt buckle. One hand closed over my throat, thumb and index finger a steady pressure on my jugular, giving me a pleasant light-headed feeling. The other slid between us and unbuttoned his shirt. The hand at my throat slid down to my breasts, squeezing the most tender parts of them every time he loosed a button.

It slid further, reaching the cleft of my sex when the one between us reached his belt buckle. I couldn't even begin to pretend I wasn't responding to him. I barely had a coherent thought.

"Step in." His voice startled me so much I cried out.

"*Fuck.*" My heart was a jackrabbit in my chest, but I did what he said.

The water was almost too hot to stand. I winced as he stepped in behind me and eased us down into the tub. I tried not the think about the part of him that was resting against my ass, but the way he nibbled on my ear made it difficult to think about anything else.

I felt his hand again on my throat and then something soft and porous. A sponge? That's right. He was washing the blood off me. Which he did quite thoroughly. *Why can't I think straight?*

"Remember how easily you succumb to swoon, Pet."

I remembered, the Vicodin and whiskey effect. "No fair."

"You keep saying that like it's supposed to be."

I was sliding. The water which had been up to my breasts was nearly to my chin. I braced my hands on the sides of the tub and pushed myself up and back against him. He growled and dropped the sponge between my legs. Before I had time to register alarm, he wrapped my damp rope of hair around his palm, pulled my head to the side with just enough force to hurt, and buried his fangs in my throat.

This time when the spinning and falling sensation came, he was holding onto my breasts with one hand and my hair with the other while I was holding onto the tub for dear life. "Oh...Jesus."

I can't get enough of you.

There's only so much of me to take, though.

He tore his fangs away from my neck, unwound my hair from his hand and snatched the blindfold from my eyes. I blinked against the steam as I felt him stand up behind me. I wanted to ask him what I'd done, but that would mean I *liked* what he was doing, and that wasn't possible, was it?

"Yes, you liked it. And you didn't do anything wrong. But you're right, there is only so much of you. I don't want to use it all up in the damned bathtub. Get out."

He didn't even look at me when he handed me the towel. "Put your shorts back on, and get into the bedroom. Quickly."

I watched him leave in a state of shock. My head cleared, and I assumed the swoon was wearing off. Fuck, what had I gotten myself into? I pulled my boxers on while my skin was still wet and searched my surroundings for a weapon. Desollador shoved the door back open, grabbed me by the hair and pushed me out into his bedroom ahead of him. "You agreed to this, remember?"

Tony's body sobered me up immediately. Someone had died here, and I had offered myself up in exchange for another. That's right, I agreed to it.

"Do you see me fighting?" I took a step back when I saw how red Desollador's eyes were. "But if you hadn't noticed, there is a very dead vampire bleeding all over your hardwood floor."

"A reminder. The choice was her or him. By taking away my control, you chose her. His death is on your hands."

"Fine, but do we have to look at him?"

Desollador pulled the duvet from his bed with a flourish and covered up the body. "Better?"

I contemplated the bundle, grateful the fabric was a rich, dark red so the blood wouldn't show. "Yeah."

"Usually a lady shows some gratitude when a gentleman lays down his coat for her."

"You are no gentleman."

"Diane," he warned.

"What do you want? I told you I give. Do what you're going to do." I crossed my arms over my chest and stuck out my chin. *How bad could it be?*

He laughed. Not a chuckle, but a full on cackle. "That's something you don't want to know, Pet."

"Fine. I get it. You're a badass. Just get it over with."

All humor faded from his eyes. "I am beginning to think I should have hung on to the shrinking violet in my hope chest. She at least was civil when she wasn't balling. Maybe I should bring her back?"

"No! I told you I would give myself to you. I am. What do you want me to do?"

He nodded to the bed. "Lie down."

Tough to do with my arms crossed, I ended up with one draped over my body to cover myself and the other balled in a fist at my side. Desollador noted my body language and said, "I am not feeding from your neck this time."

He peeled my arm away from my breasts and kissed my throat. Maybe he would change his mind and just…

His hand cupping my breast cut off the thought and, with it, my breath. His teeth scraped too close to the sensitive bud I willed him to avoid. I trembled under his lips. I held the picture of the girl from the hope chest in my mind and tried not to struggle.

"Close your eyes," he ordered.

Guilt crept up into all the places Desollador touched, sucked. I came so close to breaking. Poor girl. He'd hunt her down because of me.

"Spread your legs," he said.

I pressed them together.

"It's not what you think. But even if it was, you made a deal. Spread your legs."

I complied, but only a little. He coaxed them further apart, and I squeezed the sheets for dear life to keep from closing them again.

"Don't open your eyes," he said. I started at a sudden noise — like a small jet engine or a storm in a bottle — close to my ear.

"What are you doing?"

He didn't answer, not for a while, leaving me alone with the frightened rabbit thump of my heart and that strange whirring sound. I felt almost grateful when he touched me again, his hand a vice around my leg, spreading me wider. "Brace yourself," was all the warning he gave before pain — a searing white heat — bloomed against my inner thigh.

I screamed, writhed. My eyes flew open, but his hand clamped down on the back of my leg, holding me still for the agony to consume me. Then in place of heat, ice, which hurt as much but I instinctively knew to be less damaging. He was right. I did whimper, but then he'd just mutilated me. I didn't have to see my leg to know it.

I squinted into the candlelight. Desollador held a small metal skewer with the hand not holding my leg and, on his end table, I saw a blowtorch. No, not a skewer, a brand. What the hell? *Vampires don't brand their victims!*

"I am more than a vampire, Diane."

I tried to sit up to survey the damage, but he pushed me back into the pillows and started wrapping my thigh in inch-wide strips of gauze. "Let's save the surprise for later."

My teeth chattered so hard I wondered if they'd crack, and I couldn't stop myself from trembling. My eyes welled with tears, though I held my breath to stop them from falling. "What did you do?"

He climbed over me, pressed my wrists into the pillow, and answered, "Marked you."

I heard a mewling noise and only realized it came from me when Desollador whispered, "I told you you'd whimper."

Before I broke, he bit, and everything stopped — the pain, the dread, the tears. My body burned for him. My blood sang for him.

His hands wandered over me as he drank, pulling the hem of my shorts into the cleft of my buttocks, thumbs pressing into my hip bones, fingers teasing my waistband. I didn't miss the fact that the part of me not scared shitless was getting frustrated.

I passed out not long after that and woke again in my own bed as the sun came up. I could have mistaken the whole thing for a dream if not for the mother of a headache racking my brain, the ruin that was left of my bedroom door, and the Mark on my thigh in two-inch letters that read: PET.

CHAPTER 4

The brand was exactly as tall as the putty knife that I found in the closet was wide, but only about half as long. I found a fifth of brandy in my pantry and swigged it straight from the bottle while I cleaned every trace of mud off the knife and set it on the stove burner until it glowed.

The alcohol didn't prepare me for the pain that came when I pressed it against my already once-burned skin. When I pulled the knife away, off with it came all trace of that word. In its place, a fresh hell of agony drove me to my knees. I held onto consciousness just long enough to turn off the stove.

I awoke on the floor of a nightclub, red and blue spotlights pulsing to a techno beat. Roger stood over me, hand extended. His face cracked apart in lava-colored fissures when he smiled. I didn't want to be impolite, so I tried not to look. The dancers around us burned too, not even strangers, but people I knew, or had known once upon a time.

Karena and Tony were there, and Trina, even Renn with her pixie cut and mauve lipstick, head thrown back in a laugh that bellied her small stature. Her brothers—the twins—were there too, smiling at me and setting all sorts of butterflies in my stomach to fluttering. My aunt, wearing an enormous gold-plated bulldog pendant between her ample breasts. All of them burned.

I heard a voice with a distant bluegrass twang calling over the music, "Hey y'all, bow to your partner. Bow to your corner, and that ain't all."

I groaned and curtsied to Roger, then to Renn. She paired up with one of her brothers. Trina paired with another. Tony and Karena completed the square.

"Circle to the left with a hee and a haw!"

Skirts spinning, the eight of us locked hands.

"Now here's the plan, get ready to do a right and left grand. Grab a pretty girl, and grab your friend. Head back home, and take off again."

We passed off hand to hand and somehow ended up in the same place we began.

"Heads to the middle, sides to the back, now square it up like an old Pontiac!"

I wondered if my aunt felt left out of the revelry when Tony and Karena ducked out and she whirled in, partnered with a tall red-haired man. Rams horns curled from his forehead, and his hoofed feet made clodding sounds on the floor. When we promenaded, I noticed wings that sprouted between his shoulder blades. Our fingers touched as we exchanged partners again, and I wanted to snatch my hand away. I racked my brain trying to place him.

When the song ended, I found myself partnered with the stranger. I decided he was a party crasher, but at least his presence gave us an extra partner so Aunt Sandra could dance too. A slow song picked up where the techno beat had left off.

"Where are you from?" I asked the stranger.

"I am a wanderer. You would say homeless."

"How do you live?"

"I have not done that since the time of Adam."

I looked to my left and right, searching out a friendly face for reassurance, but found an empty dance floor around us. "I'm sorry," I said to him, and meant it.

"Does that make a difference?"

"What?"

"Offering apology." I searched for some way to explain the comfort of offering sympathy, but he didn't wait for an answer. "Is your 'I'm sorry' proof against Yetzer Hara?"

His words clashed against the music, an unfamiliar chord of

dissonance. "Yetzer Hara?"

"It desires you, as it desired me. Maybe you will make more of it that I did."

The dream broke up around us, polished wood floors giving way to damp green grass behind an office building. I recognized it as the place I once died. "I don't understand. What does that word mean?"

"Yetzer Hara is the very bottom of your animal soul."

"My soul is human."

"What are the pieces that make a human soul, Diane? Do you know?"

I took my hands from his shoulders and stepped back. "Who are you?"

"My name is Kayin."

I considered his hooves and horns. "Are you a demon?"

"Not quite, but nearly," he said. "Though once I was mortal."

"How long ago was that?"

"For a long while I was just a ghost, before I became a what I am now." I stole a glance at his horns again. He noticed. "Those I bore while I was yet mortal, a Mark to protect me from beasts that would slay me in my wanderings."

A fleeting memory I could not quite place bothered me like a sudden toothache. "Why are you here?"

He knelt and pressed his palm against the grass, which wilted where he touched. "Even in a dream, it will not bear fruit for me."

We stood in a patch of earth cordoned off by caution tape. "This is a sad place," I said. "An innocent woman was killed here."

He turned his face to the sky, awash in an eerie red glow. "Does her blood call out from the ground?"

It came to me in a rush. "Kayin. Cain."

"I wondered if you knew my story. I suppose it would be too much to hope you did not." His eyes met mine again. "Has he told you how beautiful you are, how powerful? Has he said why he must possess you?"

"Who?" Dreams make normal even conversations with legends.

"Desollador."

"No, he hasn't told me."

"Desollador is in love with you. But Edward needs your soul and wants me to help him get it."

"Edward. Catherine's creation? Are you linked to him too?"

Kayin bristled his wings. "Be careful when you meet him; he was once the eater of souls." He smiled. "Though I do not think he can consume you, not even with all his children feeding him your pieces."

"Why would he want to consume me?"

"Your soul does not know the limits of flesh. He needs it to feed himself."

"Are you going to help him?"

"I should, shouldn't I? He gave me pure form."

I looked at those horns again. How could I not? "Are those unpure?"

The dream broke up around us again and when it came back together I stood with him in my kitchen, my sleeping body curled in tight over my burned thigh.

"No, but they are unclean," he answered. "Edward gives me the gift of unMarked flesh. Else I can only have an ordinary form when I find one sleeping, and I can only stay until the owner wakes. It is not enough time to live."

That said, his shadow consumed my empty shell, wings making a cocoon around it. When the shadow dissipated, my body awoke without me in it. That puzzled but didn't alarm me, not quite. I'd remember to be afraid when the dream ended.

Possessed, I picked up my cell phone from the kitchen counter. The battery indicator flashed red like a warning. I was both a passenger in my own body and an observer outside of it. I could feel the touchscreen under my fingertips and the throbbing heat in my thigh. My consciousness split in two, I watched myself thumb through the contacts in my phone, landing on the last name I ever wanted to call.

It rang three times before someone picked up. "Hullo."

"Hi, Roger?"

The first thing Desollador noticed upon his return home was that the hallway mirror was leaning up against the wall, reflective side down.

In the living room, he found the intruder with his feet propped up on his coffee table, where a double vodka on the rocks made wet rings on the polished wood. He was eating Thai food with a fork straight from the box. "You want some? Oh that's right. You'd rather have the delivery girl. I can call her back. All I could find in your stash was a hundred, so I am pretty sure she'll make a second trip."

"What are you doing here, Salli?"

"Nice to see you too, brother. I heard you found a hot new piece in your toy box. Came to see her for myself. I ran across the one you let out of it earlier. She is something to look at, but not sure there is much up here." He tapped his temple.

"What did you do to her?"

Salvion plunked the takeout box on the coffee table and downed the vodka in one gulp. "Damn, this is some smooth stuff. I didn't think you drank."

"I entertain. What happened to the girl?"

"I set her arm — geez you wouldn't believe the pipes on that one — but she could probably use a real doctor."

"What do you mean 'real doctor'? I sent instructions for her to be taken to the emergency room."

"Yeah, about that. Your boys are under the impression she made it there safe and sound, so go easy on them."

"Where are they now?"

"I don't know. I met them in the driveway when they were leaving with the girl. They ended up circling the block a few times on the way to the 'hospital' then handing her off to the 'ER doc'." He made finger quotes at the end.

"That would have been you."

He nodded. "Haven't seen them since."

"What did you do with the girl?"

"Go see for yourself. She's back in your toy box."

"Damn." He marched to the bedroom and threw open the lid. The girl wasn't restrained, but she made no move to escape.

Tears streamed down her cheeks, and she'd gouged the wood until her fingernails bled. "What's wrong with her?"

"Shhh. She can still hear you." As if on cue, the girl shrieked, but didn't make direct eye contact.

Salvion closed the lid again and sat on it. "She was under the impression she was buried alive, or undead rather. She's not very imaginative." She pounded against the lid from inside the box. "I am afraid you have shattered my illusion now."

"Please let me out. Please. I'll do whatever you want. Please, I'll be good."

Salvion pounded back. "Been there, done that. Got the t-shirt." To Desollador he said, "The ability to go from substantial to insubstantial and back again really scares the shit out the ladies in the sack."

Desollador shoved Salvion off the box and opened the lid again. "Knock it off, Salli. She needs to see my eyes."

"Why? She's a toy. Get a new one. Oh, that's right. You have a new one. Why isn't *she* in the box?"

Desollador crossed the room in three yard-long strides, tore a gold-framed mirror the size of a big-screen TV off the wall above the dresser, and hurled it at Salvion with bone-shattering force. "I said knock it off. I know how to hurt you, brother."

He missed, scattering glittering shards across the floor at Salvion's feet. "Whatever. Have it your way." He waved his hand and vacated the room at a pace not quite fast enough to be considered fleeing, but close enough.

Whatever illusion the girl saw, went with him. Her eyes focused on Desollador, then filled with tears. "No, no, no, no."

Desollador pulled her out of the box. "You are OK. You will survive this. I gave my word on it."

She shook her head in silent pantomime. Desollador moved his hands from her arms to her face and said, "Sleep." Her eyes rolled back in their sockets as she fell forward against his chest. He carried her to the bed. When the twins returned, he would have them take her to the hospital.

He would have them scour her memories of tonight as well, replace them in her mind with a vivid recollection of a back alley assault (she had been asking for it) and the idea that her whoring ways had finally driven her husband away. She'd never stop hoping for him to come home again, a fitting fate for the little slut.

A few minutes later, he joined Salvion in the living room.

"You and that word of honor crap. What is that?"

"What are you doing here, brother?"

"I told you already. I heard you found a new toy and came to see her for myself."

Desollador's gaze slid to the bedroom.

Salvion shook his head. "Not that toy. I believe her name is Diane."

Desollador upended the coffee table. "You will stay away from her."

"Down boy. This was Edward's idea."

"Fuck Edward. I don't care whose idea it was. It is not going to happen. Diane is mine, and I-do-not-share."

"Don't know what to tell you. Take it up with the old man."

"Get out of my house."

Salvion spread his hands, palms out. "Now just wait a minute. You've got a freaking mansion here. There's room enough for both of us."

"Not nearly."

"Besides," he said with a smile. "Edward and Kayin should be here by morning."

"What? Why?"

"Probably same reason as me, to help you work on your sharing skills."

"Salvion, if you don't leave my sight right now, I am going to earn a century of bad luck breaking you. Gladly."

He grabbed the vodka bottle and yawned. "I'll be in the guest room. One of the ones on other end of the house. Wake me when the gang's all here."

Desollador gave the coffee table a solid stomping, which reminded him of the girl on his bed. He had given Diane his word he'd free her. Nothing saying he needed to be gentle with her in the meantime. Torturing the little slut just might temper his rage before Edward arrived.

After that, there were not enough sluts in the world to take the edge off.

Before giving my body back to me, Kayin set me up on a date, and I didn't have the heart to cancel it. That's how I found myself at 'Eighties After Dark' at the Masquerade that night. Roger wore a navy blue Henley and fashionably faded blue jeans, and looked out of character without his red t-shirt and whistle. My entire wardrobe consisted of camisoles and white button-up shirts. They were easy to swap out if they got bloody, and commonplace enough that no one ever noticed the quick change. Black would have been more forgiving, but it was too damn hot for it. I added a pale blue scarf to my usual uniform to hide Desollador's bite and put on a bit of red lipstick.

"You look nice," Roger said.

My stomach knotted. "Thanks. You too."

Small talk would have been awkward, but the music played nearly too loud to talk over, so we didn't have to do too much of it. I ordered a vodka soda in a tall glass, and he ordered a Bud.

"So what made you change your mind?" he yelled over George Michael.

"What?" I leaned in.

"I asked what made you change your mind? About hanging out?"

A demon possessed my body and changed it for me. "Rough couple of days. I guess I just thought this would be good to take my mind off it."

"What's going on?"

"Just stuff."

He bit his lip. I willed him not to push. "Sorry to hear it. I'm here if you wanna talk about it."

"Nah. It's okay."

"Well, I'm glad you thought of me."

I pretended not to hear, but didn't ask him to repeat himself.

"Hey, you wanna dance?" I started pulling him out to the floor before he could answer.

"I don't really—"

"Sure you do. Just bob your head and move your feet from side to side. You can't mess up."

I threw my hands in the air as the chorus began and demonstrated the side-to-side movement. Turns out, he really, and I mean really, didn't dance. I laughed at his attempt to follow my movements. It felt so damned good to laugh.

"I tried to tell you!"

"Yes, you did."

"I'm just going to go sit over there." He nodded to the bar.

"Uh-uh. Not so fast. I'm not going to dance alone. You just keep on doing your chicken thing over there. I'm sure no one will notice."

"My chicken thing?"

I laughed again. "Shut up and dance."

For a while, we did. I forgot about the dreams, about the demon and the prophet. For a while, I got to be just a girl. That girl wasn't even very uncomfortable with the way Roger watched me move, in a way that said he hoped the night would go somewhere it just couldn't. He only touched me a few times, a hand on my shoulder, my waist, at the curve of my hip—safe, friendly places, but exploratory in a way I knew I should shut down. In a minute, I told myself. I couldn't remember the last time I felt a safe, clean touch. Not since I got the calling.

So it was my fault that he kissed me.

I enjoyed the sweet, chaste comfort of it for the span of a heartbeat before opening my eyes (his were closed). Then I leapt back from him. He reached out toward me. "I'm sorry. I shouldn't have—"

"No, it's my fault. Shit! I shouldn't have come here. It was a mistake."

The cruelty of my words registered in his eyes. "I can handle a little rejection, Di. It's no big deal." He held his hands up and away from me. "No more kissing, promise."

"It's not that. I can't have a relationship with you."

"I said no more kissing. It's cool. We're just friends." I could swear his lips were on fire when he said it. Was I dreaming again?

"No, we're not. I don't have friends. Shit! I'm sorry. I'm really sorry. I'm just gonna take off."

He stopped me. "You don't need to go anywhere right now." Part of his forehead blackened and crumbled away. I was going crazy right there in the middle of the dance floor. He kept talking like he didn't feel the fire. "I'll leave, OK? We'll talk later, next time you're in the park."

A rivet of fire opened up in the hand that he placed on my shoulder, tunneling up his sleeve. I tried to keep my voice steady. "OK, yes. We'll talk. Just go." His arm looked like a smoldering log now. "Just leave. Please." I squeezed my eyes shut, but couldn't get the image of him burning out of my head.

"I'm leaving. Are you going to be OK?"

I made the mistake of looking at him. His mouth made a gaping maw of embers. "Go!" I screamed.

A hole opened up in the mob on the dance floor. I stood alone in it. The embers that gusted from Roger's mouth lit all around me, threads of fire weaving through the crowd. Some dancers stared at me; others carefully avoided looking in my direction. But not one of them seemed to be aware that flames were eating them alive.

Bree Conner poured four tequila shots in a row and looked up just in time to see Roger blow past her, red-faced. "Hey Rog, you OK?"

He stopped short and looked behind him. "Oh hey, I didn't know you were working tonight. Yeah, I'm alright."

"You don't look alright."

"I seriously misinterpreted an invite to dance and got my ego bruised is all."

She grabbed his collar, pulled him over the countertop and pushed her tongue into his mouth. He was such a sweet boy, letting her have her way with him for at least ten seconds. Finally she pulled away, wiped a smear of hot pink lipstick off his chin. "There, ego all better now?"

He staggered back a little. "You do remember you used to kiss my brother with that mouth?"

"Old news. But I'm telling you right now, you're gonna have to get your ass all sorts of torn up if you want sympathy sex from me." She thumped the first shot in the line. Four glasses danced down the bar, landing one after the other in front of customers too drunk to care how they got there.

"You are one strange girl, Bree."

"Yup, and don't you forget it."

Roger looked over his shoulder, fingering his lips. "Would you mind keeping an eye on my, um, date?"

"The one that dissed you? Yeah, I'll keep an eye on her alright."

"No, she's cool. She made it clear from the get-go she wasn't interested. I pushed way too hard."

"Uh-huh, sure you did."

"She's a friend. I like her, and she was pretty upset, so I would appreciate it if you just make sure she doesn't leave until she's calm."

"You are such a sap. What does she look like?"

"White shirt, braid down to here." He gestured to the seat of his pants. "Wearing a blue scarf. Name's Diane."

"Alright, but you gotta do me a favor. Give your brother a call. He's going dark and moody on me lately."

"It's that time of year."

"I know. Sucks."

"Look, about you two, I could talk to him —"

She held up her hand. "I've told you, I love him to death, but no. My ass isn't nearly lily white enough to live up to his moral code."

"That's not true. You're a catch, and he knows it."

"We're fine as friends. I don't have to take any of his shit, and he pays half my rent," she said. "You holding up?"

"Yeah, it never did get to me the way it gets to Mace. It's not like we ever knew him."

"Right." She sent another shot spinning down the counter. It dodged a couple of longnecks in its path, but no one was looking.

"Just watch out for Diane, will ya?"

"Fine…but call me if you need a shoulder."

After he left, Bree called for another bartender to cover her station and wound through the throng until she spotted Diane. Strobe lights flashed in time to the music and painted the girl's white shirt a neon blue. She spun in a slow circle, trembling, mouth open. Bree followed the direction of her gaze and saw nothing that would warrant her reaction.

"Jeez, Rog." The pushers in these places sold pharmaceuticals laced with rat poison or Drano, guaranteed to cause hallucinations, but more of the 'jump out the window trying to escape the hoard of giant, mutant cockroaches' variety. Whatever the girl thought she saw, she was in trouble. Her fear almost tangible, a circle of empty dance floor had opened around her and stayed that way.

Having experimented too much with, well, everything in high school, Bree could write a book on bad trips. While she never tried to peel herself like a banana, she knew from firsthand experience that your face will fall off if you look in a mirror when you're high on LSD. She once dropped acid before dinner and watched in fascination while her foster mother sliced the mushrooms for lasagna—every now and again popping a piece into her mouth—because the top of her head unhinged like a Pez dispenser to accommodate slices of fungus the size of basketballs.

Bree gave up the habit when she started hallucinating man-sized moths. Moths scared the bejeezus out of her, like the Donnie Darko version a butterfly. With a sigh, Bree marked a straight line through the dancers to Diane.

Laying a hand on the girl's shoulder, she began, "Are you all ri—" before a vision of fire engulfed her.

B.K. RAINE

It disappeared as soon as she jerked her hand away.

Diane still stood transfixed in the middle of the floor, shocking blue eyes red-rimmed and cracked with tears.

Bree reached out to her again and again saw flames as soon as she made contact. Charred dancers whirled around them, stirring ashes with their feet. She pulled her hand away and exhaled in relief as the real world came into focus.

"What the hell?"

A man entered the circle of space around them. He draped a pale wrist over Diane's shoulder and leaned in toward Bree, spilling over his eyes a streak of pale hair, not blond or even white, but a chameleon color that changed with the lights above him. His skin looked like a translucent version of Diane's shirt.

"Go away," he ordered.

"I don't think so."

"You would do well to mind your own business."

"Mind my business? What are you, three?"

The man grabbed her shoulder with bruising force, and the sky began raining fire around them all.

Diane gasped, swung her head from Bree to the stranger. "Who are you?"

"I can see why he doesn't want to share you," the strange man said to Diane.

She pulled a dagger on him. Who carries a dagger to a nightclub? Hell, who carries a dagger? And how did she get past security with it?

He looked at Bree again. "Last chance. Leave."

After a split second of deliberation, Bree grabbed Diane by the arm and ran. She pulled up short when the man appeared again in the parking lot smack dab in the middle of their flight path.

"You are a freaking idiot," he said.

Bree drew a knife of her own, thumbed up the fifty-fifty serrated blade. She kept her voice steady. "You are a dead man if you don't leave us the fuck alone."

Diane went ahead and plunged her dagger right between the

stranger's ribs. Without so much as a grunt, he dissolved like a ghost and reappeared a moment later behind her.

With a thought, Bree tossed Diane's body out of his reach, which happened to be into the side of a parked car, setting the alarm to howling. Which set off half a dozen others nearby.

The stranger winced at the noise, but started advancing on them again. Bree spread her arms and a wave rolled out around her. Every car in the parking lot tipped on two wheels. They came down with a collective clamor and a symphony of alarms. The doors to the Masquerade opened, and first one, then a dozen club-goers poured out in response to the sound.

Salvion glanced at them, then back at Bree. "That show in there was not for you. But if you want to play, we'll play." Then he spread wings, gray as dust, and took flight.

A long while later, after the cars had stopped screaming and the lookie-loos had gone back inside, Bree peeled her eyes off the empty sky to glance back at Diane, who still lay half-sprawled on her ass beside the car, eyeing Bree like she was as much of a monster as the moth man. As soon as they made eye contact, Diane sprang into a crouch, blade tucked against her forearm.

"Seriously? I just saved your ass."

She looked from Bree to the woman-shaped dent in the Honda Civic she'd landed up against and back again. "Did you throw me into a car?"

"Yup."

"Without touching me?"

"Two for two."

She nodded towards the circle of cars; a few were still wailing. "And the rest of them?"

Bree flicked her fingers and the dagger flew out of Diane's hand. "I'll give you three guesses and the first two don't count."

"You're telekinetic."

"Yes. I move shit with my mind. I also saved your ass tonight, and I would really appreciate an explanation as to just what I saved it from. Who the hell was that man?"

"I was going to ask you that question. I saw him at the same time I saw you." She eyed Bree with just enough suspicion to piss her off.

"Did you miss the part about me saving your ass?"

"I don't know you."

"Small fucking world, huh. Roger asked me to keep an eye on you."

"You know Roger?"

She ignored the interruption. "You were wigging the hell out when I found you. When I touched you, well, I don't know what I saw."

"I should have stayed away from him."

"The weird silver guy? Yeah, I'd say he's from the wrong side of the tracks."

"No, Roger. I should never have come here. I knew better than to put him in this kind of danger."

"Oh yeah? This kinda thing happen to you often?"

"No. This was something different."

She exhaled hard enough to lift a lock of hair over her eyes. "Different. That's one word for it. So what's the usual?"

We stood in a parking lot slick with rain and peppered with starlight, both of us sullen and suspicious, while I debated how to answer her. In the end, I asked her to follow me to the Majestic for eggs and coffee.

We shared the restaurant with three others—a kid about eighteen with greasy hair wearing a Meatloaf t-shirt, and a fifty-ish couple who sat reading the *Journal* without speaking to each other in a corner booth close to the bathroom.

"What's your name anyway?" I asked her as soon as we slid into the booth.

"Not much for small talk are you?"

I didn't answer and figured that would be answer enough.

"Bree. My name is Bree."

"Well...I don't know where to start."

She held up one finger for me to wait, retrieved a cigarette from a depleted pack of Marlboro's and fished a lighter out of her left jean pocket.

"I don't think you can smoke in here."

"Ask me if I give a shit." After she had taken a deep drag, she said, "You can start by telling me how you know Rog."

"He's got nothing to do with this."

"We aren't talking about whatever this is yet. How-do-you-know-him?"

"He's a friend."

"I've met all of Roger's friends."

I shrunk a little. "I go to the park sometimes to sketch. We met there, but this is the first time I've seen him…out."

"Yeah, how was the date? I mean, before the whole roof is on fire thing."

"It wasn't a date."

She studied me with her fingers templed for a while. I wondered if she would press me further. "In the parking lot, what did you see?"

"A man becoming insubstantial when my blade cut him. Cars lifting in a circle around you."

"I mean at the end. What did you see when he left?"

I shrugged. "He just vanished."

"That's not what I saw. I saw him turn into a moth the size of a man. It's a long story, what the whole moth-man things means to me, but I'm guessing the burning people means something to you."

"Yeah." It came out like a croak.

"Always thought I was freakishly endowed in the supernatural aptitude department, but apparently this asshole can make people see shit that isn't there. How about you? You shoved a dagger—not a knife, a damn dagger—hilt deep into his chest like it was an everyday thing for you. Stab first, ask questions later. What's your special power?"

I snapped my gaze to the window, to her reflection, my eyes drawn to random blue and pink strands peeking out from underneath her platinum-blonde ringlets. She looked like a rockstar. Bile burned the back of my throat. "I don't guess I have one. I just…. I have no idea how to explain any of this to you. Or if I should even try. You could be hurt. Killed."

"I could kill you right now if I wanted, and I wouldn't get caught. I could kill everyone in this place just by thinking about it." I tensed. She held up a hand. "But I don't, because I'm an OK person. That son of a bitch was *not* an OK person. So I would appreciate knowing just what the hell I've gotten myself into."

"He doesn't want you."

"No, he *didn't* want me. He wanted you and told me to get lost. I didn't. Now I am pretty sure he wants me too."

"I told you this wasn't my usual." I took off my scarf and set it on the table beside me, lifted my head to reveal the twin puncture wounds Desollador had left there. "This is my usual."

She leaned over the table to look at them, spilling cleavage out of her leather tank top. I flinched away when a soft fingertip touched my throat. She didn't seem to notice and probed the wounds anyway. "Are these real?"

"It's a vampire bite."

"I can see that."

"I've been hunting them for three years. A week ago, one started hunting me. Apparently he brought friends."

The waitress had filled our coffee cups. Bree cracked four sugar packets into her coffee like eggs, then stirred in three containers of half-and-half. I munched on my toast in silence, sipped coffee after each bite just for something to do while Bree considered my story.

I heard a throat clear. "Toast and coffee. Really, how many times do I need to tell you to take care of yourself?"

Desollador sat at the table beside us, straddling a chair.

I tried to hide my surprise and then tried to figure out if he had entered without me noticing because I was that distracted or if he had some way to cloak his presence when he wanted. How many more powers could he have?

Bree looked at him with some apprehension, but not even half as much as he deserved. "Get lost. We're in the middle of something."

Ignoring her, Desollador got up and slid into the seat beside me, traced a finger down my throat. "Showing off?"

"Is this supposed to be the vampire?" Bree pointed.

I fished a syringe from my purse. The bullets hadn't worked, but salt in his veins was the only way I knew to kill him, so I had to try. When I plunged it into his femoral artery, he caught my hand in his. A surge of hope coursed through me when he began to shake, but it was only a spasm, which he endured with a growl. As a rule, vampire's scream and puke when they die, so I knew that wasn't about to happen.

Then he smiled, his mouth predatory. "I take it you *like* me angry." In a move so swift I didn't see him make it, he took me, right there in the middle of a diner, none the wiser but the two of us and Bree. Under the table, his fingers with mine slid between my thighs. Then he withdrew. The asshole had taken a *sip* from me. "We'll explore that in more...depth...the next time I visit. Soon."

Bree grabbed her cigarettes with one hand and the edge of the table with the other. "This is too much."

Desollador winked at me as his eyes turned red. To Bree, he said, "Stay."

"Get the fuck out of my mind!"

"My brother said you were a stubborn one."

"Your brother?" I asked, my pulse surging.

"One of them." He studied Bree. "Not a smart move on your part pissing Salli off, but I'd like to see you do it at least once before he kills you."

"What are you doing here?" I asked.

His fingers clamped around the back of my neck. "Reclaiming what's mine."

The waitress noticed he had joined our party and swung by to ask him if he'd like to order. Bree spoke before he had a chance. "I need the check."

Desollador opened his wallet, which seemed like such a mundane thing for a vampire to carry. "The coffee is on me. And bring my friend a plate of eggs and a tall glass of orange juice."

When she left, he said to me, "You know the drill."

I clenched my fists to keep from shaking, and nodded.

I didn't watch him leave, but Bree did, craning her neck as if she could still see through the concrete walls. "So that was the vampire?"

I nodded again.

"What the hell have I gotten myself into?" I thought the question might be rhetorical. She spun around in her seat again to face me. "Will they come after my friends? My family?"

"I don't know." A lie. "Yes."

"I gotta get out of here. I...hell, I don't know what I gotta do, but whatever it is, it's not here. You coming?"

I took a few slow steady breaths, unclenched my fingers. "I can't."

"What do you mean you can't?"

"If I don't finish the damn orange juice he ordered for me, he will follow our waitress home tonight and kill her."

"You got all that from 'you know the drill'?"

The waitress dropped off the orange juice and promised the eggs would be up soon. I waited until she left to answer. "I've been down this road before."

Bree watched me spin the glass in slow circles, my vision blurring. If the sour liquid hit my tongue just then, I'd puke, I just knew it. I didn't know if that would mean an innocent girl's death.

"I have to go," she decided.

"Maybe you should stay with me tonight."

"Really?" Her laughter was unpleasant. "You think I would be safer with you? No thanks. I think I'll try *not* hanging out with a monster magnet for a while."

I wrote my number and address on the back of her receipt.

"Call if you change your mind."

She didn't even look at it, just crumpled it up and stuffed it in a pocket. "Don't take this the wrong way, but stay the *fuck* away from Roger."

I nodded and buried my nose in my glass, sniffing back tears until she had gone, but just barely. Then I cried. The guy in the meatloaf t-shirt and the couple sitting in silence reading the paper pretended not to notice.

I pulled out my phone and scrolled through my contacts until I found Roger's name.

Are you sure you want to delete this contact?

Yes, I'm sure.

Assassins don't have friends. Neither should blood toys.

Bree drove with the windows down, hair lashing at her face. She got Roger's voicemail for the sixth time and this time opted to leave a message.

"Damnit, Roger, call me back. Do not, I repeat, do not go anywhere near Diane until you've talked to me." She tossed the phone in her passenger seat and cranked up something loud and heavy on her radio, then worried she might miss his call, so she turned the radio off. She called twice more before she made it home.

A low-hanging limb in her driveway scraped the top of her car and dropped a leaf through the sunroof, triggering a scream. Her house, a three-bedroom cottage she shared with her ex, was too dark despite the cloud-shrouded moonlight. She swore out loud that Mace still hadn't remembered to replace the damned porch light. "Shit, do I have to do everything myself?"

Her voice sounded too loud, an assault to the silence. When she felt someone watching, stalking her, as she started across the path from driveway to porch, she walked faster. When she imagined matching footfalls, she began to run in earnest, fishing in her pocket for house keys as she went. She was scratching at the lock with the wrong one when a light came on inside.

The front door swung open. Mace shook his head. "Problems? It wasn't even locked."

Bree chanced a look behind her and saw only the distorted shapes of trees, less ominous in the fluorescent light of reality. Mumbling an apology, she slouched into the nearest armchair, welcoming the squeak of leather. "I've had the weirdest fucking night."

"Oh really?"

"Did you know Roger was seeing someone?"

"News to me." He disappeared into the kitchen and reappeared with two beers. Handing one to her, he asked, "Is she hot?"

"What? I dunno. He was at the club with her tonight. They had a thing, and he asked me to look after her."

"A thing?"

Bree waved her hand around her face as if batting away an errant fly. "Thing, ah, fight or something, I'm not sure. I went down to check on her and things got...scary."

Mace leaned back against a trio of cheap terry throw pillows and pressed his palms together. "Is that what you'd call it?"

"Oh, believe me, that's putting it mildly. When I touched her, everything was burning. It looked so real."

"A wonder you made it out alive."

"No, that's the thing, it looked real but I could only see it when I was touching her. Touching: fire. Not touching: no fire."

"Maybe you should have stayed the hell out of it at that point."

Bree slammed her beer down on the side table. "What the hell, Mace?"

"I'm just saying if the party was meant for Diane, maybe it would have been prudent to mind your own damn business when you had the chance."

"I told you, Roger asked..." Bree got it then. "What have you done with him?"

The thing that looked like Mace whistled. "You catch on quick."

"What. Have. You. Done. With. Him?"

Not-Mace shushed her. "There was no one home when I got here."

The hand resting on the sofa back lengthened, paled, translucent skin over ice-blue veins.

In a single move, Bree upended the sleeper and lunged for the door. Salvion did his disappearing act again, reappeared nose-to-nose with her moments later, and slammed her into the upturned furniture. Broken springs punctured her skin in half a dozen places. When she screamed, the world went wild.

The television sputtered through channels possessed, volume increasing with each splenetic flicker. When the noise reached its zenith, a bookshelf opened fire with paperback ammunition. A dog-eared copy of Machiavelli's *The Prince* passed right through his selectively insubstantial form. The coffee table jettisoned its collection of ceramic ashtrays and assorted beer bottles. Then the coffee table itself went flying. Pictures abandoned the walls and broke against hardwood floors. She flung at him anything that wasn't nailed down. Well, it didn't occur to her to throw Mace's recliner. You just didn't mess with a man's recliner.

Salvion kept coming, like a ghost squaring off against a poltergeist. He just wasn't tangible enough for her to hold, even with his fingers wrapped around her throat.

"I usually don't get up close and personal like this. It's kind of nice," he said.

It was by sheer coincidence that a sharp stiletto of broken mirror caught in the maelstrom and pierced his throat. It rendered him substantial in an instant, roaring in pain or anger or both. She scanned the debris and found half a dozen more reflective slivers close at hand. Now that he was solid, she could hold him, though it proved a damn sight more difficult to toss him off of her than it had been to pick up even one of the cars in the Masquerade parking lot. With her last reserve of energy, she threw the remaining shards and him with them. He landed by the front door, ripping at the stiletto protruding from his throat. He vanished the moment he pulled it out. No theatrics or threats that time. He just retreated.

Right about then, Mace opened the door. His dark eyes surveyed the chaos, widening when he saw her. "Are you OK?"

Bree rubbed her hip and winced. "Yeah, I'll live."

"What the fuck happened? Have you called 9-1-1 already?"

"No, and I'm not gonna."

He pulled his phone from his back pocket.

She got to her feet, using the broken couch like a crutch, and took it away before he could finish dialing. "And neither are you."

"The hell I'm not."

When he tried to take his phone back, she stuffed it in her bra. "I know what this looks like. OK, no, I don't know what this looks like, but it isn't whatever you think it is."

He stalked through the mess, lifting delicate pieces of artwork from shattered frames. "Please tell me it isn't about drugs, Bree. Is it about drugs?"

"No, it isn't drugs, but I have a problem. And I'm afraid that might mean you have a problem too."

Mace looked at her through a thick fringe of hair as black as a raven's wing. "You think?"

Bree pulled a crumpled receipt from her pocket and smoothed it between her fingers. "There's someone you need to meet."

CHAPTER 5

How many times had Renn made this trip? Four years? Hell, she was still driving on an intermediate license the first time, nobody but family allowed in the car and not one of them willing to come with her. What for? Hadn't they all wanted out of this little town too? Main Street was the only road running through it, and even that was doornail dead these days. The twins had just been the ones to finally make it out, hopping in Tate's Monte Carlo and hightailing it the hell out of dodge. By now they'd be living the good life in the big city.

Never mind they don't call, they don't text, they're Benevolence's own happily ever after. So what if they left a little sister at home sick with worry? Boys will be boys. Be happy for 'em, Renn. Maybe they'll come back for you one day. Rescue you from a life of topping off coffee cups at Emmie's Place for fifty-cent tips.

Only they didn't leave that day for the big city. They left on some stupid treasure hunt up on Serpent Mountain and, if nobody else would, Renn meant to find out what happened to them up there.

She slowed down for a curve. Her daddy used to say a horse could eat out of its own cart on these turns. She sniffed; *he* would have come with her. Though it was hot as sticky buns outside, Renn drove with the windows down and the heater on high to keep the engine cool. The radio didn't work, but it wouldn't have picked up anything up here on the mountain anyway. No cell reception either. For the tenth time, she looked at her phone.

"9:10," she said to no one.

She dictated the hour twelve more times before she arrived at her destination. It rose up ahead, the driveway grown over with creeping vines, crisscrossed by tree roots the size of railroad ties. The house looked like it once belonged on a plantation, not up on some mountain in the middle of nowhere.

Renn marked the time again, stuffed her phone in her pocket, and got out of the car.

Wind whispered through leaves like the crowd filling the back pews of church on Sunday. Above that, she heard a low scraping. Not a nature sound, but something purposeful, manmade.

It didn't sound like it came from the house, but around the side where an unsteady footpath led to a stairway into the ground. The scraping sound got louder. Shaking, she brandished a can of mace, her finger poised on the trigger and, with careful, silent steps, descended.

The trapdoor stood open at the bottom of the stairway. Renn lowered herself onto her knees, hooked her hands on the doorway and poked her head into the hole. Past the door, a ladder led into a room about the size of a walk-in closet, ceiling so low a tall man would have to bend his head to stand. Sheets of mosaic tiles were stacked up against one wall. She wouldn't have seen them at all if their mirrored surface didn't catch the sun filtering in behind her just so.

The sense of déjà vu, growing since she started the Jetta to make this trip, reached the tipping point as she peered into the cellar. No doubt about it. *I have been here before*, she thought.

That's when he stepped out of the darkness. Trowel in hand, covered in dried grout, he stooped to keep his head of golden brown hair from scraping the ceiling. Renn screamed and jumped away from the door, her tailbone landing forcefully on the bottom stair. The man climbed the ladder with startling quickness.

"Renn."

Her name, coming out of this stranger's mouth, sounded damned familiar but she couldn't quite place it. In fact, she heard a buzzing static where the memory should be. She scrambled backwards, upwards, still on her hands and backside.

He followed her, making shushing noises with his hands. "It's OK. You don't have to be afraid. But you can't keep coming up here."

I knew it. "Who are you?"

"It's better that you don't know."

"What do you know about my brothers?"

He touched her arm, and she wanted to slap his hand away, but sensed he was about to say something intimate—important—and she didn't want to ruin it. "They're gone."

"No. No!"

He pulled her into his arms, and she felt torn between anxiety about a stranger hugging her and the growing certainty that he was not a stranger. "Your brothers are dead. I'm sorry."

She realized then that she knew that too. "I want to see their bodies."

"We've been through this all before, Renn." He heaved the cellar door shut, pulled her up the staircase out into the brutal sun. "I didn't want to have to do this again, but you've left me no choice."

She looked up into his eyes to see what he meant and watched them turn from a pleasant hazel to a deep, alarming russet. She tensed to run, but he held onto her wrist and lifted it up to his lips, like he would kiss her there. His hair fell over his face. Then came an intense sting, and she began to fall. Not literally—as he held her upright—but above and around her, the world spun away. Her reason for being there spun away.

"Renn, look at me." His russet eyes filled up her vision. "That's it."

Those eyes were too close, too far inside her. She squirmed.

"Shh-shh. Your brothers just took off one day, up and left. But wherever they are, they're happy now; you know that in your heart. They are so, so happy. And you are happy for them. That keeps you from missing them too much. You have no need to come up here ever again. Do you understand?"

Is that right? "Happy."

"That's right. Your brothers are happy. And you are going to leave this place and never come back."

"I'm ... I'm leaving?"

She didn't remember him walking her to her car, but he must have because he opened her door. "That's right. You can't come back here. Every time you do, you put yourself in danger."

Renn figured out how the key fit into the ignition and started the engine.

"Forget this ever happened," he said. "Forget you were ever here."

"Forget…"

"And get out of this town, Renn. Something bad is coming. You've inconvenienced me for years, but I don't want to see anything happen to you. Just leave."

She drove back down the mountain at twenty-five miles an hour, in second gear all the way and riding the brakes hard enough the rotors were glowing by the time she made it to level ground. She could smell them just sitting in her driveway now.

Slumped over the steering wheel, she sobbed. How many times had she made this trip in four years? How many brake pads replaced? How many tanks of gas wasted on a drive she couldn't even remember making?

She went inside and bee-lined it to the kitchen for a granola bar. When had she last eaten? What time was it anyway? She grabbed her phone from her pocket, looked at the screen, a red flashing circle in the middle looking back at her. She tapped it once. The circle turned black, and underneath it these words:

Recording length – 1 hour 38 minutes.

I was sitting on my bed trying to figure out how many changes of clothing to cram into my suitcase when a barrage of fists came at my door. I stood up too quickly; imaginary gnats blinked in and out of my vision. *Whoa.* Figuring my enemies wouldn't bother with the formality of the knock, I opened without checking the peephole. Bree stood in the hall, platinum-blonde ringlets dripping rainwater, rouged lips set in a tight grimace.

"You don't answer your phone," she said.

I shrugged. I'd been busy. "I'm not used to anyone calling."

"Can we come in?"

"Who's this?" I nodded at the man beside her. Short black hair framed a harsh, chiseled face.

He advanced a bronzed forearm toward me. "Excuse me. *This* is a friend of Bree's."

I looked at his outstretched hand and back to his eyes—his scowl—before turning away from them both, flinging the door away from me as I went. I didn't see who stopped it from slamming, but Bree spoke next.

"Don't be an asshole, Mace. Diane, this is Roger's brother."

I ignored the wrenching pain in my gut and glanced back over my shoulder. "Sooo nice to meet you."

He still scowled, with both arms locked over his chest now. "Sorry, rough night."

"Huh, it's going around."

"Can we come in?" Bree asked again.

"Sure. Yes." Was I supposed to offer them a drink? That's what always happens in the movies. "I've got tap water and V8...if you're thirsty."

They shared a look I couldn't quite read. *Crap, I must be doing it wrong.* I gathered up an armful of laundry from the sofa and tossed it into my bedroom. The movement made the gnats come back. Just for a second. "Have a seat. If you want."

Mace sat and covered his nose with the back of his fingers. "Jeez. Do you have stock in Clorox?"

"Huh?"

"Never mind. Bree, tell her."

I had only one sofa in the living room. Was I supposed to sit on it with them? That seemed weird, and I wasn't sure the coffee table was sturdy enough to hold me, so I grabbed a chair from the kitchen table and sat in it sideways, hooking one arm through its back to keep myself from swaying. Desollador was right. I did need to take better care of myself.

Would it be impolite if I had a glass of juice if they didn't?

"Tell me what?"

"Bad news. Salli knows where I live. Where *we* live."

"He came after you tonight?"

"He came after me wearing Mace's face."

The gnats this time came with a buzzing too. "Damn. Did he let you go, or did you fend him off?"

"No, I hurt him, but it was pure effin luck. Get this. I throw a couch at him, and it goes right through him like he wasn't there. But I hit him with a few pieces of broken mirror, and he's bleeding. Figure that one out."

I needed to get that juice. "That's more than we knew last night. That's good."

Mace got up, moved toward the balcony until he stood in the path of the open door, and took a deep breath. I never noticed the bleach fumes were so strong. Was I just accustomed to them after so many years?

"What about you?" I asked him. "Did he come after you?"

"Nope. I came in, the house was thrashed. Bree tells me she's in trouble and since this guy 'borrowed' my face, that probably means I am too. I can't decide if she's batshit or messing with me."

"Great, he's a skeptic," I said to Bree. "I don't have the time — or the desire — to prove to someone else that vampires are real. And, quite frankly, that would be the easy part. That's the only one of these *things* I even have a name for."

"Vampires aren't real."

"Mace, is it? OK, I'll go through this as quickly as I can. No, I don't have stock in Clorox. I get a lot of blood — mine and vampire — on my clothes, and a gallon of bleach is cheaper than replacing my wardrobe. This," I said, lifting my hair off my neck, "is a real, honest to goodness, vampire bite. Your friend here saved my ass tonight from a monster that can apparently manipulate reality so you see your worst nightmares come to life before your very eyes. And she can also, in case you didn't know, pick up a few hundred cars with her mind. Are you following?"

Now he laughed. "I was worried, Bree. I really thought you had gone batshit on me. And you better be glad I love you, or I would be so pissed right now that you trashed the house for the sake of a prank."

"Mace, don't hate me."

"No, I told you, it's cool. I'm just glad you're not crazy." He shot upwards with such momentum that watching him made me feel like I was falling. One minute he stood in the doorway, the next he clung to the ceiling like Spiderman. "What the—"

"She's telling the truth," Bree said. "We are both telling the truth."

He went still, his voice very, very low. "Put. Me. Down."

When she did, he didn't move for a long while, and it seemed wrong—dangerous—to be the one to break the silence. He stared at Bree, his hands clenching and releasing. Then he started to pace, or something that was like a pace, but more threatening for the way he kept swinging that wary expression between her and me as he walked.

Bree finally broke the silence. "Talk to me, Mace."

"I've known you for how many years? I slept in your bed for two of them...and you never told me."

"It's not something I tell people."

"You didn't tell *me*!"

"Hey, hey, don't do this here. Please." I scooted over to the sofa and sunk against the armrest. "I've been bled three times in the last twenty-four hours, and I haven't had a good night's sleep in two weeks. I can't deal with human crap on top of that."

"Human crap. Really," said Mace.

Bree chewed on the stem of her sunglasses and drummed her fingers on the sofa. "I don't believe this."

"That makes two of us," said Mace. But he did. He believed it, because he started pacing again.

"Can I smoke in here?" Bree asked. "I mean, I can go out on the balcony."

"No, it's OK. Hold on." I took that opportunity to grab the bottle of V-8 and fetched her a coffee cup I never liked much anyway. "I don't have an ashtray."

"Thanks. So do you know anything about this guy? I know you

said you didn't, but obviously vampire boy knew him, so there has to be something you can tell me."

"I have dreams that tell me where to hunt, a voice that tells me how to fight. But I never knew where it came from until yesterday. She's...." I wrapped a strand of hair around my finger and let it go. "She's dead now, but she was a witch, and she accidentally created a monster."

"How do you accidentally create a monster?"

"She was trying to make a man."

Bree blew a long streamer of smoke. "Oh, well, in that case."

"But she created a monster instead, one I haven't actually met yet. His name is Edward."

I looked at Bree to gauge her reaction. She raised a fist in the air and mouthed 'yay'.

"It was a mistake; she's been trying to fix it ever since."

"As a ghost," Mace clarified.

"This Edward has linked himself somehow to the other creatures, monsters," I continued. "Desollador, Salvion, and a demon named Kayin. If they were immortal before, now they are invincible. If there is a way to kill them, she doesn't know it. Which means I don't know it. But she says there may be a way to stop them."

"How do you stop what you can't kill?" Bree wondered, then let out a bitter laugh. "I cannot believe I am having this conversation."

"It gets less surreal over time."

"That sucks."

"Yeah."

"So how do we stop what we can't kill?"

I was about to tell her when from the kitchen, Mace exclaimed, "I'll just be damned."

We both turned to look at him. "What is it?"

"Your last name is Woods?"

He held a large Priority Mail envelope. I nodded. "Yes, why?"

"D. Woods."

"Yes, my last name is Woods. Why is that important?"

He spun the envelope. I recognized it as Protector. Pointing at the mailing label, he said, "McClain Designs."

"Yes?"

Bree gasped. "No way."

"Small fucking world, ain't it?" he said to her.

"What are you talking about?"

With a laugh, he tore open the envelope. I started to protest, but decided I'd just let it play out.

He slid the cardboard out with a reverence that surprised me and placed it on the counter. With index fingers and thumbs pressed at ninety-degree angles against two corners, he lifted the top layer to reveal the piece. "What are you calling it?"

"Protector," I answered. Bree joined him at the counter in examination of it. I stood, but didn't follow.

Mace turned, gave me an unsettling smile, and closed the distance between us. He extended that bronzed forearm out to me for the second time that evening and said, "Mace McClain. Terrible to finally meet you, Ms. Woods."

I stared at his outstretched hand like it might bite me. "Holy crap."

Catherine had been a ghost so long, she could scarcely remember being anything else, had been stuck not quite in this world or the next, invisible except where barriers of consciousness were weak. Even after so many years gaining strength and learning the limits of her ghost flesh, she remained an incomplete apparition in the waking world—a disembodied voice, a spectral image with no voice at all, or just an icy manifestation of emotion.

In absence of tangibility, Catherine observed. She stalked and plotted, moved her pieces around like pawns on a chessboard. With great, patient effort, she influenced her soldiers with myriad whispers that planted themselves like seeds in their subconscious minds. These bloomed into vast orchards disguised as accidental forests. From within the design, her pieces could see no discernible pattern, but Catherine hadn't been on that side in a long while.

She didn't have time for such subtleties now. She didn't have time for Diane to sleep, for the veil to lift so they could speak. One of her trees would be cut down tonight, and she must stop it.

Catherine reached for Diane and wished, not for the first time, that she possessed a poltergeist's ability to manipulate matter. *There is somewhere you need to be. Now. You must hurry!*

"Terrible to finally meet you, Ms. Woods," Mace said.

Hurry. You have to hurry.

Diane showed no sign of hearing her. "Holy crap. Mace McClain?"

Mace nodded. "Gotta say, I always thought your art was seriously twisted. I pictured some goth chic with bad makeup and lots of candles."

"Is that who buys it?"

Bree snickered.

He shot her a dark glance and answered, "Some of it."

"He keeps most of them," Bree said.

There is somewhere else you need to be right now!

Diane's brows furrowed. She glanced away and then back again. "I'm glad someone likes them. I despise them, but they're important."

You have to save him! Hurry!

"Why?" Mace asked.

You are wasting time!

"They remind me why it's a bad idea to have friends."

Bree rolled her eyes. "Give me a break. Get over yourself."

Hurryhurryhurryhurry…

"We got off subject anyway. Catherine said there is a way to stop them."

Mace closed his eyes and rubbed his temples. "By them, you mean the vampire, the demon, the moth-man and the undefined monster named Edward?"

"How do we stop what we can't kill?" Bree asked for a third time.

"I have no idea, but I know where to find the answers. I have to go back to Benevolence."

That's right, Benevolence. Remember the dream, Diane. There was more to it than answers, than going home. What did you bring back with you? Where are they?

"Benevolence?" Bree asked.

"You wouldn't know the place. But that's where I'm headed."

Mace still held his head. "Because of a dream."

Look at what you brought back!

Diane rubbed her thumb across her palm and fingers, once, twice, like trying to feel for something that wasn't there.

Yes, you held them in your hands. You brought them back. The little toy car, the plastic fruit, and my note.

"Yes, because of —"

Go get them, Diane. You need to hold them in your hands again. Read my words.

"Yes, because of a dream. I...hold on a minute."

No matter what. Hold on. Holdonholdonholdon.

Diane left Mace and Bree staring after her as she made a dash for the bedroom and scooped up the objects from beneath her bed. She scattered the plastic fruit across the covers, picked up the toy car and gave it an experimental roll across her palm. Finally the note was in play.

"What are you doing now?" Bree stood just inside the doorway with her hands on her hips.

"It wasn't just a dream. I brought things back with me from it."

"Things?"

"Toys and a note...from the prophet, Catherine."

"From a dream?"

Diane flipped the note over, read the four new lines on the back. "Yes, from a dream. Do either of you know how to get to Winterville Drive?"

Mace joined Bree in the doorway and barked, "Why?"

"Because that's where I'm going to kill a vampire...maybe more than one."

"That's Roger's place," Bree answered.

The note read:

> *205 Winterville Drive*
> *Salt in their veins to kill*
> *Hurry*

I felt for a brief moment elated. Finally, a vampire I knew how to kill!

Then I noticed the wicked anger in Bree's pretty green eyes. "That's Roger's place."

I popped a snap on my belt and tossed her my backup knife, hilt first. "You're welcome to come."

"Damn right I'm coming." She examined the serrated blade. "Will this kill them?"

I shook my head. "The amethyst makes them weak. Salt is the only thing that kills them."

A syringe went into her back pocket, the knife in her waistband. She raised an eyebrow at Mace. "You still think I'm batshit?"

He pointed at me. "I think *she's* batshit."

"So you coming?"

"Why not? Let's go trash Rog's place next."

The storm that had been threatening us for days rained down holy hell as we departed. A steady, driving torrent carved streams from ditches, made rivers of highways. The wind blew in stuttered gusts. Traffic lights, held parallel to the ground by squally, invisible hands, watched the pavement with flashing yellow eyes. Fangs of lightning punctured the sky. Thunder came with a low growl that rumbled in the darkness until proximity made it a roar.

Roger opened the door in bare feet, hair tousled, wearing a lopsided smile. "Diane. How did you know where I lived? I mean, it's good to see you." His expression faltered when he saw who was with me. "Oh, hey guys. You wanna come in? Get out of the rain?"

I pushed past him and scanned the living room for signs of anything amiss. Finding nothing, I started clearing rooms, shutting and locking windows and doors behind me. Roger followed me as far as the hallway. "Uh, what's going on?"

"There are vampires coming here tonight to kill you." Slices of sky lit up through his mini blinds, the scent of sulfur close behind.

Roger's gaze swung from me to Bree to Mace in silent inquiry.

Mace shrugged. "You got me, dude."

Roger opened his mouth, but I held up my hand before he could speak. "Does your attic have stairs?"

"Uh, no. Just a pass through."

I knelt and opened my duffel, withdrew a roll of duct tape and ran long strips along the joints of the bedroom door. I did the same to the attic access.

Roger watched me redecorate his place with an expression of awe, like he wanted to ask me what I was doing, but feared the interruption might scare me away. Mace and Bree watched too, but Mace laughed silently at me and shook his head while Bree rubbed her hands on her thighs and paced.

Roger broke the silence. "Is this going to keep the vampires out?" He spoke to me like I was a child going on about monsters in her closet.

I rolled my eyes and tore a strip of tape the length of my forearm, pressed it to the outside of one of the door frames, then tore it away, stuck it back down, then tore it away again. "Nothing's going to keep the vampires out. This is going to make them noisy."

"OK, this is a joke right?"

"Why do people always ask that question?" I said to myself. "This is why I can't have a relationship, Roger. This is what I do."

"You're a vampire hunter."

The wind howled outside, echoing my frustration. "Just, Christ, just let me work."

"Shouldn't we leave? Why would we just wait to be attacked?" Bree asked.

"Do I look like I'm just waiting?"

"If you know vampires are coming here, why not be somewhere else when they get here?"

I grimaced and ignored her. Another reason not to have relationships. They required too many explanations, too much talking in general. What's the problem with silence? "I tried that. And ended up on a date with Roger I had no business being on in the first place and putting three people in danger that shouldn't even know vampires exist. I know where these things are going to be tonight — here — and that gives me an advantage. Leave, and I lose it. You wanna help, grab some furniture and block the doors and windows."

I jumped when the sofa stood up and slammed into the front door. Bree made furniture seem pissed-off.

"What the hell was that?" asked Roger.

I let Mace bring him up to speed on the whole telekinesis thing.

Once I rigged the place sufficiently for alarm, I finished doling out syringes. Roger held his like I'd given him a heroine needle. "It's saltwater," I said. "This is how you kill a vampire."

He slid it onto the kitchen counter. "Sure it is."

I let it go. It would be nice if they could defend themselves, but aside from Bree, these were potential victims — who wouldn't be in this mess if I had stayed the hell away from Roger. I owed it to them to eliminate the threat.

Mace made a shushing motion and bent his ear to one of the doors. "I'll be damned. I think something just broke a window in there." He narrowed his eyes at me. "You know, you could be behind all this."

"We don't have time for me to prove I'm not."

"Fine, but I'd rather face a burglar with a gun than a needle."

I pulled the Judge from its holster. "It's loaded with shot, so mind the spread. At three yards, that's about two feet. Use it up close or not at all."

I favored shotgun shells because of their spread, but knives and needles were almost always more effective. The problem with guns is that they are best suited for distance combat, and the only way to kill a vampire is up close, so close you have to kill or be killed. The other problem with guns is that they make noise when you chamber a round, when the cylinder or magazine advances, when the trigger breaks, and when the hammer drops. Vampires can move faster than sound, so if you make noise, they will dodge or disarm you.

Mace took up a position beside the door. Over his shoulder, he whispered to Roger. "I don't know what's coming through that door, buddy, but we are not alone."

Roger glanced at the syringe, but didn't make any attempt to pick it up, instead hefting a baseball bat from the hall closet. I suppressed an eye-roll.

The front door bucked with a groan; the sofa toppled. My pulse slowed, vision sharpened. I took a deep breath and said, "Stay close and tight."

Mace shook his head and held his ear to the door. "He's not in there anymore."

I wanted to ask how he knew that, but we were out of time. As much as it galled me to do it, I had to trust his instincts. "They're trying to scatter us. This is just intimidation."

As if to prove my point, the attic access door came crashing down between us, a gaping void of duct tape and darkness. Mace fired three times up into the hole. Apparently he no longer suspected he was the butt of a joke. The house went quiet again, or maybe I just couldn't hear any noise over the ringing in my ears.

The lights went out. Emergency flashlights plugged into several wall outlets popped on, illuminating us in a soft white light. Roger made to grab one.

I held his arm. "No. If you hold the light, it only makes it easier to find you and ties up one of your hands. Take. The. Syringe."

"What do I do with it?"

"Keep it palmed until you have no choice but to use it."

Mace sniffed the air. "They aren't up there anymore either."

I would have asked that time, but Bree slammed the sofa back into the front door before I had the chance. She took up position in the living room, the static in the air making her hair stand on end, eyes wide and searching. The ceiling bucked above her like the door, but this time it gave. A dark shape fell, landing on her back. Mace and I abandoned our post in the hallway at a dead run.

The vampire pinned her hands and drove his knee into the back of her head. Mace lifted the Judge, his finger on the trigger.

I knocked it out of his hand. The shot went wide. "Idiot! You'll kill them both. Mind the fucking spread."

The look in his eyes declared he wanted to kill me instead. I drew my dagger and leapt into the fray. The vampire rolled, pulling Bree in front of him like a shield so that the tip of my dagger aimed at her breast.

I flipped my wrist to lay the blade against my forearm, but she took the hilt in her sternum anyway.

The vampire grabbed both of my elbows, pinning Bree and my dagger between us. I lifted my feet—straddling her—and braced them on his thighs, pushing with all my strength in an effort to gain leverage.

Mace dove for the gun, rolled, and came up with it pressed against the vampire's temple, who let go of my arm—unfortunately not the one holding my dagger—and launched Mace across the room before he could take the shot. At the same time, I heard duct tape ripping and screamed, "Roger!"

Bree looked at the blade between us, then at me with an expression of anger—I couldn't decide if she meant it for me or the vampire—then back at the blade. It peeled out of my fingers and slammed into my free hand. I laid the blade across her shoulder under the cover of her hair. When the vampire seized my elbow again and pulled it towards him, the blade sank into his throat.

He released us both and tried to pull himself off the dagger. Bree sidestepped and slipped out from between us. I closed the distance, pressed him up against the sofa, and heard Roger scream behind me. Bree abandoned me then, presumably to save him.

I was sliding a syringe from my duty belt when I first heard my attacker's voice. "Hi, Diane."

I almost dropped the needle. My chest constricted. It had been four years since I heard that voice. "No. Can't be."

My dream came rushing back to me—Renn with pointy pink ears peeking out from her pixie cut, then later wearing a black dress of mourning that looked all wrong on her, pushing a toy Monte Carlo into my hand. How could I have forgotten?

Tate. My first crush, my ride to school when I missed the bus, my best friend's brother. I looked up to meet his eyes, and my vision blurred. "No, please. Not you."

"It's been a long time. You grew up pretty."

"What's happened to you? Why?"

"I had no choice."

"Oh Christ, it was your Monte Carlo that Desollador was driving."

He smiled in a way that broke my heart. "It's his now."

"I don't...." My mind reeled. "I don't understand."

"He is my Sire, Diane. He created me; he controls me. If you let me go, I'm gonna kill all of your friends." He paused. "You can't let me go."

I wanted to explain that I didn't have any friends — not anymore, not since Benevolence. "No, you don't have to do that. You don't have to kill anybody. We can—"

He covered my hand, the hand holding the syringe. "Everything is Desollador's now."

Christ, how could I fix this? My tears flowed uninhibited. What was I supposed to do? "Not everything is his. Not you. Not anymore."

I plunged the syringe home with an anguished cry and watched him convulse. His body contorted in what I imagined to be mind-blowing agony. He started to vomit in great heaving spasms. The sounds of the fight behind me filtered through my grief, and the identity of the second vampire dawned on me.

"No,no,no,no," I chanted as I sprinted to the other end of the house. I wanted to be the one to do it. The twins deserved to be put down by someone who loved them. I owed at least that much to the best friend I left behind.

The three of them outnumbered the vampire. Though Roger hit walls more often than flesh, he wailed away with that damned baseball bat with the futile determination of an attack poodle. Bree threw anything that wasn't structurally necessary to the house at him. I wondered why she didn't just throw *him*. Then Mace raised the gun.

125

I screamed at him to stop, saw his finger on the trigger twitch, and knew I would be too late. I needed to be closer. I needed him to listen. I needed to have that gun instead of the damned syringe. I needed him to waste the last bullet.

With that thought, the syringe tumbled from my hand. I lost all feeling in the hand holding it, and gained it in the hand holding the gun — Mace's hand. I could feel the weight of it in my palm, the pressure of my finger on the trigger.

Just as I felt the break, my will and those physical sensations merged, and the shot — the last round — missed.

I exhaled, and sensation flooded into my arm through the tips of my fingers. *My* fingers. I drew another syringe. The vampire watched me advance with hungry, brick-red eyes.

The next sequence of events happened so fast. He slammed Bree's face into the wall. The debris under her command fell to the floor the moment she lost consciousness. The vampire clamped a hand on Mace's shoulder. I blinked, and he was feeding. I blinked again, and he was doubled over spitting blood from his mouth.

He shook his head and said to Mace, "Cousin. Why didn't you say so?"

Mace looked at me, holding his neck. "What the hell?"

I shook my head. I knew he wasn't a vampire, else his wound would be healing already. Maybe he was some distant relative of the twins? That made no sense, and anyway, if family was off-limits, I'd never heard about it. I filed it away for later consideration.

"Noah." Our eyes met; a spark of recognition lit in his and then died.

He lunged, and I let him take me down. He was too hungry for strategy. If I appeared to submit (or be defeated), he would cease to consider me a threat. That meant letting him feed. I turned my head to the side.

"Nice. Gentle." I heard him whisper, and he tried. Still, he did not have Desollador's power to take away my pain, so it hurt, a lot.

I tried to be gentle too when I slid the dagger into his side. He gasped, drew back. He offered no resistance when I rolled him onto his back. "Noah, look at me."

He did, and he recognized me. "You're some badass vampire hunter now, huh?"

"I'm sorry."

"It's not your fault. Is Renn doing alright?"

I felt the corners of my mouth droop. "I don't know. I haven't seen her since I started hunting."

"Don't tell her."

I nodded. "When did this happen to you?"

"When we woke them up."

I wanted to save him. I wanted to figure out some way he could live as a vampire without killing, but I remembered what Tate had said. Desollador turned them. Everything was his. They were his. The only freedom I could give them was death.

"I'm going to put them back down, I promise."

Then I killed him. One of the few and last friends I'd ever had.

Diane's house did not have the settled feeling of a home. The closets looked seldom used, her clothing sorted and dumped in plastic laundry baskets. She had some leftover Chinese takeout and two bottles of V8 in her fridge. Desollador smiled at that and felt his teeth throb.

The bathroom smelled of lavender and blood. His teeth throbbed again, and that wasn't all. He wanted to see his mark on her thigh when he spread her legs. But she had mutilated herself to be rid of it. He was contemplating whether he ought to try again when he felt the death.

One of his own, there and then just…gone. It felt like a memory slipping away, so fast he couldn't quite grasp the details. Who had he lost? He'd have to make another soon. His breed line increased his own power, and already Diane had come so close to decimating it. Rage would have been appropriate considering the loss, but he could rebuild an army. If he lost Diane, she would be *gone*. He wanted to taste her again, never satisfied with what little she could yield before her heart stuttered.

Then he did taste her on his tongue, not just the thought of her this time; one of his own was feeding. From her! His fingers tightened on the sink until the porcelain shattered under them. *Mine!*

Desollador reached his mind out to her, searching. *Where are you, Pet?*

An icy fear crept into his chest. Toiletries shattered on tile as he swept them off the vanity.

Slim white button-up shirts rained down like feathers, and half-finished sketches made sounds like sails flapping as they hit the floor. When he found among the mess the note bearing Roger's address on her pillow, he ran.

My new companions gawked at me while I cried over Noah.

Mace—who between the three of them had the most cause for anger—knelt down beside me and asked, "Did you know him? I mean, before…."

I nodded, but didn't trust myself to speak.

Roger hugged the baseball bat. "Shit, we have to call the police."

Bree sat him down. "Shut up Roger."

Mace pressed on. "Both of them?"

I nodded again. "Their sister was my best friend."

"So they're from your hometown?"

"They woke him up. It makes sense now. I mean, why me and why I have to go back there to end it."

He put his arm around me. I went still. Part of me wanted to tuck my head into his shoulder and cry. The other part—the more familiar part—wanted to bolt. We stayed like that for a long while, until my eyes were dry and my breathing had steadied. I felt his weight shift like he was about to get up, and couldn't decide if I felt relief or disappointment. Then he leaned close to my ear and said in a low voice, so that no one else could hear, "If you ever possess me, if you take control of so much as a finger of mine again, I will rip your fucking head off."

I remembered the gun—remembered the feeling of it in my hand—and looked at him with wide eyes. "Is that what I did?"

He lifted his arm off my shoulders and rubbed his temples in a familiar show of frustration. His tone was less threatening when he said, "Just don't do it again."

That was how Desollador found us. Shoulder to shoulder, kneeling over a dead vampire.

"I see you saved me the trouble of killing him, Pet."

I resisted the call in his voice to look at him. Or even to look behind me as I heard the house caving in on him.

"Quit it," he snapped at Bree. "Sleep." And just like that, she did.

Damnit, was there any one of us the vampire could not control? He didn't bother to swoon Mace, just snatched him up from beside me, slammed a fist into his head, and dropped him in a boneless lump on the floor. I looked for Roger, but he was gone. He must have hid when he saw Desollador. Just as well. He couldn't help me anyway.

I still crouched over Noah's body when Desollador wrapped my braid around his fist and pulled me to my feet. I aimed my dagger blind. He disarmed me and told me to open my eyes. I refused. My cheek exploded in pain, and I did as he told me. Then I saw something in his eyes that terrified me.

"Take off your clothes," he said.

"Go to hell."

"You are covered in Noah's blood. I will not allow his scent to remain on your body. Take them off."

"What? No." Was the vampire jealous?

"If I have to ask again, I will kill one of your friends for my trouble. And you will *still* take them off!"

"You aren't asking at all."

"Diane," he warned.

I stole a glimpse at Mace and Bree, both still out cold. Then I turned my back on the vampire and started unbuttoning my blouse. When I made it down to only my underthings, he decided I was naked enough, or else he had just waited as long as he was willing. He pressed himself against my back and me against the sofa, which still leaned on its side against the front door. I trembled at his breath on my neck.

"Mine." Threading his fingers through mine, he commanded, "Lay your head on your shoulder."

My gut twisted. "Desollador, please."

"Diane, you *will* submit. This is one time I suggest you do it the easy way."

I trembled with humiliation when I gave him what he wanted, wincing with pain when his teeth broke skin. Like a caught bird, I flapped and fluttered in his palms.

Be still, Pet. I am not in control of the hunger tonight. This is why I killed that little whore before coming for you the first time. It is dangerous for you.

His admission did nothing to assuage my fear. I wasn't ready to die. Not when everything had just started to make sense.

Fangs withdrew, lips trailing across the back of my neck, then sank in again on the other side. I flinched, cried out. He pressed my hand to my mouth to silence me. His other found my belly and pulled me hard against him. With the pain came a sudden twisting, lower, where his palm rode my pelvis. He pulled his mouth away and turned me to face him, nudging his head under my chin. I tensed for it and he chuckled, which somehow relieved me, even when his teeth broke skin again. When he bit me on my breast — through the thin satin of my bra — I realized he wasn't feeding, not much. He was marking.

His teeth grazed a nipple, then came a searing pain — the sharpest yet — that didn't last. The vibration of his laughter against that tender bud nearly undid me.

You like a little pain with your pleasure, Pet. Or didn't you know that?

As soon as he released my breast, he demanded in a low voice, "Tell me you like it."

I steadied my breathing. "No."

"Lie down."

When I hesitated, he turned toward Bree.

"OK, OK. I'm doing it."

I clenched my fists as he laid himself on top of me, rolled down the waistband of my panties and nipped at my pelvis. "Tell me you like it."

"I don't know what I like."

He did not look pleased. "Then let's find out."

He spent the next hour, the next very long hour, doing just that. Sometime later, I passed out, having lost a little too much blood to care about minor violations.

I woke to the sound of Bree, Roger and Mace arguing. I had not known how lonely my life had gotten until then. It was a comfort to be surrounded by people, so I decided to play dead a little longer to enjoy their company.

"We can't call an ambulance. What will we tell them?" Sounded like Mace.

"That she was making out with a vampire, and he got carried away." Definitely Roger, a very bitter Roger.

"I think she's fine." This from Bree. "She's breathing steady enough."

"With this many bite marks? How would she be fine? How would she even be alive?"

"She's alive because he let her go. We're alive because he let us go."

"Why would he do that?"

"I don't know, because he's bored? It's just a damned game to him."

"Like hell," Roger said. "You didn't see them. They were...intimate."

"How would you know?" I asked, finally opening my eyes to join the conversation. "Were you watching?" He didn't answer. "Because if you were, you saw him force me. You saw him threaten to kill all of you if I didn't play."

"You didn't look forced to me."

I felt my eyes start to water and tapped the tears back down with anger, a lot of it. "Well you sure as hell didn't try to be my knight in shining armor, did you?"

"You brought these things into my home. You let them hurt my friends—"

"I killed them to save you!" I screamed. "They were *my* friends, and I killed them."

"Your friends, huh? I thought you said you couldn't have friends."

"Roger—" Bree started.

"No, he's right. Look what happens to them. For what it's worth, I'm sorry I ever spoke to you that day at the food truck."

He looked for a moment injured, then insulted. "Right back at ya."

Mace held up a hand between us. "So where are the bodies? If what I remember happening tonight actually did, we should be knee-deep in gore. Did it all just vanish?"

Despite the movie myths, vampires do not turn to dust when they die. They leave awful messes. "Desollador must have cleaned up after."

"Why?" I decided it must be Mace's favorite word.

"They—or he—always clean up after me. I guess dead vampires might attract the wrong kind of attention."

Mace considered my explanation and nodded. "How do we know we can trust you?"

I shivered, remembering I had little more than my own blood covering me. "I don't know what to tell you. Do or don't. I will be in Benevolence by sundown and hopefully by morning it won't matter. But first I gotta go back to my place and get some rest."

Roger sighed. "Crap, sorry. I don't mean to be a jerk. Do you wanna borrow some clothes?"

I nodded, grateful for his offer, and followed him into a small bedroom where he started rummaging through piles of dirty clothes in search of something clean. When he'd found a crumpled pair of Levi's only a little worse for wear and a faded Henley, he asked, "So those are bite marks?"

"Yes."

"There are a lot of them."

"Yes."

"Shouldn't you have lost more blood? Couldn't he have killed you?"

"I guess."

"So how come—"

"He wasn't feeding. He was playing."

"He didn't...."

So I guess he didn't watch the whole thing. "No, he didn't."

"That's good." Strange small talk. "Do they hurt?"

"A little."

"Hmmm.... Seems like they would hurt. What about when he's...you know...drinking."

"Sometimes he blocks the pain."

"Why would he do that?"

Small talk had started to feel like a good cop interrogation. I could have lied to avoid self-incrimination, but saw no point in withholding the peculiar dynamics of my monster/Assassin relationship now, only to be deserted when he found me out later. "So I'll like it."

For a few seconds, he seemed too stunned to speak, his eyes fluttering over me, recalling the places he'd seen teeth marks before he'd covered me up. Then he stammered, "Oh...well...oh." He presented me with clothes, stretching out his arms to avoid physical contact with me, attempted a casual smile and ducked out of the room while I dressed.

Desollador had left me pocked with bite marks, aching in body and soul, a little lightheaded and weary to my core. Just getting dressed seemed like such a laborious task that I fantasized about crawling into a pile of Roger's dirty clothes to sleep until he came for me, but I had to get to Benevolence before Desollador attacked again. I shoved myself in the borrowed outfit so I could hurry off to fight a battle I had no idea how to win. To do less would be to abandon three innocents into whose homes and lives I had delivered this evil. That may have been the very reason Desollador had let them go, to ensure I would play his game. Otherwise I might have just given up.

In the hallway, outside the bedroom, I heard Roger's voice. "...actually liked it, him biting her, and not just on her neck you know. It's not like I was looking, but I saw." A sound that might have been a shiver. "She gets off on him drinking her blood."

"I don't know what you saw, but I watched her kill two vampires here tonight," Bree said. "I did not see her enjoying herself."

"I don't trust this girl, Bree. One look at her artwork and it's apparent that something is deeply broken inside her.

"If she did enjoy what that vampire did to her tonight, well, even if she is on the right side of the line now, how can we know she won't cross it later?"

"She's been at this all alone for years. Would you blame her for being a little...confused?"

"You mean crazy," Roger said.

"I mean lonely."

"But she actually liked—"

The squeak of the bedroom door cut him off. "Don't ask questions unless you can handle the answers," I said. "I don't give a damn what you do, any of you, but stay the hell away from me. Whatever opinion you have of me, save it. I don't want your allegiance. I've bled too much for people like you over the past three years to listen to this crap. I will not explain every dirty, shameful feeling to people who have spent less than twenty-four hours in my world."

I sighed, shook my head. *Life is too short to hate people I barely know.* "Keep saltwater and amethysts on hand, and try to survive. I'm going back home now...alone. I hope this is the last time I see any of you. I hope none of you have to die because you met me."

As quickly as I could make it to the door, I left. Quickly, because I couldn't be sure how long I could go without blinking, which I knew would open the floodgates. All I could do was cry. Cry as I backed out of the driveway. As I cranked up the volume to Garth Brooks—because there is no better music to cry along to than country music—and tried to sing along to distract myself from the sadness. As I jiggled my key in the lock and pushed the door open with my shoulder.

I was still crying when Desollador covered my mouth with his palm and pulled me inside.

CHAPTER 6

Eric paid Charon, the ferryman, his coin. In paintings, the ferry is a small row boat or flat-bottomed ferry with one or two souls aboard, but this ship was massive. Also, Charon didn't man these oars. Of the seven castes of Purgatory, the first made their home right here on the ship. The Prideful cleansed their souls on this vessel with the sweat of hard labor, shepherding the penitent to and from its shores.

The final caste lived here too, making the ship an unsettling and salacious monstrosity. The souls of the Lustful made up its planks and sails, doing the things lustful creatures do for all to witness, but for once making good industry with their deeds.

The Envious, aching in limb and heart for a ride, followed the ship like dolphins as it made its slow passage.

Of course it only looked that way to him. Each man or woman's path to purity was unique and most not quite as morbid as his own. For one woman he met in crossing, Purgatory appeared an endless game of musical chairs; presumably she'd be free to move on once the music stopped and she had no chair to fill. Another man forever pruned the same twenty-story office building where he worked in life, now blooming with flowers of every imaginable color and variety, in search of the single white rose that would gain him entrance to Paradise.

To Eric, Purgatory seemed a Roman tragedy because he'd been a scholar before he became a warrior and always had a bug for Virgil. Later, he discovered Dante and read the *Divine Comedy* often enough to commit it to memory. He wondered why his own Mount Purgatory was an ocean instead of a mountain.

Some hours after his journey began, Eric debarked at the island of the wrathful, a communal farm with no fences, where every soul worked in suffocating closeness with his neighbor, where the seeds of their anger took root in the soil and sprouted into manna and all who ate of it found peace. Centuries ago, he'd buried the Athame in that soil.

He brought it back up now from the soft, black earth, though it felt like a triggered weapon, hang-fired, a live round sitting in the barrel…waiting.

He paid Charon another coin to take him back to the realm of the living and came back to himself with a gasp, clutching the thing to his chest. The thing that could turn Edward, the abomination, into the Eater of Souls again. It would have been safer to leave it in Purgatory. Shoving it blade-first into the damp clay floor, Eric wished not for the first time that he could destroy it, but an Object of Power could not be destroyed. Where it came from or how Catherine acquired it in the first place, she never would say, but it could not be broken. Like Edward himself, it could only be banished.

Only for now it served a purpose.

Bait.

"Where are your friends, Pet?" Desollador uncovered my mouth.

"I have no friends."

He touched my cheek with the back of his hand. "You're crying."

"Didn't you hear me, vampire? I have no friends. Yes, I'm crying." Some tough-girl Assassin I turned out to be.

"Because you have no friends?"

"That's what I said."

"All the suffering you've known, why would you cry for that?"

"Why the twenty questions?" I shoved him, which would have been satisfying if he had moved. "What does it matter?" I shoved him twice more. He didn't even have the courtesy to stagger. "Why are you here? Did you come to kill me this time or just play? Whatever it is, why couldn't you do it an hour ago, huh? Will you just get it over with so I can get some rest?"

A muscle in his jaw ticked. He hooked a hand behind my neck and tilted my head up to his eyes. Darkness flooded the depths of them, ink and blood.

"Careful, Pet. The only reason I haven't taken you already tonight is because the weasel was watching, and I wouldn't give him the satisfaction of watching you come. Ask me again why I'm here."

I hated myself for it, but couldn't quite keep my lower lip from trembling. "I know why you're here. King of vampires and all you can think about is getting in my pants."

His eyes went obsidian black, a more unsettling color than all the shades of red I'd ever seen. That muscle in his jaw was tick, tick, ticking away when he said, "I want you to choose. If you want me to go, I'll go. This time."

Not to look a gift horse in the mouth but, "Why?"

"Or I will stay, and we finish." He took my face in his hands, walked me back against the door, and grasped my still-trembling lip between his teeth.

"You mean—"

"If I stay, I am going to fuck you."

My ass hit the door hard as he stepped between my legs. My voice sounded all wrong, like I was panting for him, and no way in hell that's what was happening. "Then why would I want you to stay?"

His teeth tugged at my earlobe, nibbled the tender skin behind it. "There are so many ways I can make you scream for me. We will get to them all eventually. I may not be as inclined to consider your pleasure another night."

OK, maybe I was panting for him. "Why would you consider it tonight?"

"Because your apathy is unacceptable." He wrapped his fingers in my hair and wrenched my head back, so I wasn't looking when he slipped his free hand into the waistband of my borrowed jeans. "I can make you forget them, Pet."

I shook my head, wondering if he really would leave if I asked.

"You don't want me to leave," he said.

Christ help me, I didn't. He devoured me with a kiss. I let him. I did more than that, splaying my fingers across his biceps and tracing the grooves of rigid muscle across his chest.

"If you keep touching me, you're not going to have a choice, Pet."

My whole body trembled. "This is so wrong."

"I like wrong." His fangs peeked out from behind his lips. Staring at them felt something like checking out his package. He made a sound between a moan and a growl low in his throat, before inviting, "Touch them."

My breath caught, and I shook my head again. He let go of my hair and guided one of my hands to his mouth. "Touch me."

I let my fingertip caress the length of one ivory blade. It pulsed under my touch.

"It's…a turn-on?"

Another moan/growl. "Yes."

His thumb traced the pulse at my wrist and, never taking his eyes off mine, he struck. I was surprised it didn't hurt, though a creeping heat slid down my skin like fingers. I whimpered.

I can make you forget.

When he let me go, I fell back against the door. I wondered if it was true. Could I forget my loneliness for a while, and if I did, could I ever forget my sin? His eyes burned for me again, those invisible fingers sliding lower. I turned my back on him so he wouldn't see my face when I moaned. I took three slow breaths staring at the deadbolt.

Before I locked it.

I held my breath, let it out again, waited to see if he understood my consent.

"So we are perfectly clear," he said, turning me around, crowding into my space again, "this is the point of no return."

"And if I change my mind?"

He placed a fist on the door on either side of my head. "I'm going to fuck you anyway." His voice sounded husky, full of sex and blood. "But

I don't plan to give you a reason to change your mind."

"Is this a trick?" It came out a whisper. I ached with need, but the idea of baring myself to him, of tempting him with such an opportunity for cruelty, made my teeth chatter.

"No, Pet. No tricks." That mental touch trailed lower.

"I can't think when you're doing that."

"I've told you before, for this you don't have to think."

"Christ, I'm scared."

"I like scared."

He speared my hair, raking his fingers through its length from scalp to waist. I winced, but resisted the urge to shrink from his touch. I had agreed to this. My own blood and tears flavored his lips—salty and metallic—but I didn't care, didn't allow myself to consider anything but the wonder of not having to fight him or do anything but feel.

His hands groped under my borrowed Henley. I leaned in to him—the vampire, my enemy, the one who would keep the loneliness away for tonight.

"The weasel." He hissed in my ear as he ripped the shirt over my head and shoved Roger's jeans, my panties with them, to the floor.

Wearing only my bra, my hands covering the bare V of flesh at the root of my thighs, I trembled against his anger.

"Shower, now."

That reminded me too much of the last night I scrubbed the slick feel of him off my body, the night I ended up inside Trina, the night he was *inside* her. And the bath, with dead Tony in the next room. How could I be doing this?!

Maybe I tensed at the thought, or maybe he read my mind. He pinned my arms to my sides and hoisted me over his shoulder. "Oh, we're doing this."

He pressed me against the back of the shower, his hand flat against my chest to keep me from bolting as he removed his shirt. I flinched every time he popped a button. He noticed and started to grin and, for the first time, I allowed myself to admit: damn that grin was *hot*.

When he unbuckled his belt, I started to hyperventilate.

"Desollador, we can't. This is…I'm supposed to kill you."

He tore my bra off like it was made of tissue paper. "You can't kill me."

He caged me with his arms, his bare chest against mine, my flesh tightening. He swiped my soap and slid it between us, working the lather into my breasts, my hips, and lower.

I tried to mirror his touch, but when I got to his hips, denim obstructed my path.

"Your jeans are getting wet."

He plucked the top button open, opened his zipper a slim inch. "So they are."

I didn't hear the rest of what he said, the damp, dark trail of hair that followed the path of that zipper fascinating me to the point of distraction. He took my hand, fed it into the opening until my palm and wrist were flat against his member. I heard him groan as I practiced closing my fingers around him. Next thing I knew his jeans were on the other side of the bathroom and my legs were wrapped around his torso, my palm the only thing separating us…and then not even that.

He stretched my wrists over my head with one hand, the other cupping my buttocks as he pushed against my entrance.

I whimpered. He kissed me.

I could see he was on the ragged edge of control when he let me come up for air. "Point of no return, remember? Your body is mine."

I wanted him so much I felt my desire as pain, sharp and throbbing, in that tender place where our bodies met. "I'm not ready."

"Better get ready." When he pressed even deeper, I held my breath waiting for the pain I knew must come, but he held me there, perched on the tip of him, my maidenhead just a hard breath away from destruction. He let go of my wrists, slipping a hand between us, and pressed his thumb against my center, making deliberate circles that soon got me panting and twisting against him.

I wrapped my arms around his neck to keep from impaling myself by accident. "You're making it hard to stop."

"We aren't going to stop."

"I just…" I hauled his hand back up.

He slammed my wrist against the tile with a snarl, and thrust against me hard enough to make me wince.

"Wait. I just want—" He kept pushing. "No please."

"Mmm, I like it when you beg."

"Can I just have one normal thing?"

"What's that?"

"I want to do this in a bed."

He didn't move for a while, and I tried not to breathe. We were so close. Any closer and it wouldn't matter what I wanted. Then his head dipped, and his teeth grazed my throat. "What's in it for me?"

"Um, what more do you want?"

He lifted his head again, tugged my lips open with his teeth. "I want you on your knees with your mouth around my—"

"No, I didn't agree to that."

"And I didn't agree to do this in a bed."

"No fair."

His laughter was like a promise. "What does fair have to do with us?"

No matter what I gave him, the vampire would always take more. "Just stop."

"Not going to happen." He rocked his hips against mine to make his point.

I gasped. "Ultimatums aren't nice, vampire."

"I am not nice. So what's it going to be? Do I pop your cherry in the shower? Or do you get on your knees for me?"

I looked into his eyes, and they were all brown. He was, in that moment, just a man. Who wanted me. And damnit, I wanted him. I made a decision. "If you want me on my knees, ask. Nicely, like a gentleman."

"You don't want me to be a gentleman."

"About this, I do."

He kissed me again, then stepped back, letting my feet touch the floor. I resisted the urge to touch myself where our bodies had connected, but I must have been thinking it because he grinned in a way that said he knew.

He turned off the shower and stepped out, grabbed a towel from the rack and stretched it in front of him. "Come."

I wanted to pull the shower curtain to cover myself, embarrassed by the battle scars that mapped me.

Yellowed bruises, old cuts pink and white against pale flesh, and dozens of bite marks, but those I guess he could damn well excuse. Christ, I was ugly.

"No," he said. "Come."

He issued the command with a nudge of compulsion that I didn't even bother to fight. I let him wrap me in the towel and admired the body that held mine. His muscles were like supple stone, marbleized by the blue mist threads of his veins shimmering beneath his skin. Why did he have to be so beautiful?

That's when he whispered into my ear, "I have fantasized about those lips since the day we met in Harlin's office."

"Not the sweet talk I had in mind, reminding me of one of the worst days of my life."

"I am obsessed with you, Pet. You are all I think about, and I want to know every inch of you. I *will* know every inch of you, but before I make you bleed, I want you to make me come. I could tell you it will help me maintain some measure of restraint when I deflower you, but the truth is I just want to feel that pretty tongue on me. Will you give me that pleasure, Pet?" He punctuated his request with a husky "please".

Damnit, I *wanted* to get on my knees for him. I could only nod. Foreplay was over. He led me to the bed, where I knelt between his legs and he taught me how a woman pleases a man...and where I discovered how much power I held over him. Even on my knees. He didn't come though, not before threading his fingers through the hair at the base of my neck and pulling me away.

"Enough. My turn."

He kissed the bite marks, scraped his teeth down the fall of my breasts and the juncture between my abdomen and thighs. As I spiraled into a dizzy madness, aching for fulfillment, he clamped down my hips and whispered into my center, "Now it's time for you to beg." When I didn't, he pulled ever so slowly away. "I'm waiting."

I wasn't sure I could even speak, but managed to curse. "Son of a bitch."

"Now that's not nice."

"Screw you."

"Happy to. Just tell me what you want."

"You," I moaned, aching, writhing, spinning farther and farther away.

"Me what?"

"Damn you, I want you inside me."

Lifting up on his elbows, he said, "Ask me nicely, Pet."

I screamed as I raked my fingernails across his back. "Please!"

"Please what?"

"Please…"

"The word you are looking for, Pet, is 'fuck'."

"Please f-fuck me."

He climbed up me then, pressed himself against my entrance. His eyes colored, and the hunger in them drove me into a panic. I slid up the bed, just far enough that he was no longer knocking at my door.

"Oh no you don't," he scolded. "We are well past that."

I went rigid under him as he slid me back in place.

This is really going to happen!

"Pet," he said against my cheek.

Even my voice trembled. "Yes?"

"Look at me."

I did. His chest and shoulders made a thick wall above me. His mouth opened enough for me to make out the tip of both fangs. His eyes were black eclipsed in red.

"Brace yourself." He pulled me down the length of him. The pain came fierce and quick, wrenching a scream from me that he covered with his hand.

Be still.

No, please. Out. Out. Out.

I could no longer see his face through the thin veil of tears that welled up in my eyes, but I felt him moving inside me, out at first, then back, deeper than before.

It will subside.

His rhythm told me he would not wait on it though. He wasn't gentle, but used me with the fervor of a creature long-deprived of his desires. But he was right, the pain dulled into an ache and then eased altogether. Cautiously, I lifted my hips to take more of him. That's when I found out he had been waiting after all. The next time I screamed for him, he covered it with his mouth.

A long time later, I curled into his chest and reveled just for a while in the feel of his arms around me. I may have dozed off because the sun was bright when I came to my senses. Desollador's arms were still wrapped around me. I wonder still if he would have eventually cast me off or if he would have held me as long as I let him, but how could I let him?

When I opened my eyes, he smiled at me. I could not smile back, felt too much like a whore and a traitor. I scampered to the pile under which my borrowed clothes had disappeared, and picked up Roger's Henley.

Desollador crossed the room in two strides and tore it from my hands. "I will not be gentle removing his scent a second time."

"You are not my boyfriend, vampire." I started crying again when I said it. "There is no relationship between us, so you have no right to be possessive of me. You are a mistake. This was a mistake."

He backed me up against the wall. When I pushed against his chest, he pressed my hands over my head. "No, I am not your boyfriend. I am your Master. That was me claiming you. Let me be clear, you will suffer if another man's scent touches you. Do you understand? You will suffer, but he will die for it."

"Fine," I said, "please just let me get dressed. You got what you came for. Can't you just leave me alone now?"

His expression softened. "Yes, I can go. I would have gone...before...if you'd asked."

"Jesus, I'm a whore."

He shook his head. "No, you're not and you did nothing wrong. In fact, I'd say you did some things pretty damned right."

I trembled at the joke.

I'm going to hell, straight to hell, burn in hell.

"Will you listen to me? You're not going to hell, not for this. There is no higher power up there that knows or cares what happened here tonight. You may regret what we've done, but not because of the judgment of some deity with more important things to do."

No, no, no. I'm damned, ruined. Straight to hell. In love with a vampire, fergodsakes!

Desollador staggered, stared at me for so long I thought he might be deciding to kill me then and there.

"Do you want me to?" he asked. "After all this, do you still want to die?"

My turn to laugh, as absurd as I felt doing it. "Was that what this was supposed to be? My reason to live?"

He shrugged as if to say "well isn't it?" but didn't really mean it. "No, honestly I don't know what this was. Do you love me, Diane?"

My name sounded weird from his lips. It distracted me. Had I thought I loved him? That didn't make sense. Christopher Desollador was a *monster. But he does not run from you, he does not* judge *you*, the girl in me pressed. I blinked. "You were my first."

"I told you I would be."

"So you did," I muttered.

"Did you enjoy it?"

He kept the loneliness away. "It doesn't matter."

He ran a hand through my hair again with a tenderness that now felt perverse. "Did you?"

I closed my eyes. "Yes."

"Then don't forget it."

I opened them again. "I have to, Desollador. I'm going to kill you."

"You can't kill me. I am trying to make you understand. You would be wise to submit, or next time you *won't* enjoy it."

"There won't be a next time."

"You do remember what I told you when we first met. What I told you would be your fate? I haven't lied to you. Don't mistake kindness for weakness."

145

"I'm not your damn toy."

"Funny, you feel like a toy." He pushed me back on the bed, raked his nails across still-sensitive flesh.

"Why did you let Roger watch?"

He pinched me until I yelped. "Not a good time to mention that name, Pet."

"You could have put him to sleep with the rest. Or killed him, but you didn't. Why?"

"You let him kiss you." Eyes so black they scared the living shit out of me. "I am going to do a lot more than make him watch. But that was a start."

"Let them go." I almost said 'him' but stopped myself.

"Asking for mercy on his behalf is only going to piss me off."

"I'm going to kill you one day," I said.

"No you won't." His lips crushed mine, fangs scraping against them hard enough to draw blood, while his fingers went about their terrible business. "But next time you try, I am going to hurt you, love. And I am going to enjoy it."

Then he left...and I discovered that more than being lonely, I missed him. In that moment, I felt truly lost.

The Athame was here. Well, not *here* precisely, but there. *In Benevolence.*

"Let me get this straight," Salvion said, placing a tumbler of Desollador's expensive vodka on what was left of his coffee table. "You want to take a field trip to the place we got our asses handed to us two centuries ago?"

Edward ignored the impertinence, said with condensation. "Not that it matters. There is no danger as long we go there alone."

"Right, all for one or none at all. What about Kayin and Desollador?"

"They've made themselves scarce since we arrived, so I assume

Desollador will continue playing catch-and-release with his little mouse and Kayin will do whatever it is Kayin does."

"Stare at wildflowers and bitch about not being able to make them grow. Got it. Do we tell them where we're going?"

"I am certain Desollador is not going to approve of me killing his toy, so no, I think I will leave that alone until I have the Athame back."

"Desollador is going to be pissed."

"Probably, but at least we know he will be here preoccupied with her until then. I don't imagine Kayin will care to follow, but to be safe, make sure he knows to stay here."

"You tell him. I don't want to talk to that freak. He creeps me out."

"It is best if I avoid him." At the quirk of Salvion's brow, Edward explained, "When I found him in the wilderness this time, he was as far gone as I have ever seen him. He made a reference to the way we met. Not a threat exactly. It was a casual, almost careless mention."

"What, like 'hey remember that time I tried to steal your body?'"

It wasn't a joke, so Edward didn't crack a smile. "Something like that."

"Fuck."

"If he tries it again...well, you know what happens to you if I lose."

"Why didn't you just leave him freezing his balls off in Antarctica or wherever he was anyway?"

Hindsight is a bitch. "It was Alaska, and the Athame had been gone so long, I never thought to get it back. Kayin is not much more than a soul himself, so I hoped he might be able to help me capture Diane's."

"I don't get it. Why all this trouble for her?"

"My blood turns to lighting when Desollador feeds from her."

Salvion whistled. "Well, that sounds painful."

"More than that," Edward continued with a glare, "there is something within me that sparks to life every time it happens. I want, I need, to complete that circuit permanently."

"Awe, she completes you. That's sweet."

Edward clenched his fists. "Kayin was a Hail Mary."

"Yeah, how's that working for you?"

"Never mind. I won't need Kayin when I have the Athame."

And if his suspicions were right, once he had Diane, he wouldn't even need that.

Mace decided he needed some space. In one night, he'd been possessed by his favorite client, bitten by a vampire, and betrayed by his best friend. Shit happens, he got that. Reality as he knew it was fucked, and he had couldn't quite figure out where to draw the line between right and wrong in his new reality. But he knew one place he could go — where good and evil lived side-by-side — to remind him of the difference. Home.

He knocked quietly. She would hear. She had to hear.

The smile she flashed when she opened the door didn't reach her eyes.

"Hi Mom."

"Be real quiet. Your father's sleeping."

"Not my father," Mace reminded. He kicked his shoes off in the foyer and padded silently — always silently — into the kitchen behind her.

The smell of Pine Sol clung so strong to the air, he wanted to gag, but knew it would only worry her, so he held it back.

"Are you staying for lunch?" She worried at a strand of dyed brown hair. "I don't know if I made enough mashed potatoes. And I'll have to put on some more biscuits."

"No, I just stopped by to make sure you were doing OK."

She scrubbed some imaginary filth from the counter with a disinfectant wipe that made his nose sting. "Oh, you worry too much."

"Mom, why don't you leave him?"

She glanced at the doorway with panicked eyes. "Shhh, don't say things like that! How about some pie? I can heat you up a piece, with some whipped cream."

"I don't want any pie. I want to know you're safe."

"Of course I'm safe. How about a glass of sweet tea? That'd be nice."

He sighed. "Yes. That would be great."

She poured one for herself as well, but didn't sit down to drink it. She polished the faucet until it gleamed and wiped fingerprints off the refrigerator. "How about you? Still liking the city?"

He snorted. "Any place is better than here."

"Job? Girlfriend?"

She knew he owned the design firm that brought in a steady, if small, paycheck, but held out the hope his talents would one day land him at some Fortune 500 company with a nice cubicle and a 401K. He'd sooner eat his own arm.

"No girlfriend yet. Don't worry. There's plenty of time for me to settle down and make grandbabies for you."

A shadow crossed her eyes, but she brightened before he could remember where he had seen it before. "Well, your father would have liked that." His real father. "He always wanted a big family..."

"Why don't you ever talk about him?"

"Because I'm a married woman. Your father hasn't been in my life since you boys were little, and besides, he's not the one who raised you. You have to give David some credit for taking on a woman with no money, no skills, two small children and —"

"And never, ever letting you forget it."

She sniffed and turned her back on him. He trailed her into the laundry room. Jesus, why did it have to be the whites? Again with the bleach. When she leaned into the dryer to pull out an armload of linens, he saw it.

"I'll kill him."

She bolted upright, tugged down her blouse in the back where it rode up just enough to give Mace a glimpse of the bruise hidden beneath it. "It's nothing. I took a spill in the bathtub. Why, if David hadn't been here, I don't think —"

"Stop it. Just stop it, Mom." He picked up a towel, folding first widthwise, then left side toward center, right side toward center, so they overlapped. Turned it lengthwise and did the same. She stacked another

149

towel on top of his. They looked like they belonged in a store display, not a linen closet.

"How many times did we fall down the stairs, or have an accident riding our bikes, or walk into some imaginary door when we were growing up? Don't lie to me."

"I'm sorry. I should have protected you boys better. But—"

"I know, Mom."

"It's not so bad now. I really did take a spill in the tub." Which meant he pushed her in it. Mace knew how those word games worked, too.

It wasn't her fault. She had tried once to escape, and once was enough. When David found them, he dislocated Mace's arm dragging him out to the station wagon, stuffing him into his booster seat, pulling the seatbelt too tight. His mom begged and pleaded and promised, but in the end could do no more than "Get the hell in the car." She couldn't strap Roger in, could only clutch him to her chest as they sped off.

Mace remembered headlights and horns blazing and the terrible feeling that David was driving wrong. Seemed to him like they should be driving on the other side of the road, not so many cars on that side to dodge. His mom screamed and cried until David made her stop. Her head cracking against the passenger side window made a sound like a bowling ball hitting pins. Her arms went slack and, in the next turn, Roger slipped into the floorboard, bawling.

After that, they all learned how to walk softly, speak when spoken to, smile like they meant it, except when smiling may be mistaken for mocking, laughing, sassing or any other inappropriate emotion. Roger ran before the ink dried on his high school diploma without a second glance, but Mace hung back, felt guilty for even thinking about leaving her. That's when David made it clear the house was only big enough for one alpha male, and Mace would just make it worse for his mother by staying.

Unless he killed him. Killing another human being would be a terrible, inexcusable evil, but he was willing to accept the burden of sin on his soul for her, and when he saw the new bruise on her skin, he told her so.

She shook her head. "No, my boy. You aren't going to do any such thing. I couldn't bear to see you ruin your life like that."

"It would be worth it, knowing you could finally live yours."

"No. I've already seen...just no."

She starting setting the table. Biscuits straight from the oven into a basket lined with a red and white checkered kitchen towel. Mashed potatoes in a clear glass bowl with a serving spoon crossed on top.

"Oh no." She gasped.

"What?"

"I've run out of butter. I...oh, I know it was on my grocery list. How could I have forgotten?" She cast a furtive glance at the clock. "It's OK. I can fix this. I have time. I'll just run to Mrs. Mason's and borrow a stick. I'll be back in ten minutes. Would you mind checking on the ham, so it doesn't burn? Just be sure to take it out of the oven as soon as the timer goes off. Can you do that?"

"Yes, Mom."

"And cover it so it doesn't get too cool."

"I know."

"If David wakes—"

"It's OK. I'll take care of it. Just go."

When she left, he decided. The world had already turned on its end. He had the puncture wounds to prove it. He would save his mother, though it may be the last thing he did. He took a carving knife from the block; it made a metallic zing as it slid from the sheath. He knew without checking that it would be sharp.

In the living room, he found David standing with his back to the doorway, staring out the window. How long had he been awake? How much had he heard? It didn't matter anymore. Mace's hands tightened on the hilt of his blade.

"Come stand beside me. You should see this," David said.

"I'm fine where I am."

David glanced over his shoulder, a pointed look at the knife in Mace's hand. "You will have to get much closer for what you intend."

"You know you asked for this, old man."

"You are not the only one who thinks it. Come see."

What game did David play? "I told you —"

The man turned around and regarded Mace with a calmness at odds with David's personality. "Do you know he never leaves his car parked in the driveway?"

"What?"

"Always in the garage, so he doesn't have to be out there unprotected." He nodded to the window. "Not for even a moment."

"Who's *he*?"

"He makes your mother rake leaves and take the garbage to the curb on pickup day and even check the mail."

Oh, David had lost his ever-loving mind. "*You* have always made Mom do all the work."

"He will circle a parking lot for hours to find a spot within sprinting distance of the door and has not taken lunch outside since the day your mother tried to escape with you and your brother. He is a large man inside his walls, yet he is terrified of what is waiting for him out there."

"What are you talking about?"

"I told you to come see."

Curiosity won. Mace tightened his grip on the knife and joined David at the window. "Holy shit."

A wolf stood in the shrubbery, front paws on the windowsill, close enough its breath made hazy circles on the glass. Yellow eyes near glowed against soot-gray fur.

"Your mother was right. Killing him will ruin your life," David said.

"What the hell? You mean killing *you*?"

David leaned closer to the glass, closer to the wolf. "If you can get him outside, I believe this wolf will do it for you." He tilted his head in Mace's direction. "I wonder why that is."

The wolf looked at Mace now too, his hind quarters trembling, his ears flicking back and forward.

David looked back out the window. "Did you know that vampires are shape-shifters? Desollador's other form is a dog.

He told me he mated with a bitch one time while in that other form just to see what would happen."

At the mention of vampires, Mace began to suspect his world was about to be upended again.

"She gave birth to humanoid children, a litter of them. Can you imagine that? It took the bitch two nights to whelp them all."

David had never told a ghost story in his life. He considered celebrating Halloween tantamount to worshiping the devil. He and Roger had never once gone trick-or-treating. "You're not David, are you?" Mace asked.

The David thing ignored him. "The children were not immortal like their father. In fact, one child succumbed to a wasting sickness when he was still a boy, but a few grew to manhood. One of them, the only one born after moonrise of the second night, even learned to speak and took a wife, eventually had a child of his own."

"Why are you telling me this? Who are you?"

The man who looked like David held up a hand for silence. "One evening not long after his son was born, the man was robbed. During the assault, he acquired the form of his mother, the she-wolf. He never took the form of man again."

Mace stepped away from the window, the presence of the wolf outside it now unsettling. "How would you know that?"

"Desollador, who sired the pups, became my brother."

"You're the demon."

He shrugged. "If you want to call me that, it's as good a name as any."

Mace wondered if killing David would kill the thing inside him, too. "What do you want?"

"Shape."

"Huh?"

"You all take your clean, mortal forms for granted. It is the way of humans. Once it was my way too."

"So that's why you steal bodies?"

David fell to the carpet like a deflated balloon. A monstrous winged shadow, that at the very least looked like a demon, stood in his place. "I steal because I covet."

Mace backed away, raising the knife in front of him like a shield. He made a shooing motion at the shell of his stepfather. "Well, you can have that sorry sack of shit," Mace said.

The demon thing shook his head, then nodded to the window. "No, that one wants his flesh more than I do. If I were you, I would give it to him."

With that advice, the shadow dissipated, and the demon thing disappeared. Mace returned to the kitchen to re-sheath the knife. The ham had burnt to a damned crisp. David would beat her for that, more severely than for forgetting the butter. Mace finished off his mother's glass of tea and returned to the living room. David still lay passed out by the window, the wolf still looking in.

It wasn't a hard decision. It wasn't much of a decision at all. It was just time. Mace hefted the deadweight over his shoulder and opened the door. The wolf whined, but Mace tried his best to ignore it. He took his burden into the woods, deep enough the trees obscured his view of the house and hopefully any view from the house to him.

"What the—?" David began.

Mace heaved David off his shoulder and onto the ground like he was swinging an ax, though his muscles groaned for it. "Good, you're awake."

David rubbed his back and said, "You sorry piece of shit, I'm gonna kick your ass for this."

He started to stand when the wolf pounced—snout to face—and growled. David screamed. It was about damn time for that.

"I don't think you're going get a chance."

"Wait! You can't leave me here with this thing."

"I'm not gonna leave." Mace smiled. "I'm gonna watch."

The wolf gnashed his teeth once and then squeezed one of David's ears between them. That ear might as well have been made of wet tissue paper the way it came apart.

Unnatural shadows converged on David like a swarm of flies. Growling, the wolf pounced on them in a fit that gave Mace the impression the canine was interrupting something. The shadows scattered as fast as they came, their gift withheld. When David screamed again, the wolf took his tongue. In two juicy red bites.

Mace sat down on a log while the wolf tortured and ate his stepfather. It took fourteen minutes for David to stop moving and then another ten for the wolf to drag his body away into the forest. Somebody would find the old man's bones when winter came, he guessed, after the wild things picked them clean.

Back home, his mother sat in the kitchen, sobbing over the ham. She didn't even pretend to perk up when she saw him. "I told you to take it out as soon as the timer went off."

"I was busy."

"I don't know how to fix this. Oh Lord, how do I fix this?"

He put his arm around her shoulders. "It's OK, Mom. It's over."

She looked up at him with wide eyes. "No, Mace, you didn't."

"No, I didn't."

"Then what?"

He fingered the silver ring he'd worn at his neck since he was a child and answered, "I think my father did."

Roger wiped off a trail of spit from his chin with the back of his hand and yawned, stretching his arms over his head. He finished the motion off by plucking the bleeping alarm clock from the nightstand and stuffing it under his pillows. He stumbled from his bed with eyes closed and felt his way to the shower, the few hours of sleep he'd managed to get not even close to enough.

He opened his eyes long enough to adjust the temperature knobs and wondered about the frothy pink swirl of water draining between his feet.

That's when he remembered the blood, the vampires. Diane. He groaned, clutching his stomach and the knot forming there.

What possessed him to be such a jerk? Diane denied the vampire, more than once, before giving in. Sure, he saw that. But he also saw how she moaned and panted under the vampire's lips. How often had he imagined her making those noises for him? He turned on her for no better reason than jealousy.

"Such a gentleman, Rog."

Maybe she'd be at the park, and he could apologize. Maybe they could figure out together what the hell was going on before the sun went down again. Vampires could only come out at night, right?

When he finished his shower, Roger finger-combed his hair and made a few passes at his chin with a disposable triple blade. Grooming complete, he ambled back into his room to don his "uniform", a pair of Wranglers with more holes than pockets (holes he'd earned, not bought thankyouverymuch), a primary red t-shirt, and a whistle. The latter was more like a nametag than a tool.

After grabbing his cooler and a few beers from the fridge, he took a step into his ruined living room and gawked. "Holy crap." When superheroes and villains fight, they make a mess.

He wondered if he ought to call Bree and Mace, but decided he needed to see Diane first and figured he might find her at the park. He was sitting on his cooler, eating a sandwich when he felt a warm tongue and fangs on his neck. He scrambled to get away, kicking over the cooler in a panic. A flash of rust-colored fur wearing a pink collar in skull-and-crossbone print followed his lunch to the ground and ate half a sandwich—baggie and all—before the petite redhead holding the leash could pull her away. "Molly, no."

Roger did his best not to vomit. "You scared the crap out of me."

"Sorry." She wore a tennis skirt the same shade as the dog's collar. "Please say you are the dog man."

He bent over to catch his breath, pretending to take a closer look at the dog, a young Visla. "Her name is Molly?"

"She probably thinks her name is 'No'."

Molly bounced again, but Roger shook his head and said, "Settle down."

She tipped her head back and howled. "Ah-ah, no talking back. Sit."

Molly howled again, wagged her tail half a dozen times, then plopped down beside him.

To the petite redhead said, "I am the dog man."

She introduced herself as Cassie and passed him a fifty-dollar bill. Half an hour later, Roger handed over a Visla that still howled at every command and wagged her tail with such enthusiasm her hind-end never stilled, but could pass a basic obedience test even if surrounded by overturned coolers and ham sandwiches.

Cassie clapped her hands, then stooped to rub one floppy, amber ear. "I can't believe it. You know, I took a class with her once at the canine academy, but they couldn't teach her in two months what you just did in less than an hour."

Roger shrugged and rubbed the other ear. "Maybe she just wasn't ready to learn. They settle down as they get older."

Cassie slipped him another twenty in a handshake to show what she thought of his modesty.

His mood had improved by the time the next client—a man this time—approached. Roger averted his eyes to avoid staring. "You the dog man?" An albino maybe?

The monster of a dog at the man's side made a sound like the clearing of a throat, so Roger looked up and forced a smile. "That's me."

"Well, this gig really isn't a big step up from begging on a street corner with a paper cup and a cardboard sign, is it?"

"Excuse me?"

The man extended his hand and introduced himself. "I'm Salvion."

"I don't care. What the hell do you want?"

"I can imagine how disappointed your mother must be to know her son is a beggar and a sorry waste of space."

Roger hauled back and threw a haymaker, but when his hand

should have made contact with the asshole's jaw, Roger hit air.

A cold crept into his heart, but he told himself he must have misjudged the distance. "Do I know you?"

"Not me. But him." The man indicated the dog with an affection pet, a gesture of familiarity to which the dog responded with a clipped snarl. "Him, you've met."

The dog rose up and placed his front paws on Roger's shoulders, then leaned forward until their noses touched.

"Down," Roger commanded.

Roger was known as the "dog man" for good reason, but this dog just curled his lip and rumbled. When Roger reissued the command—punctuating it with a firm shove—the dog grabbed a mouthful of hair and hauled his face into the ground, then lifted a leg. The acrid scent of ammonia suffused the air, and Roger felt a moist warmth creep into the thigh of his Wranglers.

He hurled another command, this one directed at Salvion. "Get your damned dog off me, man."

The albino cackled. "He's not my dog. Get him off yourself."

Marked. He thought of Diane and the events of the previous night, but a heavy insulation of humility muted the warning bells that should have been ringing. He risked a glance back at his attacker and saw the man crouched where the dog had been.

"Do you remember me now, Roger?" Red eyes. That voice. Couldn't be. Vampires can only come out at night, right?

He considered the likelihood of vampires in broad daylight for about three seconds, then took off. Certain there would be greater safety in numbers, he cut a path to the lake. There were kids in the water despite the weather, watched over by couples reclined on beach blankets and plastic lawn chairs. Roger looked back to see if the vampire followed. When he saw no sign of a pursuer, he let out a breath so hard it sounded like a cough.

Still breathing heavily, he slouched into a vacant park bench to collect himself.

Beside him, two little girls with wind-tangled hair nibbled on muddy pebbles and chattered at him, taking turns grinning and waving.

A little boy waddled up to the pair and pecked at one girl's hair, tearing out a snowy clump with a crooked, toothless grin. Roger braced himself for her scream, but she just spit the pebble from her mouth like a grape seed and claimed a finger-thick tuft from behind the boy's ear instead.

Roger watched with mounting alarm as a feathery pile began to grow around them until a man—maybe the parent of one or more of the young cannibals—shoved off his picnic blanket to intervene. That man's brown and gray mottled beard looked like he'd trimmed it with hedge clippers, shafts of curls protruding at odd angles from his chin. He looked more like a cartoon character than a human.

He cooed to the boy while he scooped him up in wiry arms and tossed him—squawking—into the pond. The child stayed under long enough for Roger to grit his teeth in worry and start to stand, but before he could launch himself into the filth, the boy surfaced, dripping thick, snotty water and flashing green teeth.

Roger curled his lip and averted his eyes, wondering if the pond was even safe for kids to play in. He looked back in time to watch the child scoop a flitting grasshopper into his mouth and start to chew. Roger imagined he could hear the crunch and slurp as the bug went down, and the sound made him wince.

Then a voice—half-forgotten in the disturbing picnic display—said, "Jeez, I hate birds. Disgusting creatures."

Roger slid to the edge of the bench, away from the creature who joined him on it. "Birds?"

Salvion pointed at the pond; Roger looked off the end of his finger. Geese. Geese in the water. Geese on the crusty bank. Geese crunching pebbles and crickets and plucking errant feathers from each other's wings. Just geese.

Not one man, woman or child in screaming distance.

"None of it was real."

Salvion shrugged. "You wanted a crowd. I gave you one."

Roger tried to bolt, to find himself another crowd to hide himself—

a real crowd — but Desollador's hands on his shoulders prevented it.

The vampire shared a private glance with Salvion and nodded. Salvion blinked out like starlight on glass.

Without preamble, the vampire hooked his elbows under Roger's shoulders, lifted him backwards over the bench and tore into his throat. Roger's feet scrambled to find purchase on the damp grass; his arms windmilled in panic. Then he started to suck. It made Roger moan.

Do you want me to stop?

He couldn't answer, couldn't think beyond the pressure mounting in his groin. He understood then; the vampire's venom is lust. No one ever sucked him like this. Oh fuck, he was gonna —

Who's the sick bitch now?

Desollador drank for no more than ten seconds before Roger got hard. That's when the vampire stopped. Roger's gaze locked with eyes that glazed black from iris to pupil. He didn't know it then, but that was the color of pissed.

Desollador spat out blood he hadn't swallowed and growled. "Fucking hypocrite." Shifting his grip, the vampire pulled Roger down off the bench and drove a booted heel into his groin. "Pathetic. I'm not giving you the satisfaction of drinking you to death. But I will gladly make confetti out of your entrails."

Shadows converged and, when they scattered, the Dog charged. True to his word, he sank his teeth into the soft flesh of Roger's abdomen. "Off!" he screamed, shoving his will against the animal form that contained the vampire intellect. "Off!"

The Dog staggered backwards, shook his head as if to clear it, and charged again. This time, he thrust his nose in Roger's face.

Roger trembled, but managed not to look away. "Fuck off."

The Dog barked.

Roger yelped, but held his ground. "Off!"

The Dog backed away growling, then feinted another charge.

Roger screamed, "Go! Get out of here."

After one more bark, the Dog did just that.

Roger threw up for a long time after he left.

As soon as he left, I stripped the sheets and tossed them into the wash with two cups of bleach. I scrubbed my bathroom until it sparkled. I even mopped. If I destroyed the proof, I destroyed the sin. At least as far as it made a damn iota of difference to my future. That I had sex with Desollador didn't change the fact that we were enemies. Or that I'd still have to fight back when we met again.

After I cleaned up, I ordered delivery—an enormous spread of five-cheese pizza and hot wings, veggie lo mein and crab rangoon, egg rolls and sugar donuts. The single most confusing night of my life left me hungry, though I didn't really plan on eating all that food.

I coaxed each of the delivery guys (and one woman) inside one by one under the guise that I had misplaced my wallet, and talked their ear off until the next showed up to take his place. I pretended we were friends and didn't even feel pathetic doing it. If I could have no greater connection with the human race, I'd make the most of it.

After all the delivery people left, I stuffed my face at the kitchen counter watching *Big Bang Theory* and wishing I had a friend half as funny as Sheldon. I read somewhere that people should eat sitting down, at a table, TV off, to savor their meal. I decided after my experiences with Desollador in the diner the night before and the café what felt like years ago, I would just as soon stand.

I was hefting a tent bag filled with weapons into the back of my Jeep when Bree pulled into the driveway. I grimaced and went back in the house for another bag, leaving the front door open. When I saw Mace and Roger file out after her, I opened another bottle of bleach and decided the kitchen sink needed a good soak. I couldn't decide which motivation moved me most: annoying Mace or disguising any lingering scent of sex in the air.

I smirked when I saw him hold his nose against the fumes when he crossed my threshold. To be fair, he wasn't the only one.

"Wow," Bree said. "I think the scene is clean. Who died here anyway?"

"I'm leaving. My poor landlord is going to have his hands full repairing the damage I've done to the place." I nodded to the bedroom door, splintered to hell and back with buckshot. "The least I can do is get my blood out of the floorboards."

Mace took in the spread set out on my kitchen counters. "Where's the rest of the cleaning crew?"

"What are you doing here?"

Bree pushed him back. "We thought you might be gone already."

"Yeah? Give me an hour."

"We were wondering if you'll let us tag along."

I raised an eyebrow and plucked a shrimp dumpling from the depleted box. "That depends."

"On what?"

"On them." I nodded towards Roger and Mace.

Both mouths opened at once. Roger spoke first. "I had no right to say what I did. I am so sorry. You couldn't help what that vampire did to you."

He started toward me, arms out like he wanted a hug, and I damn near leapt over the counter to put distance between us. That little maneuver put me within arm's reach of Mace. I heard his sharp inhalation, then, "Fuck me."

Bree and Roger said at once, "What is it?"

I didn't need to ask. At his expletive, I realized I had scrubbed everything in the house except me. "I need to talk to Mace. Alone."

Something flashed in Roger's eyes—jealousy?—but Bree tugged him outside before I could decipher it.

"Go ahead. Out with it," I said when they were gone.

"Can I trust you?"

"With your life."

"Everything in here smells like bleach except you. You smell like him, a lot more than you did when you left us last night."

I just nodded. I felt no shame, no need to offer explanation.

He looked me up and down, then changed the subject. "I am pretty sure Roger hates our mother."

I tried to keep my face from registering my surprise.

"After our father disappeared, she married a man who beat the snot out of all us every day of every year until we were old enough to leave. She tried to get away once, and it went bad. So she never tried again. Rog and I, we got out, knowing full well we were leaving her alone with a monster."

He shook his head. "I felt so guilty, so pissed with myself for abandoning her there, but Roger gives all his anger to her, because she stayed."

"Does she love him? Your stepdad, I mean?"

"I never asked. It would be a shame if she did."

"Why?"

"Because I let him die today. I watched a timber wolf eat him alive."

"A wolf?"

He nodded once and clutched a sphere of silver hanging on a leather cord in the hollow of his throat. "I am afraid to know what will happen if I take this off. Your demon—Kayin?—told me a story today about werewolves." He said it like he wasn't sure if that was the right word. "Then I let a wolf that—if Kayin's story holds water—has been stalking my stepfather for years, rip him to pieces in front of me."

There were so many questions I wanted to ask, but I couldn't form the words for a single one. "Maybe you should leave the necklace on for now."

"Ya think? My point is that lying down with a monster doesn't necessarily make you a monster too." I winced. "But Roger will despise you if he ever finds out."

"It's none of his—or your—business. You don't know me."

"You're right. I don't know you. That's the problem. But I do know you smell like sex. And him. You tell me what I should make of that."

"No."

He nodded like he expected it. "Can you keep us alive?"

"I don't know if I can keep myself alive. Honestly, you may all be better off getting as far from me as you can run."

"Roger had another visit from your vampire today. I don't think running is an option."

"How did he get away?" Or did Desollador let him go?

Mace shrugged. "Rog is the dog-man. Just hope the vamp doesn't have rabies."

A tentative knock came at the door. Bree popped her head in. "Everybody still alive in here?"

"Don't make me regret keeping my mouth shut," Mace said close to my ear. "Cross too far over the line, and I will kill you."

"You can try," I said, then raised my voice. "We're fine. You can come back in."

Roger's gaze shifted from me to Mace. "What was that about?"

"Mace said you had a visit from Desollador," I said. "Are you OK?"

He lifted his shirt to show off the rows of ACE bandages wrapped around his torso. "I'm gonna have a nasty scar where he went canine on me, but I'll live."

For now, my mind supplied.

We didn't talk much after that. Roger and Mace fell onto the remains of my breakfast when I gave them leave and I finished loading up for the trip, shuffling several bags from the backseat into the luggage compartment. I wondered how many times we'd have to stop for bathroom breaks and what in the hell we were supposed to talk about for ten hours.

"Do you have any more of that duct tape?" Bree called from the doorstep.

I opened my duffel and threw her a roll. "Why?"

"You said your landlord is already going to have to fix the place up again when you leave, right?"

"Right..."

"OK, good."

With that, she disappeared inside. The exchange intrigued me enough to follow her.

I entered just in time to see every mirror in my rental shatter. She collected dozens of curved shards and wrapped the ends of each with a four-inch band of tape, strange daggers with makeshift hilts.

"Salvion's weakness apparently," she explained to Roger. "These make him bleed."

"What about knives or bullets?" Roger asked.

"He turns insubstantial," I explained. "They go right through him."

"We're fighting poltergeists," he muttered, then, "We're going to die, aren't we?"

He wasn't looking at me when he said it, so I chose not to answer. If I gave too much thought to those kinds of questions, I might just give up. I could see no possible way that we might survive, not all of us anyway. What was the point of driving ten hours just to die? We could just as well do that here and with a lot less effort.

And without having to face the ghosts waiting for me in Benevolence.

B.K. RAINE

CHAPTER 7

Kayin studied the blood on the ground. The old poacher's skin felt like a roomy coat after wearing the slight build of the one Mace called Old Man and David. Kayin did not expect to find the werewolf when he followed the brooding one home.

That one reminded Kayin of his own brother. Stark and righteous, with his sacrifice of blood and bone. And his mother — so much like Eve — ruled by her husband, rearing her children in pain. David, though, was a poor substitute for Adam. Maybe Mace's father had been a righteous man before he became the Wolf. Mace, like his father before him, would be blessed with not one pure form, but two.

Kayin might have envied that.

Hadn't he known envy as a young man, and hadn't Sin crouched at the door in waiting for him to act upon it? Hadn't he been more cursed than the fallow earth, soaked in his brother's blood and forever barren? Hadn't Sin ravaged him in the end, and yet, did the Lord not proclaim he could be its Master?

"Are you sure you're going to be OK?" Mace asked, one foot in his car and one on the ground beside it.

"Go," his mother said. "I can be at Sissy's before dark."

"Call me when you get there. I don't like the idea of you being alone right now."

"You worry too much. Besides, are you sure…?" Her eyes scanned the tree line.

"He's not coming home, Mom. He's never coming home."

"But if he should, what'll he think when he doesn't find me?"

"He's dead."

She twirled a lock of hair around her index finger. "I know, hon. It's just going to take time to get used to the idea, is all. You drive carefully going home."

He gave her a stiff nod and sat down. "You're going to be OK now."

Her smile didn't reach her eyes. "I love you."

Kayin watched the boy drive away, watched through the kitchen windows while the woman picked at the ham, carving off the blackened edges before wrapping the honey-colored center in transparent cloth and placing it on the counter. She made herself a plate of fluffy potatoes and flaky leavened bread and sat down to eat it alone. That's when Kayin decided to join her.

He frightened her at first. Kayin reminded her not to commit the Sin of taking the Lord's name in vain. When she took up the knife, he feared she would cut out her tongue for giving offense. Instead, she offered it to him blade-first. She brought blood, but he forgave her for it. When he took a place at the table, he asked her to say the evening prayer.

She cried over her blessing. "Lord, thank you for this day...and this meal and the company of...new friends. Um...give us this day our daily bread. And forgive us our debts, as we forgive our debtors. Lead us not into temptation, but deliver us from evil. For Yours is the kingdom and the power and the glory forever. Amen."

He ate a slice of ham from the tip of the knife. "That was beautiful, Eve."

The corners of her mouth turned down just a little before she found her smile. "Th-thank you. I don't know your name."

"My name is Kayin. Will you call me by it?"

"Kayin. It is..." She took a deep, cleansing breath. "It is nice to meet you."

"Do you know the Wolf that hunts in these woods?"

"I don't understand."

"I believe the Wolf that killed the one called Old Man was once a

167

man himself. Do you know him?"

She took a sip of tea and swallowed with care. "Yes."

Kayin tipped his head. "Tell me."

"What is there to tell?"

His reaction was puzzling. Rage surged up from his groin to his hands, which slammed down into the table hard enough to rattle the china. "Everything!"

She shrieked, "He is my son's father!"

He tried to smile to ease the sudden fear in her. "Go ahead."

"He always wanted children." Her eyes were glassy. "Tom was such a good dad."

"What happened to him?"

"He had this silver ring, his class ring." She shrugged. "He wore it on his thumb. I used to hate how it rubbed against my knuckles when we held hands. He told me he dreamt he should give it to Mace."

"Did he?" Kayin prompted.

"I was never quite sure what happened next...what actually happened. But it must have happened, right?" That shrug again.

"He became the Wolf."

"He took the ring off, put it on a cord. He had just tied it around Mace's neck...when he got this look on his face, went completely white, and then he just...changed into..."

"The Wolf that avenged you tonight by feasting on the bones of Old Man?"

"I think so, yes."

"And your son still wears your husband's ring?"

"On a chain around his neck."

Kayin speared another slice of ham and chewed. "What will happen if he takes it off, Eve?"

She flinched. "He can't take it off."

"Did Tom have a brother too?"

"No, he has a sister, but I haven't seen her since our wedding. She owns a ranch out in Montana, trains horses or something like that."

He steepled his fingers under his chin. "Doesn't Roger train dogs for a living?"

"How do you know that?" She lunged for him. "Leave my baby alone!"

He caught her and pulled her into his lap, tucking her arms against her side.

"Eve, haven't you ever wondered if the reason your son and your father's sister possess this gift of compelling animals is the same reason your husband, and possibly your son, possess the ability to become wolves?"

"Who are you? What do you want with me?"

"I told you, my name is Kayin."

"Cain? And you call me Eve. What is your brother's name?"

"My brother's name was Abel."

She cried in great heaving breaths. "I don't want to die."

"Shhhh. I would never hurt you, not like I hurt him. Mother, I am so sorry. If I could return to that day —"

"I am not your mother!"

"You are the Mother of all men. And I am your firstborn."

"I can't be your mother. You must be older than me. Please let me go. I will never tell."

"No, no, this is just borrowed flesh. See." He shed his skin again and, as Spirit, stretched his shadow wings for her. "He Marked me, lest I be killed on my wanderings."

She scrambled off the poacher's lap and fled deeper into her home. Kayin followed. She cornered herself in her bedroom behind a locked door that she probably thought would keep him out. When he stepped through it, her hand fluttered against her mouth. "I must be going crazy. This can't be real."

He had to show her, to make her understand. He opened the bedroom window and called the wind through it, and with it, his flesh and bone. Flesh and bone that would never return to dust, never return to the earth from which Hashem exiled him. When his own body clothed his spirit again, he said, "Eve, I am real. I am Kayin."

"I am not Eve," she whispered.

He knelt and touched her face, pretended not to notice her flinch. "I know. But I do miss her, and I have been here so long, sometimes I forget."

"You are really Cain?"

"I hear the stories. I try not to. I cross oceans to escape them. I know ours is a cautionary tale, and I am the most hated man ever born to this earth. The first murderer, kin killer, cursed. I am not going to hurt you, Mother."

"OK." She drew a shaky breath. "I believe you."

He swiped his thumb across her cheek, drying a tear that stained it. "I would like to be redeemed for my sins. Do you think that is possible?"

"The Bible says in Christ all things are possible."

"Do you think that is true?"

"Did He really rise from that tomb?"

"He was a doomsday prophet causing much grief to the Romans. I learned some time after his death they crucified him. Two hundred years later I heard his followers proclaim he rose from the dead. I do not know if that is true."

"Then I don't know if redemption is possible."

He sat back on his haunches, balancing on hoof and tip of wing. "Your firstborn has your husband's gift."

"Don't you mean curse?"

"No. Mother. This" — he gestured to indicate the whole of him — "is a curse. To have two pure forms, man and wolf, is a gift. Do you think it is one he can bestow on another?"

"You mean like a werewolf?"

"Yes," though he hadn't known it until that moment. "That is exactly what I mean."

Renn slipped into the stairway and paused just beneath the kudzu, listening for footsteps that might belong to the man on the recording. She held her breath as long as she could, but her heartbeat was the only sound. After a few minutes, she switched on her flashlight and aimed the diffuse beam down the stairs. The cellar door was padlocked shut.

Pulling two bobby pins from her hair, she muttered, "Thank you, cable TV."

Ten minutes later, she stood in front of a massive wooden door, in the center of an earthen pit with less floor space than her bathroom.

"Creepy kidnapping cellar. So not where I want to be right now."

On the opposite end of the room, behind the ladder, the ceiling necked down into a cramped space not even tall enough to allow her five-foot-two frame to stand upright. That's where she found a pair of what appeared to be two-foot by two-foot trap doors set right in the earth.

"OK, let's try door number two."

Propping her flashlight on the ground beside her, she heaved the closest one open with two hands. At once, the beam ignited swirls of dust motes in a deep purple glow.

"Amethysts?"

Hundreds of uncut stones were inlaid in the trap door, each of them secured with four small metal prongs. Thousands of prongs. On a door.

Renn snatched the flashlight and aimed it into the hole. "What the hell?"

She'd found a coffin, a space so small it made her gorge rise, encased on all sides with more jewels, crowded edge to faceted edge so that no bare space peeked between them. Her heart beating like an unbalanced washing machine in her chest, she closed the lid and rocked back on her heels to stand. That's when she saw it, something shiny in the corner, peeking out from the dirt and cobwebs. She held her breath as she stretched across the top of the second door to grab it.

A cell phone. Tate's cell phone. She pressed the power button. Dead. Of course it was dead. It had been down here, what, four years?

Cell phones being just too damn expensive to trade out every time a new one came along, she had the same model. Except she carried it in a case with an external battery because she always forgot to put it on the charger. She swapped cases, flipped the charging position to ON and wondered how long it would take to get a four-year-old phone to charge up…or if it even would.

She would have left then except for the fragmented memory of a stack of reflective mosaic tiles and a man covered in plaster holding a trowel. Had to be him. Had to be the voice on the recording, the one who warned her away from this place with its secret rooms and lost cell phone. Tate had *been* here.

What looked to be a railroad tie barred the door. Renn spent a good five minutes shoving her bodyweight into the damned thing to coax it into moving, expending more four letter words than she could afford to pay the swear jar before managing to shove one end through the iron hanger that held it in place. The weight of the thing did the rest. It hit the floor with a heavy thunk and a cloud of dust.

It took much longer to pick the lock behind the barricade. Her light started to dim by the time she got the door open. In spite of that, the beam nearly blinded her when she shined it inside, magnified by its many reflections. The room, about the size of the dunking booth at the county fair, was tiled floor to ceiling in one-inch by one-inch mirrors.

"And I thought the coffin was weird."

For all she expected to find up here on the mountain, she couldn't fathom what any of *this* might mean. She was contemplating going into the mirrored room for a better look when she heard engine noise and the crunch of tires on gravel. Heart hammering in her throat, she crept back up the stairs, peered through the kudzu. And almost forgot to breathe.

"Dude, I can't decide who looks more out of place here, you or me." Salvion chalked a cue and took a look around. The men in the pool hall wore flannel like a fashion statement. "On second thought, definitely me. Look, I know beggars can't be choosers, but next time you might want to nab a body that knows its way around a razor."

"Sin knows no degree. Vanity, envy and murder, they are the

same."

"Is that so? Hot damn then, pick one. I got sins to spare. One-way tickets to Hell all around!"

A few flannel shirts glanced their way. A few swigs later and they were back to their pool games.

Salvion chalked the stick again, but never put cue to ball. Kayin shook his head. "There is no Hell, Vain one. There is Earth and there is Sheol. And there is punishment befitting our crimes."

"Really, you got stuck on this rock for a few thousand centuries looking like a gargoyle. That was fitting punishment?"

"I was the first man born on this earth to a woman. I killed the second. What do think fitting punishment should have been for my sin?"

"Get over yourself. So you killed your brother, and your mother singlehandedly brought about the fall of mankind. We all got family issues."

Kayin took up the sugar dispenser from the nearest table. It was the size of a Mason jar, beveled glass with a reflective aluminum lid. A waterfall of white crystals showered from it as Kayin drove the mirrored end over and over into the back of Salvion's skull. Salvion held up a hand to ward off the blows, but the poacher outweighed him by fifty pounds. He tried running instead, backing away in three-foot strides and putting as many tables between him and Kayin as possible.

Creepy son of a bitch didn't make a sound while he pursued, just ate up the ground between them as fast as Salvion could cover it, twisted meaty fingers around the collar of his hundred-dollar button-down and drove the sugar dispenser twice more into his face. The first blow broke his orbital socket, the second one his nose.

When one of the other patrons pulled him off long enough for Salvion to become insubstantial to heal himself, he remembered to throw up an illusion first so the human would not notice the disappearing act.

"What the hell?" he asked between pants.

Kayin shrugged off the restraining arms and said with a quiet warning, "You will not speak of our Mother thus."

"She's not my mother, freak."

"She is the Mother of all men, even you. And for that she will have your respect."

"Whatever, sorry." He fingered the lump on the back of his head. "Shit, is that how you killed Abel?"

He didn't nod, didn't flinch. "I beat him to death with my bare hands in a field where his flock grazed alongside my crop. It was a terrible deed, and I should not have done it. Yet, my brother should not have been so bold with his tongue. Do not make his mistake."

"Yeah, got it. Look, I didn't bring you here to reminisce about the bad old days anyway. Edward and I have something to do. We are going to be out of town for a few days."

Kayin tilted his head, but there was a disconnect in the almost feline mannerism and that brawny frame he wore. "We have only just arrived."

"I know that. Looks like we have to go back to Benevolence."

"Is that wise?"

"Hell no. It's probably a trap, but we gotta all be in the same place at the same time to get caught, right? So as long as we don't all go, we should be fine."

"Hmmm, your reasoning is somewhat flawed. For my part, I do not think I have to be in Benevolence at all to be bound to one who is. Witchcraft" —he wrinkled his nose like he might sneeze at the word— "makes use of a fetish, a fetish that Edward has in his possession."

"Yeah, well, maybe he'll leave it here. And anyway, Desollador won't be going either. We need to split up."

"But you will go."

"Yes. Edward thinks Eric is waiting for us, planning something. He wants backup."

"Would it not be wiser for Desollador to go then?"

"Desollador is thinking with his dick at the moment instead of his brain. So let his little Pet keep him busy while we're gone, and you keep an eye on him to make sure he stays well the hell away from Benevolence until we get back. I have no intention of going down again for a two-hundred-year nap."

Kayin rubbed his stubble with vacant eyes. "Yes, me neither."

There isn't a kid to grow up in Benevolence who hasn't taken at least one dare to break into the house at the head of the Serpent, so I had seen our destination before, but found it no less threatening for all my familiarity. With three stories and three-dozen windows, the place might have once been a grand mansion, but compound was a more appropriate term. Except for two Goliath marble columns and a single stone lion guarding its entrance, it was devoid of ornamentation. Not one decorative bit of crown molding. Not a single shutter on any window, though all thirty-six were barred. Not even an urn that might have cradled a topiary in better days. Not one small thing to prove it had ever been a home.

I raised my fist to knock, wondering why I bothered even as I made the gesture. *No one lives in this house.*

"I thought I'd never see you again," came a voice behind us.

I drew on her, heaven help me. Bree tossed her into a tree before I fired.

"No, it's OK," I called when Bree would have uprooted them both. "She's a friend."

Renn grunted and picked herself up. "I don't feel like a friend."

Bree looked at me for an explanation while Roger snorted. "For someone who has no friends, they sure do seem to be coming out of the woodwork. Are you sure we don't need to kill this one too?"

"Shut the fuck up," I said before he could mention the twins. To Renn, I asked, "What are you doing here?"

She folded her arms. "Nice to see you too."

Crap. I didn't have time for this. "Well, of course, it's great to see you. I'm just shocked to run into you here, is all."

"I live here," she said as she brushed bark off the seat of her jeans. "But I'm shocked to run into you at all. Much less in Benevolence. Even more shocked you pulled a gun on me. But what shocks me the most is that I somehow landed upside a tree when no one was close enough to touch me."

I didn't have an answer for her, not one I could tell her anyway, so I diverted. "What *are* you doing here, Renn?"

"Looking for my brothers."

I winced. The memory of killing them was still fresh in my mind. "But the twins have been gone —"

"Four years. Yeah, I think I remember the general time frame, thanks."

"Why are you still looking for them?"

"You aren't the only one who lost someone, Diane. Only I didn't get to bury my brothers."

"I know that," I sighed. I didn't want her here. I could almost accept all the blood on my hands up until then, but not hers. "Why would you think you would find them here? After all this time?"

She gave a bitter laugh. "This is where they were headed the morning they disappeared. That stupid metal detector!"

"Oh honey —"

"I've been trying to get to the top of this mountain for years to look for some clue to explain why they never came home that day. But every time I make the trip, I get about three turns up the mountain and suddenly I'm back in my driveway, hours passed and no memory of where they went."

"You've been losing time?"

"Until a few days ago. I think I made it here that time, and whatever I found, someone didn't want me to see."

"You *think* you made it?"

She fished in her pocket for her phone. "The first few times I tried this, the recording was so bad I couldn't hear anything at all." She selected a file, tapped a point midway through the recording and passed the phone to me.

A man's muffled voice said, "Renn." Garble. "Keep coming up here."

"Who(inaudible).... What do you know about my brothers?"

"Gone." A rustling sound, then static, then, "Dead. I'm sorry."

"I want to see their bodies."

"We've (inaudible) before." A metallic clang, then more rustling, though there was a cadence to it, like jogging or climbing. "I don't want to have to do this again." Then, "No choice."

A gasp, intimate and feminine, a sound Renn would make with a lover. The man's voice came again after a prolonged silence, and it was louder now, closer. "Renn, look at me. That's it. Shh-shh. Your brothers just took off one day, up and left. But wherever they are, they are happy now, you know that in your heart. You have no need to come up here ever again. Do you understand?"

"Happy."

"That's right. Your brothers are happy. And you are going to leave this place and never come back."

"I'm...I'm leaving?"

More rustling, what sounded like a car door. "That's right. (Inaudible) danger." He said a few more words, but they were drowned out by the sound of the car starting.

Renn snatched the phone back from me. "There's nothing else on the recording. This strange man tells me to fuck off, forget about my brothers, and I drive home like it never happened. If I didn't have the recording, I wouldn't believe—hell, I wouldn't even know—it ever happened. So I come up here today to sort it out and stumble on some kidnapper's wet dream." She pointed back towards a vine-covered path that seemed to lead to nowhere. "And you. After all this time, you!"

The others watched the events unfold in respectful silence. Then Bree asked, "How do you know each other?"

"Renn was my best friend in the world until my parents died, and I started..." I exhaled through my nose and wished somebody would give me a vampire to kill so I wouldn't have to deal with this conversation any more.

Renn narrowed her eyes at me. "Started what? Running away?"

Bree ignored her. Putting two and two together, she whispered, "Her brothers...?"

I didn't trust myself to speak, so I just nodded.

Renn answered, "Disappeared just before Diane's parents died."

"Who was that on the recording?" Mace asked me.

I shrugged. He might be the one we came here to see, but if my suspicions were correct about how he managed to turn Renn away and wipe her memory of the visit, I wanted to vomit. Only one type of creature I knew could control someone like that, and if Catherine sent us here to find him, this was a trap.

I nodded towards the path. "What did you find over there?"

Renn passed a wary glance to my companions, but in the end led us to the cellar. While we were investigating the mirror room and the amethyst coffins, she pulled another phone from her pocket.

I was preoccupied with those coffins, wondering why there were two of them, when I heard Noah's voice. "This is some medieval shit."

I jumped before realizing his voice had come from the phone.

"Found this down here today," Renn said. "I can't believe it actually powered up."

Mace watched the video over Renn's shoulder, eyes widening when the camera panned on Tate's face. He made eye contact with me and inclined his head in a gesture that seemed to say, *Sorry you had to kill him.*

Renn's fingers were trembling hard as she selected the next video. The mirror room looked very different four years ago. Someone had been busy bringing it into the 21st century.

The video showed a brief glimpse of Salvion in the reflection of one broken mirror, then the phone slipped out of Tate's hand. The camera angle showed fragments of what followed. A pale hand the color of ice lifting the coffin lid and something crawling out. A body landing hard at the bottom of the ladder and the close-up sounds of feeding.

"What are you doing? Get off him!" Noah's voice, followed by a rifle report and an answering laughter. Then Noah appeared in view, the camera close to his face.

Roger gasped, "Holy crap, is that —?"

Mace elbowed him in the ribs. "Shhh. That must be one of her brothers."

Renn didn't hear. She watched the phone in stunned horror, one hand over her mouth, tears welling in her eyes.

Noah's head slid out of the picture again. He screamed once off-camera, then fell silent. That was the last visual on the recording, though sounds of sucking and scraping went on for a long while afterward.

I put my arm around my friend, though it felt awkward to do so, like I no longer knew how. "I'm sorry."

She grabbed onto me so tightly I wondered if she had forgotten how I left her alone to deal with her loss. "What happened to them?"

"I don't know, hon," I lied.

"He told me they were dead. He knows. He has to know. I have to find him." The man on the recording. I knew Renn would never leave it alone, would never give up until she had her answers.

"OK, I'll help you," I decided. "But first, let's get out of this hole. Bree, can you get us in the house?"

"Depends. Do you want the door to still be attached when I'm done?"

Renn wiped her eyes. "I can get us in."

After digging into the lock with a twisted pair of bobby pins for the better part of an hour, the door finally opened on a collapsed staircase, peeling floral wallpaper, mismatched bits of furniture and old rugs that were more fleas than threads. The house felt like a corpse as we tiptoed through it, afraid it might wake.

"This isn't creepy at all," Bree said.

"Remind me why we drove ten hours to get here. I think I felt safer at home." I wanted to slap Roger, but he was right. The place afforded us no protection, no modern conveniences and so far only yielded obscure clues about how to save ourselves: the mirror room and the coffins.

"There has to be more here," I said. "We just have to find it."

"What exactly are you looking for?" Renn asked.

We tiptoed through an empty room, anchored by a small brick fireplace, into what must have been the dining room.

Several ladder-backed chairs faced the wall in one corner, a three-legged farmhouse table pushed against them.

In the center of the room, where the table should have been, we found a hinged door set into the floor.

"That," I answered.

"What is it with this place and hidden rooms?" Renn asked under her breath.

Mace went down first, more to clear out the spiders than to protect us from any lurking demons. I knew the demons had been set free years ago. Bree and Roger stayed topside to keep watch.

It was a pit, two heads taller than any one of us and as large as the room above it, dug into the shape of a circle. A thick white line of powder ran the circumference of its walls. I dipped my finger in it and touched it to my tongue. "Salt."

"How very CSI of you," Mace said.

"What is this place?" Renn held the flashlight on my hand as I reached up to trace a passage carved into the earthen wall.

"None without a soul may leave," I read. Someone had written that line on every inch of every wall of the space, even on the underside of the floorboards above us. "This place is meant for Edward."

"Diane, who's Edward? I don't understand. The mirror room, the coffins, this place. Do you know what this is all for?" She lowered her voice to a whisper. "Do you know what happened to my brothers?"

I was wondering how to tell her, how much to tell her, when Bree called down, "We've got company!"

I scrambled back up the ladder, heaving myself into the dining room at the same time he entered. I touched my shotgun to reassure myself it was clear in its holster, but didn't draw it.

The man in the doorway inventoried us with a glance, hazel eyes pausing on mine long enough for me to see a twitch of recognition and maybe grief, then named me, "Diane."

It sounded like someone else's name from his lips. I asked, "How do you know me?"

He pocketed his hands and gave me a wry smile. "Catherine told me you were coming."

"How do you know Catherine?" I wondered with something like

jealousy.

Before he had a chance to answer, Renn climbed out of the hole. "It's you," she said.

Something like ice slipped down my bones. This was the man who had turned her away from her search—from who knows how many searches—and made her forget she had ever been here at all. The man who caused that gasp, intimate and feminine, the kind of sound she would make with a lover. I knew that gasp.

I palmed a syringe instead of the knife, just in case I was wrong, and extended my hand. "I didn't get your name."

He grasped it in a firm shake, but before he could introduce himself, I pulled him close and plunged the needle into his torso.

"Damnit!"

I was airborne before he finished cursing at me, landing awkwardly on a legless dining room chair.

"What the hell?" he asked, rubbing his torso like he'd been stung by a bee.

Oops. "I needed to make sure you weren't—"

Bree interrupted me. "Diane. He is."

"He can't be. The salt isn't affecting him."

"I don't know what to tell you, but that man is a vampire."

"How do you know?"

"I can't touch him. Just like I couldn't touch the ones you killed last night."

"What do you mean you can't touch him?"

"I can bring this house down on top of him, but I couldn't move him if my life depending on it."

Renn watched our conversation like a ping-pong match, then turned her attention back to the stranger. "Who are you? What happened to my brothers?"

"My name is Eric Skinner. And if I am not mistaken, Diane killed your brothers last night."

Kayin hid in the shadows while the Dog crept through Diane's empty apartment, nose down to sniff the dust of shattered mirrors that peppered the hardwood floor. Desollador must have been truly distracted not to pick up the poacher's scent. Did the vampire know how his Dog whined for her?

Curious how Kayin did not feel the tug of envy for Desollador's other form, not the way he felt about the Wolf. Perhaps because the vampire never really got to be the Dog. He was always just a vampire wearing fur. The Wolf was superior, a pure form. The Wolf was not human—even if he remembered that form—and no longer burdened by temptation or conflicted emotion, by guilt or envy. Kayin could not recall how he learned that truth, but of it he was certain. The Wolf that used to be Mace's father knew no internal struggle in the face of killing his enemy, but absolute righteousness in his actions.

The Dog whined again. He wondered how the vampire lost his Pet. Her blood called to him. Perhaps distance muted the sound. The Dog picked through the sheets left on her bed, circled the mattress three times before lifting his leg to mark the center of it. Kayin shook his head. Someone needed to kill that creature.

He did not think it would be Diane. In the days of Abram, He who made Heaven and Earth would have visited upon her great suffering for her iniquity. But then Kayin could not possibly fathom His plan. Hadn't he bestowed His divine will—to create, to control—upon her? He would work a great miracle with that one. Like the staff of Moses, the ram's horn of Joshua, Jael's tent spike, she would be shaped into a mighty instrument for His work.

Tacked to the kitchen wall, at eye level where the Dog couldn't reach, Diane had pinned an envelope with twenty one-hundred-dollar bills. On the envelope, she had written:

Mr. Krise, you have been so kind to me. I hate to leave this mess behind for you to clean, but I hope this will be enough to cover it.

Thank you, Diane

PS. Don't worry about me. I am going home to take care of my problem once and for all.

He carried it into the bathroom where the Dog marked the shower in the same manner he claimed the bed. When he saw Kayin, Desollador issued a single bare-teeth bark and shifted. "What?"

"Edward and Salvion have gone."

"Good. I don't much enjoy their company."

"And me?"

He shrugged. "Stay if you want."

"Do you enjoy my company so much more?"

Another shrug. "You don't want what's mine."

"True. I do not covet my brother's Pet." Kayin tried to grin, but from the vampire's expression he could tell he'd missed the mark.

"Have you seen her?"

He held out the envelope. "Diane has gone home."

"Home? Where the fuck is that?"

"You do not know?"

He swiped the envelope for Kayin's still-outstretched palm. "I asked, didn't I?"

"Diane is from Benevolence."

"Well, shit."

"Edward and Salvion have gone home too."

"Wait. To Benevolence? Why?"

Kayin inclined his head. "I did not ask. Salvion has warned me to stay away and is quite confident you will do likewise, being preoccupied with your Pet here."

"But Diane is there?"

"I do not believe Edward and Salvion knew she would be. If you follow, there is greater risk of defeat if it comes to a battle."

A muscle in the vampire's jaw ticked. "And if I don't follow..." He shook his head. "I'm going."

Kayin tried to grin again. "I thought you would." This time, the vampire's expression said he might have gotten it right.

Whatever else Eric Skinner was, I decided then and there he was also an asshole. "Why would you say that?"

"What does he mean? Diane, what did you do?" Renn's voice trembled.

I stared murder at Eric, but tried to soften my eyes for my friend. "Your brothers died four years ago."

"He said you killed them."

Son of a bitch. "I kill vampires, Renn. I killed two of them yesterday."

She opened her mouth.

"Don't you dare say there is no such thing. One killed my parents. Another killed your brothers."

"That wasn't what I was going to say. I was going to ask if Tate and Noah were the ones you killed last night."

I nodded, not trusting my voice to hold steady if I spoke.

Meanwhile, Mace had squared off against Eric in some silent pissing match. In response, Eric lifted his chest and asked, "Have you told them your secret yet?"

"What do you know about secrets?"

"I know we don't have time for them."

"He *is* a vampire," Bree said. "What does it mean when salt doesn't kill a vampire?"

As far as I knew, it meant he and Edward shared a link. Had we walked into a trap after all? "Who are you?"

"Will you refrain from stabbing me, shooting me or otherwise inflicting harm if I answer?" The assumption of familiarity in his tone unsettled me. He had one of those faces that looked like a million others, like I could know him, but I was sure I didn't.

"For now," I said.

He seemed to consider my answer, then nodded. "Two centuries ago, Catherine collected a group of gifted humans, not unlike the four of you, to put Edward and his progeny in the ground. I helped them do it."

"Two centuries," I repeated. "So you are a vampire."

Bree bristled. "I told you that."

He nodded. "Four years ago, Renn's brothers released Salvion from the mirror room, and in doing so released them all — including me — but my connection is not like theirs. Catherine has brought us together to put things right. Well, except for her." He shook his head at Renn. "You are the most stubborn person I have ever met. I keep sending you away, trying to keep you safe, and you keep finding your way back. I am afraid it's probably too late for you to leave now."

"I don't want to leave."

Waning daylight tossed shadows deep into the corners, into the crevices between the hardwood, into the spaces between the beams of the ceiling. It turned the stranger's eyes — Eric's eyes — into a pleasant, mossy green. "We have much to discuss. I think it's best you hear it from Catherine."

"Sorry, now is not a good time for a nap," I said.

"Just because Catherine has only been able to talk to you in dreams does not mean you have to sleep to talk to her."

"Wait, you have a way to bring Catherine here?" I asked. "While we're awake?"

He turned, golden brown hair rippling over his shoulders, a hand waved in invitation. We followed him into the sitting room, which didn't have anything to actually sit on. He pulled a crude leather pouch from his pocket and began pouring a steady measure of salt around us until he had us corralled. After lighting enough candles to make the room feel like a Catholic church, he settled himself cross-legged on the floor and indicated with a stiff pat of his hand that we should join him.

Mace wrinkled his nose. "Are we going to take off our clothes and start chanting now?"

Renn lowered herself to a space close to me and folded her legs beneath her.

I was close enough to Eric to touch him when I asked, "So what do we do?"

He placed a candle in front of him and passed his hand through the flame.

"Catherine," he called. An approaching heartbeat broke the silence.

"Just like that?" I asked.

"Shhh. No, there is no 'just' to what I am doing. Catherine," he repeated, passing his hand through the flame again. Every candle flame except Eric's thinned and died in coiling wisps of smoke and the sharp, sweet tang of sulfur. The remaining flame twisted and swayed, the smoke from the other candles curling around it.

"Catherine." The flame swelled and began to take shape.

She appeared in a blue glow. The ghost in my dreams, my prophet. I thought she smiled. "You are all here. My chosen."

"Catherine," I entreated as if I might awake and lose her. "How do we stop them?"

Her image twisted again, her gaze passing over each of us in turn before settling back on me. "You take up arms, your gifts, your power."

Roger wrung his hands once, then sat on them. "What power? I don't have any power!"

But the ghost raised one gossamer eyebrow at him and flickered to Mace instead. "Take off your ward."

"What?" Mace sputtered.

"You know what. The ring your father gave you before he lost his human flesh. It wards against your beast. Remove it."

His hand hovered at his throat, patting the ring suspended in the hollow of it, the way I touched my gun to assure myself it was still there. "No."

"Remove it," Catherine repeated, clasping her ghost hands to wait.

"I said no." I was starting to recognize that set of his jaw.

"I know that, dear boy, but I hoped you would change your mind. It was not a request. I have power in this circle." The phantasm flared, lashed out a pale hand of flame and ice, and tore it from his neck.

Mace clawed at her transparent fingers and snarled.

Snarled?

The movies are all wrong.

The flesh doesn't melt and rend. Fur does not grow and spread. Muzzle and fangs do not sprout from an open mouth. Hands and feet don't split to make way for claws. Even clothes are spared in transformation. Within the circle, shadows gobbled up Mace in one quick gulp and spit him back out as a wolf, twice the size of a mortal dog and as black as the shadows from whose coupling he was born.

The Wolf that had been a man swung his head, itself the size of a small dog, between ghost and human. Eric warned the rest of us, "Do not break the circle, not for any reason. It is our protection from what lies outside."

"Outside? I am more worried about what's in the circle."

"Edward is coming, Diane, and we are not ready to face him."

I looked to Catherine, who presided over us impassive as a hologram. "Turn him back!"

She spread her hands and answered, "Even if it were my will, I do not have the power." In that moment, I hated her.

The Wolf extended his tail in line with his spine, fur bristled, ears erect. He issued a low growl, first at me, then at the ghost and back again, his tail moving with a constant and unnerving twitch. The whites of his eyes glowed stark and angry in the darkness.

When he swung his head towards Renn, she scooted backwards, acting enough like prey that he started to advance. She screamed, and he bore her down, paws bigger than my hands pinning her shoulders to the floor. His lips curled back over fangs, and she redoubled her cries.

"Shit," Bree said, her voice a ragged whisper. "I can't touch him either. Why can't I touch him?"

"The Wolf is cousin to the vampire," Eric answered. "Roger, I believe they call you the dog-man?"

"*That* is so not a dog."

"Your gifts are not random. This has always been their true purpose."

He shook his head to deny it, but when the Wolf took Renn's throat in his mouth, Roger closed his eyes and started entreating him quietly to release her anyway.

187

After a few minutes, the beast lifted its head and tilted it in his direction. Renn sobbed in relief.

At the sound, Roger opened his eyes and commanded, "Get. Off. Her."

The Wolf took a step back.

"Is this my gift? I am"—he held a fist to his chest—"the Beastmaster."

The Wolf opened a mouth too full of teeth and started to pant. Bree and I cursed, and Renn sat up on her elbows. All of us waited to see what Roger would do about the two-hundred-pound werewolf in the room.

"This thing is Mace, right?"

Eric nodded. "In a sense. Mace is both the Wolf and the man. His beast is no longer contained by the ward, and it is the dominant persona. You have to command him to give his body over to the man again."

"You command him! I teach fucking obedience tricks to dogs. I don't have philosophical conversations with them. And anyway, that is not a damned dog!"

"Don't be dense. This is your gift, Beastmaster." I couldn't tell if Eric was mocking him or just respecting his self-appointed title. "You communicate with—you control—animals through your thoughts. Change him back."

Roger scowled at Eric. "How do you propose I do that?"

Bree slammed her palms against her thighs, her eyes heavy with unshed tears. "Roger, cut the shit, and just do it."

He nodded to her and said, "I'll try." He closed his eyes again and stayed silent for a long while. "He doesn't feel like a man," he said with a frown, but didn't open his eyes. Sometimes his lips moved and once I heard him beg, "Please come back, brother." But it took a long time for the shadows to rekindle.

When they receded, Mace was himself again. He blinked and flexed his mouth, his fingers, felt for the silver absent from his neck.

A spark of memory flashed his eyes, which went wide again as they latched onto Renn. "Are you OK?"

She nodded.

To Catherine, he asked, "What have you done to me?"

She smiled and answered in the tone of a mother humoring a child with a silly question. "I removed the ward that prevented the use of your gift. While there is a risk of losing yourself in the beast, like your father did, Roger will bring you back."

Mace held out his hand. "Give me back my ring. There are enough monsters in this town already."

Her smile never wavered as she placed it in his waiting palm.

"I'm no werewolf."

"Good," Roger said, "because I don't want to be responsible for making sure you don't end up stuck that way."

Renn hugged her knees. "What if you attack one of us again?"

Mace scowled at her. "What if you scream bloody murder right in my fucking face again?" She flinched, and his face softened. He tied the cord around his neck. "I'm putting it back on, so don't sweat it."

She buried her head. "I didn't know werewolves were real."

"Yeah, well, I didn't know telekinesis was real, then my ex-girlfriend plastered me on the ceiling with her mind. I didn't know vampires existed, but hell, Diane…" He stopped himself, but I knew what he'd wanted to say. "Diane's been bitten so many times you can play connect-the-dots on every body part." I saw Eric flinch out of the corner of my eye.

Catherine silenced us all. "Everything exists. We draw our thoughts from a universal memory, a collective consciousness. There are no new ideas, therefore no thing is imaginary." She flickered to me. "Do you wonder about your gift?"

"No. I know what I can do."

That smile again. I never noticed my prophet could be so patronizing. "Do you?"

"I can become a ghost, possess people like a demon, and bring small things back from my dreams. Or at least I have done all of those things once; whether I can do them again is anybody's guess. I can kill. That's my gift."

"Why?"

"What do you mean 'why'?"

Her infuriating smile never wavered. "Killing aside, what about the rest? Why can you do these particular things?"

"I don't know. I didn't choose them."

"But you did choose them, each of them when you had the need. You dreamt of things that made you happy so you brought them back with you from your dream to give you hope. You desired to be the hand that offered mercy to Renn's brother, so you traded your arm for another's to prevent him from shooting true. You took the compulsion from a new vampire's soul, possessing his wounded bride and sending your will through her blood to do it. For all these tricks, you have no idea yet the nature of your gift."

The rest were looking at me like they had watched Mace when Renn's throat was between his teeth, except for Eric, who still wore an expression of vague pain, and Catherine who waited for me to understand.

"My soul doesn't know the limits of my flesh. That's what Kayin told me."

"You straddle the waking and the dreaming world."

"I don't understand."

Catherine spread her hands. "You don't have to understand. Not understanding is not silver to your Wolf."

"So what is?" I asked.

The blue flame-woman tossed her braid of flickering indigo behind her with an exasperation that made her seem too human to be a ghost. "Assassin. Dreamer. Girl. When you reconcile your selves, maybe you will truly own your power. Until then, I think you will just get by."

Bree was next in line for debriefing, but it turns out Bree was closest among us to owning her power.

"You are not a girl anymore. The only reason you cannot move mountains is because you have not tried it lately." Then Catherine sighed, a sound that reminded me of wind moaning against closed windows.

Her smile faltered as she finally addressed Renn.

"I never intended you for this game. Eric has exchanged a measure of strength with you along with blood."

"Blood?" she and I asked at once.

Eric nodded. "I had to. I don't have Christopher's power."

"Christopher?" I asked.

"That is his name, the vampire that Marked you."

"His name is Desollador."

He flinched again. "You call him by his surname."

"Yeah, whatever that means. I call him Desollador."

"Fine. I don't have Desollador's power. I need blood to influence thoughts. And I was trying to keep her safe."

"So you are a vampire."

Catherine's figure dimmed, sputtered. "Ghosts can only haunt for so long. My energy is spent…I must leave you now."

"Without saying goodbye to your husband?" came a voice from the doorway.

As the shadows started converging again on Mace, I spun around to face Catherine's creation. He looked bigger than he had appeared in my dream, tall, broad shoulders and a torso that could have served as the mold for a gladiator's breastplate. He wore a black dress shirt that probably cost what I spent on my whole wardrobe. Legs that reminded me of the Goliath columns at the front of the house were stuffed into tight black BDUs. Army-Navy store meets Armani. I could have sworn I had seen his face before, his likeness, in more than a few celebrated paintings and timeworn sculptures of famous lovers. Catherine had made a virile monster.

Behind me, I heard the Wolf start to growl. Before I could sort out how that was possible after Mace put the ward back on, Eric said, "Don't let him break the circle." Fur brushed my arm and the Wolf stepped between me and edge of the powder-white line, trembling with anger and barely-caged aggression.

Edward regarded him with equal parts scorn and curiosity. "This pup was a man when I entered. It's been a long time since I ate a werewolf." To Catherine, he added, "I should have guessed sooner, love, that these children were yours. Is this the whole team or should I expect stragglers?"

"You are an abomination. You cannot be allowed to continue," Catherine managed to say, though her form quivered with fatigue.

"Bring on your toy soldiers, wife, mother. You do remember your daughter's fate." He paused, his smile fading to a stern slash of mouth. "I'll take care of your little tin men."

The ghost's departure plunged the room into darkness. Within the circle we scrambled for matches. Bree flicked the useless lighter over and over again hoping it may have one last flame to give. In the blackness, the Wolf alternately snarled and whined. I could feel him against my legs, coiled up tight as a spring, but Roger held him there. I laughed — which sounded absolutely batshit in the dark — at the thought of Roger serving as intelligence surrogate for a werewolf. We were so screwed.

Finally a round yellow glow pushed back the darkness and floated in Eric's palm. A vampire and a witch? I reached out to touch the ball of light, and as my fingertips touched his, from outside the circle came a roar and a sound like shattering glass.

I turned towards the noise. Desollador slammed his fist against air that separated us, sending violet sparks flying and invoking another explosion of sound. "You will not survive the reclaiming if I have to strip his scent from you too, Pet."

"So dog is your dominant persona?" I asked.

Slam. Shatter. "Why don't you come find out?"

"Why are you here?" Edward asked Desollador.

"I am here for what's mine. And you, Father?" I didn't miss his sarcasm.

"I am also here for what's mine."

"Can they get in here?" I asked in a whisper.

Eric shook his head, but pulled his hand out of my reach anyway.

Edward tapped his feet, crossed his arms over his chest. "Where is the Athame, boy?"

Eric's eyes went black. He leaned closer to that invisible line than was prudent, so he was nose-to-nose with Edward, but instead of speaking, he just smiled. His expression said they had a history, and not a pleasant one.

Mace lashed his tail at my shins and made a noise deep in his throat that drew Eric's attention back to us. "Get him under control, Beastmaster."

Roger opened his mouth at Eric to protest, but ended up grumbling without words with our lupine ally instead. After a few minutes of apparent debate, the shadows came round again to smooth fur into flesh. I couldn't watch without feeling dizzy.

Desollador was crouched at eye level with Mace when he became man again. "You know my Dog fucked a bitch in heat centuries ago just to see what would happen? Heard she had human pups. Do you think that makes me the father of werewolves?"

Mace, still too much the Wolf to speak, only growled.

Desollador grinned with teeth. "Not happy to have my blood in your veins? I could help you out with that."

"Don't break..." Eric started.

"Don't break the circle. Sit on our asses and wait. Got it."

"What do you say?" Desollador ignored Eric and me. "My Dog against your Wolf. That is why Catherine chose you, isn't it?"

From across the circle, Edward said, "Enough. Christopher, kindly go find your Pet a good reason to come out of her glass house."

Edward turned to Desollador and nodded. The vampire looked at me, an unfathomable expression in his eyes, and left the room.

Bree watched him go and bit her lip with a frown. "That can't be a good thing."

CHAPTER 8

It took Desollador less than ten minutes in his canine form to make it back down to the base of the mountain. Though he didn't run any faster as the Dog, the meeting with Mace left him with a primal urge to prove himself on four feet.

He had met his bastards before, thought he had killed them all, down to the last of the litter. Could there be another vampire out there with his...curiosity? Werewolves. Abominations with so little humanity inside, they lost their human form forever once they turned.

Desollador spared just one of the ten minutes to ponder why the Wolf hadn't broken the circle, what invisible leash had held him in it, and how he managed to become Man again. Then the question flitted away like an errant butterfly when his nose caught the scent of meat. That it was wrapped around the bones of an eight-year-old girl tucked in between flannel sheets, snoring softly in her bed, did not matter in the least.

Watching her through an open window and the lacy billow of curtain, Desollador wondered what she dreamed about, amusing himself with the idea that her dreams were sweet-scented and bright with laughter, twinkling with innocence. If he didn't kill her, the coming nightmare would taint every good dream that came after him.

He vaulted through the open window and came to a crouch at her bedside, becoming Vampire again when he landed. He covered the girl's mouth and squeezed her jaw until her eyes bulged open. She blinked in the sparse light to identify her attacker, making out just one of his red eyes before flailing tiny fists and feet at his chest. Desollador let her struggle for a few seconds before silencing her with a hiss.

"If you move again, I will put this pillow over your head and smother you until you are dead."

The girl stopped moving at once, rigid as a statue except for her trembling.

"I have a gun," he continued. "If you scream for your parents, I will shoot them in front of you, your pretty mother first, then I will suffocate you." He waited for her to draw a tremulous breath. "But if you are quiet and do exactly as I say, they will be safe, and I won't have to put the pillow over your face. Do you understand?"

Under his hand, she nodded.

The vampire eased his palm off her lips, and when she did not scream, pulled it away. The girl tucked her flannel sheet under her chin and whispered, "What do you want?"

He answered with the truth. "I'm going to take you up to the top of the mountain."

"Wh…what are you going to do to me?"

"What is it that you are afraid I will do? Tell me that, and I will tell you if that is my plan."

"Shoot me. Smother me. Strangle me. Burn me. Or…you know, the bad thing that men sometimes do."

Desollador tapped his chin and pretended to consider. "No, I am not going to do anything like that. I give you my word."

"So…you're not going to hurt me?"

His eyes flooded with merlot and the girl's head started to buzz.

"It's time to come with me."

Desollador was holding a little girl when he came back, a little girl with round doe eyes and cheeks that glistened with tears.

"You son of a —" I shoved myself off my heels.

Eric hauled me back. "Not for any reason. She is lost now."

"Desollador, no," I begged. "You cannot be this much of a

monster. Let her go."

"Make me," he challenged.

I tried, but Eric pulled me away again, ordering, "Stop" like he expected me to obey.

Desollador slammed his fist against the invisible wall, dragging the girl behind him. I don't know which was louder, the circle shrieking or the child. "Let her come, brother."

For once, I was inclined to agree. "Let me go."

"You will not jeopardize all of us, and every life they will take after us, for a girl you cannot save."

"Watch me," I growled and fished a blade from my belt, but Eric wrenched it out of my fingers, threw me face-down on the floor and sat on me. *Well, hell.*

Desollador slammed his fist against the air again.

"Let me up! That's a little girl!"

"She was dead the moment Desollador stole her. You. Cannot. Help. Her."

Still trying to heave him off me, I howled, "You'll have to fight me all night, Eric, if you don't let me try."

His body on top of mine grew so rigid I thought he might let me do it until cool fingers found my neck, searched my spine. "No, I won't." With a quick, suffocating pressure, he flagged down unconsciousness to give me a ride, and away I went.

As the world went black, I heard Desollador raging, "Her fate is on you!"

I know, I thought, *and I am trying to save her.*

When I awoke, the cracks between the floorboards came into focus with stark clarity, but a thin white veil of fog crowded the edges of my vision, like a sunspot moving just out of my line of sight every time I tried to look directly at it. Chasing the mist brought Desollador back within my field of vision, angrier than I had ever seen him. When he wrapped his hand around her head, I feared he might rip it off while I watched. I stood and tried to scream, but had no voice.

This time when I broke the circle, Eric didn't stop me, did not even beg me to stay. Evil may have rushed in behind me to devour those I left behind, or my companions may have rushed out to seek escape.

I did not spare a single thought on either possibility, focused only on Desollador and the child.

His lips drew back over his canines. I reached for the girl, and thrust my fist right through his ribcage as if my hand was made of air. Stifling a well of rage and frustration, I tried again, but with no better luck.

Around her tiny throat, the vampire put his shining fangs and I threw myself at her, wrapped my arms—my very essence—around her like a cloak. Aware that wresting this prize from Desollador would be tantamount to parting the ocean, I meant to do it anyway.

No matter what, just hold on, I told myself. And with her tightly held within me, I ran. Desollador's roar followed me.

Out of the house now, into the brilliant night scented with rain, clouds thin enough to see the moon through them, adorned with a halo yellow and white as daisies. I ran over fields of freakishly large mushrooms, so fast that the ground below me, twinkling with wet puddles and water droplets, hardly knew the soles of my feet.

I mused that the adrenaline rush of flight must have lent me superhuman strength because the girl seemed weightless in my arms. A black owl flew with me, between trees with faces and brittle twig-arms that reached for me—whether to stop me or hurry me on my way, I couldn't fathom.

The bird asked "Who?" But I didn't waste any breath to answer.

All at once, or maybe it just seemed that way to me, the mountain ended, giving way to a valley seeded with equal parts red clay, saw grass and dandelions. We outran the rain. The wind blew myriad miniature white parasols into a mist I still couldn't quite see…so many wishes.

In this place, I sat down my burden, unwrapped her from myself and wondered where she belonged.

Those big doe eyes blinked at me. "You're so pretty," she said with something like awe.

I shrugged off the compliment. "Are you OK?"

"Are you an angel?"

I started to snap, 'Do you see any wings?' but caught myself. "No, I, uh…"

"Am I dreaming? It feels like I'm dreaming, but I don't know when I fell asleep."

I thanked the good Lord that children are so fey. "Yes, you are dreaming. Of angels and fairies and—"

"Handsome men with red eyes?"

"Yes, all a dream."

"That's my house." She pointed.

Scooping her into my arms again, I said, "I'll take you back."

When I left her tucked again in her bed beneath the flannel sheets, she told me, "This was fun."

Well, hell.

I risked my life, probably killed five others to save her, and the child thought it was all a dream. I grumbled to myself all the way back up the mountain. This time when the owl asked "Who?" I answered, "The damned sandman apparently."

The house rose black against the moon-glow clouds, not dark, but black, a box-shaped void guarded by an obsidian lion. Like a solarized photograph. Had the bad guys made it their own, then? Did I just imagine that it breathed?

I slid back in silently, expecting to hear a fight. When I didn't, I readied myself for the sight of the carnage. But my companions still huddled together in the circle while Desollador now sulked empty-handed against a wall and Edward twirled a ball of flame in his palm like the Goblin King with a crystal ball. It illuminated an ornate box suspended from a leather thong around his neck. What was it about weird necklaces lately?

My five companions still huddled within the circle. But how? Confusion thickened the fog around me. I'd broken the circle. I opened the door, welcomed the demons. Then I saw the sixth figure in the circle, face-down on the floor, sleeping, coffee-brown hair spread over her back, hiding her face, but I didn't need to see it to recognize it as mine.

I was just a dream after all.

But then how did I rescue the child?

The plastic orange, the toy car, explained a voice I now recognized as Catherine's.

I don't understand.

You took Desollador's victim the same way you took the orange.

But that was a dream thing I made real. This was a real thing I made dream.   *Oh Christ, I did make her real again? She's...she's in her bed?*

Yes, you saved her. Now, do you know how to save your friends? Better do it quickly. They are considering slim chances.

Slim chances: escape, survival. Catherine gave a vague description, but I understood. They were planning to break the circle.

Eric shook my body. "Diane, wake up." Looking down on him, I would have laughed, but I didn't see the point. Besides, Eric would not muscle me into compliance this time.

I stuffed my companions into my dream self faster than any of them could raise alarm as one-by-one they started vanishing from the circle. I took my body last because it felt strange and somewhat *wrong* to put inside my soul the flesh that usually carried it.

I felt inside-out and too full with other people when Catherine told me to take the box. *He carries a fragment of the demon in it.*

More than stealing every body and soul inside our circle, I got a thrill swiping that box from Edward's throat, like a killer collecting a souvenir of her crime. I left through the walls this time, which is what I probably did last time though I hadn't noticed then. The owl still followed me with a curiosity. When it asked its question, six voices answered.

I stopped at an unremarkable thatch of Bradford Pears, snowy blooms wilting in the damp air, and vomited up the people I had eaten. Then I settled back into my flesh and, right-side-out, and woke up exhausted. When the owl pestered me again, I told it to shut up.

"You really know how to pull a boner, don't you, brother?" Salvion asked.

"I would ask why you are here, but I assume you followed your toy," Edward said with venom.

"You did tell me to feed off her as often as possible. So you know why I am here," Desollador answered. "What about you?"

"I followed the Athame. Did you know it was here?"

A cold dread filled the pit of Desollador's stomach. "I didn't."

"We need to leave. Now. Before Catherine manages to get the whole gang together again," said Salvion.

As much as Desollador hated to admit it, "Salli's right."

Edward waved their concern away. "Kayin is on his way back to the wilderness. Catherine's cause is lost; she has no lure to bring him here. Your obsession with that girl makes you too easy to manipulate."

"My obsession? You sent Kayin and Salvion to feed from her. To feed you!"

"Easy, Christopher," Edward warned. "If I have the Athame, I won't need your plaything anymore."

It went without saying, Desollador thought, that if Edward had Diane's ability, he would not need the Athame. She just ate a *room* full of souls. Edward could only dream of that kind of power.

"So you'll have her all to yourself again," he went on.

"Make your point."

"I believe our *friend* Eric has it."

"Can't you tell? I thought it calls to you," Desollador said in tone as close to patronizing as he could manage without crossing the line.

"It's obscured. I feel it near, but I can't pinpoint where. Find Eric. Make him tell you where it is. You can still do that much, can't you?"

Where he'd find Eric, he'd find Diane. It made his teeth ache. "What I create, I control."

Edward smiled. "Me too."

You just keep thinking that, old man, he thought, and went to find Diane.

CHAPTER 9

While my body was sleeping, my soul was bone-tired, too tired to even remain fleshed. I drifted between dreaming and waking, body and out of body, until the dawn began to ease through the trees, roll over mountain and shadow mountain, turning the blackness bruise-blue. The worst part, though, were the dreams that weren't mine, that rubbed off on me from the souls I had stuffed inside me. And the worst of those were Eric's.

Naked, he knelt in front of a woman, really not much more than a girl. Lush, strawberry-blonde curls cascaded over her bare torso, casting deep shadows in the candlelight. He kissed her collar bones, and she hummed a contented sound. He caressed her shoulder and frowned at a faint scar he found there, like a white cord against her skin.

"What caused you such pain? Show me. I'll slay it."

She laughed and pushed him on his back. "I have no need of a knight to hunt dragons for me."

"Hmmm, and what is it you need?"

"You. Just you."

He breathed her name, "Angeline," and rolled her on her back again.

The candlelight dimmed, and the lovers felt their way around in the darkness, tender sighs and soft moans to mark their journey. She called out "Eric" in a way that sounded more like an entreaty than a name, and his fingers found a thin rope of skin on her thigh in the shape of his brother's crest.

Then she was standing, a fur clutched against her breast, fingers shoving love-tousled hair from her forehead. "I will not speak of this!"

Eric lunged for the covering even as she retreated. "What did he do to you?"

"He loved me."

"That is not love."

"All that loves is not gentle. Who are you to condemn his?"

"I am your husband, a man who will cherish you, who will protect you, and who would never bestow my mark of ownership on you as if you were a common steer."

She slapped his cheek, pulled off the golden band on her finger and hurled it against his chest. "Is that not a mark of ownership?"

Now he did tear the blanket from her, broad hand closing on slim thigh with bruising urgency. "And this? Can you toss this from your body as easily?" As white as the corded scar on her shoulder, but twice as large, the brand rode high up on her hip.

"You would pit me against my dead husband? Tonight of all nights?"

"Can you not see my anger is on your behalf, at what he did to you?"

"Is that true? What will you do to avenge me? What more besides leaving him bleeding on the battlefield is there to do to him?"

His hand moved in a blur and then she was on the floor, palm against her cheek, the sound of his folly still echoing about their bedchamber. Fingers over his mouth now, shock written across his forehead. "Oh Angeline. I—"

"See," she said, lowering her hand to reveal a bright red handprint. "All that loves is not gentle. "

"Forgive me."

"I will tell you something, husband. I knew more pleasure that night, being marked like a common steer," —she traced the mark on her thigh—"than on this one."

The candlelight dimmed again. From one moment to the next the world went dark and filled with blood. So much blood. Angeline lay bent at an obscene angle over the dining table, her lips parted in an expression of frozen anguish, still lovely even though they were as blue as her eyes now.

"What did you do?!" Eric screamed into the dead air and forced himself to his feet, staggering away from the carnage after the one who created it.

How long had he been out? Where was the red-eyed devil?

A sound like horse hooves on packed earth echoed through the keep. He followed the noise until it cracked against the walls, loud as a thunderstone. Was this what it felt like to die? His injuries must be mortal—a sword in the gut, an arterial wound from the demon's mouth.

What was that thing that attacked? Who? Surely, his memory was compromised, because the monster looked like—

The noise was at its zenith now, and he found himself standing in the middle of the nursery, his daughter—Angeline's daughter!—cradled in his arms. Her pulse a hammer against his breast. And not a soul left alive to protect her from the monster he had become.

Merciful daylight came and Eric—looking older now somehow, though his flesh had not aged a day since his wife and daughter died—stretched out in the grass, gazing down on another woman. This one wore her auburn hair straight and cropped just above her shoulders, but had the same striking blue eyes.

"I got carried away," he said, tucking her hair behind her ears to reveal two neat puncture wounds. "I can heal them."

She covered them with her hand and smiled up at him. "You wouldn't dare."

"Natalie, it's going to scar."

"My scars are memories, Eric. Let me have a good one."

"There are no good ones."

"You stubborn man." She pressed her hand against his chest. "I want your mark on me, so leave it be."

A shadow passed over his eyes. He dragged a fingernail across his palm and wrapped it around her neck—blood to seal the wounds—before she had the chance to pull away. "I am not a man," he said, "and this was a mistake."

"How dare you say that to me, after—"

"I'm sorry. I am poison to you, Natalie. I have already marked your soul. That is scar enough."

Daylight faded and, when the moon chased back the darkness this time, Natalie faced Desollador like a gull braving a howling sea, Eric beside her.

Desollador looked from one to the other and smiled in a way that made me scramble for consciousness as he said to Eric, "If you want to keep her, I suggest you claim her. Or someone else will."

His laughter followed me back into the forest, where I found my way out of one hell and into another. I opened an eye and squinted into the sunlight. Eric's face obscured my vision, and I frowned. "No offense, but you are the last person I want to see right now."

His expression matched mine. "I'm sorry. I shouldn't have put you to sleep."

"No," I agreed. "Especially if you can't learn to keep all your kinky little secrets to yourself."

His brows crinkled. "What do you mean?"

I sat up and tried not to puke. "Who's Natalie?"

Eric flinched when I said her name. "Natalie is why the monsters you fight have been gone from this world for two centuries."

"Who's Natalie?" Bree echoed. "Did I miss something between you eating us and spitting us out again?"

"I didn't really eat you."

"You brought us here, inside you," Mace said.

Roger gave me a shell-shocked look that made me ache for his former lightness. "I never knew you were so sad," he said.

I felt like I had locked them in my diary and knew they had read too much. I sat up, rubbed at a sore spot on my neck, caught Eric's apologetic nod, and drew my knees to my chest. "I'm sorry. I couldn't think of another way out."

"You saved us," Mace said. "But you should know, you gave up a lot of secrets doing it."

I searched his eyes. Did they all know about the night with Desollador now?

"You have friends now, Diane," he finished.

I took a deep breath and fought back a deluge. "Oh…OK."

"I won't lie, I think you're one twisted bitch, but I trust you. And I'm with you."

I shrugged it off. "I had no idea I was out of body when I took the girl, until I came back and saw myself laid out on the floor. I don't know how I did what I did."

"Thank you." Renn's eyes glittered with unshed tears.

"I told you I had no idea."

"I'm not talking about that." She bowed her head. "Thank you for being the one to do it. What needed to be done."

"What?"

"Tate and Noah. You could have just let him shoot them." She inclined her head to Mace.

"How did you know? How much did you see?"

"When you took us inside you, our souls touched yours," Eric said. "The things you saw from my past were connected to your own soul's journey. What Renn saw was connected to hers."

"You know you sound like a fruit loop, don't you, buddy?" Mace asked.

I gave Renn a hug. "I'm sorry."

"I missed you."

I didn't trust myself to return the sentiment, so I just nodded.

"I don't mean to ruin the moment," interrupted Bree, "but getting back to this Natalie chic, how exactly did she do it?"

"She did it the same way Diane got us out of that house," Eric answered.

I paled. "I don't know if I can do it again. No, that's not true. I am almost positive I can't do it again."

"Actually," Eric said. "Next time you will do more."

"Really? It's all me, huh? I am looking at a werewolf, a beastmaster, a telekinetic that can apparently move mountains if she tries, a vampire, and the—I'm quoting here—most stubborn human being he has ever met. All this power, and it's up to me? I don't think so."

He inclined his head. "You are right. Next time we will do more also."

I heard that infuriating note of familiarity again. "We need to talk," I said to Eric. "Alone."

We ventured too far away from the group, but it took some time to form the words I wanted to say to him. "You understand you are the first vampire I haven't tried to kill."

"Technically you did try to kill me. If not for my connection to Edward, you would have been successful."

"I don't understand how, or for that matter why, you are connected at all."

His jaw tightened. "I was an experiment. It didn't work out the way Edward intended, but it aids our cause greatly."

"It does?"

"I have a unique gift. I can walk between this world and Purgatory."

"Purgatory? Like 'tortured souls go to work off their debt to society' Purgatory?"

"An alternate plane of existence where the Self goes to be purified and sanctified before returning to the Source."

"Oh, *that* Purgatory." I rolled my eyes when he didn't say anything. Sarcasm is lost on some people. "Sorry, I don't follow. What's this got to do with Edward?"

"I can take him with me."

"To Purgatory."

"Yes. Edward's existence makes the other three immortal, unstoppable. In Purgatory, for the span of a few heartbeats, his link to them will be thin enough to make them vulnerable. You will have seconds to make use of that vulnerability. If you are successful, Edward will be stranded in Purgatory for as long as his children are confined. And as long as I am there with him."

"Wait, as long as you are there? Why?"

"I am linked to Edward. If I come back here, he can find his way back too."

"But what if he never comes back?" Christ, I hoped he never came back.

Eric didn't answer.

It sounded like an awful fate. "I will find another way this time."

"There is no other way. And truthfully, it is where I would rather be. This plane is full of hurt and so far from redemption."

"Well, let's assume you are a good vampire —"

"Let's not."

I raised an eyebrow. "Then I'm screwed, because I don't know how to kill you."

"You can assume — correctly — that I am on your side. But you have got to understand that there are no good vampires. Do you know why we can't survive off animal blood?"

My turn not to answer.

"You didn't know?"

"You drink from humans?" It occurred to me we were a long way from the group.

He cocked his head, and when I took a step away, he advanced on me with a quickness that made my heart skip. A tree at my back prevented further retreat when Eric planted a hand on either side of my head and leaned in to my ear.

"I drink human blood."

I pushed against his chest, but he had me pinned between the proverbial rock and hard place.

"Because it's the only way to save any vestige of humanity I have left." His breath warmed my neck. "The only way to keep the monster inside me in check."

"Who do you...? I mean, where do you get...?"

"Most of the time from willing partners and most of the time they survive me."

"Most? Oh good. Not like the vamps I've spent the last year killing then. Apparently they didn't get the how-to-stay-in-touch-with-your-humanity memo."

He gave me an unkind smile. "You find a lot of vampires trolling daycares and nursing homes?"

"Is that a no-no? Exactly what constitutes off-limits to a vampire?"

"We all have different standards."

"I'm pretty sure I know at least one with none."

He sucked in a breath he didn't need to take, then let it out and said, "Desollador kills adulterers."

"How would you know that?"

"Even Kayin and Salvion have weaknesses rooted in human experience. Only Edward has no humanity to salvage."

He wasn't the only one who could change the subject. "Who was Natalie?"

He gave me some space, not much, but enough to catch my breath. "I told you already."

"I know what she did. Who was she…to you?"

"She was my heart." He punched the flesh of the tree just once and a shower of bark chips rained down on my left shoulder. "And a vampire was her weakness. She compromised her soul for him, pined for him, died with him. She put him in his coffin, as was her duty." He squeezed his eyes shut. "Then she climbed in beside him…and went to sleep."

I couldn't stop the gasp that escaped me. "You mean you. She put you…in the ground…when your soul took Edward to this Purgatory."

He nodded.

"And she killed herself rather than be without you."

"I found her bones when I awoke. Can you imagine?"

I shook my head, but my imagination did a pretty good job conjuring up that morbid picture anyway.

"And can you imagine my horror to find we have a new champion with the same weakness?" I started to protest, but his eyes warned me against it. "I know you gave your virtue to Christopher. In the end, when you put him in his coffin, I wonder what your choice will be."

I huffed in frustration, "It's Desollador!" but wondered how I could be torn so quickly between the twisted passion of a murderer and the brooding heartache of a stranger. And why all the significant men in my life turned out to be monsters. "You don't know me," I said.

"I know you better than I know myself." He brushed an errant lock of hair from his eyes. "I have been inside your soul, remember?"

Clenching and unclenching my fists, I seethed, "My name is Diane, not Natalie."

"In this life."

"What is that supposed to mean?"

He gave me a look that said I damn well knew what he meant, but told me anyway, "You and Natalie share the same soul."

If he was going to be ridiculous, I could go there too. "And how about before that? Before Natalie?"

He shook his head. "Don't."

"Don't what? We are talking reincarnation, so let's talk about it. Are all of the women in your life the same one born again?"

"This will only end badly, Diane. Stop."

"Because if that's the case, wouldn't that mean I share a soul with Angeline as well?"

His eyes turned the color of fire and his lips pulled back to reveal his deadliest weapons. "Do not say her name!"

"Why, Eric? Because it sounds ridiculous? I am not some dead girl. No matter how badly you want me to be."

He squeezed my shoulders. "I don't want you to be. Don't you get that? I want your soul to get over us!"

"Us? You mean vampires?"

"He means brothers." Desollador ripped Eric away from me.

"Diane, run!"

I wondered if Eric had forgotten that a human could not outrun a vampire, until he charged Desollador and collided with a sound like hammer to brick. Unmoved, Desollador snatched me up by my throat and slammed me against the tree. "Seems we have some reclaiming to do, Pet."

To Eric, he said, "I told you her fate was on you. I thought you would have learned not to touch my things after that messy business with my wife." He practically spit the last word.

Understanding washed over me in icy clarity. "Angeline," I whispered.

His eyes were starless obsidian. "You should have kept my mark, Pet."

I clenched my fists and tried to sound more courageous than I felt. "I am not your Pet, vampire."

"Now that's where you're wrong."

Eric charged again, but before he connected, Desollador barked, "Stay," and Eric stopped like he'd hit an invisible wall.

"Christopher, don't do this."

Gaze still boring into me with alarming intensity, he said to Eric, "The less you say at this moment the better, brother. And you can call me 'Sire'."

Kicking my feet in a violent tantrum, I clawed at the fingers wrapped around my neck with one hand and, hoping his brother's plea would distract him, drew the dagger at my back with the other.

Desollador didn't even flinch when I slid it between his ribs, but he did smile, a scary expression, what with all the teeth.

"So my little brother thinks you are Angeline born again? My wife enjoyed a good measure of pain with her pleasure. You do have that in common." Desollador plucked the blade from his side and regarded it with a gleeful expression that I just knew meant bad things for me. "This will do nicely."

"Brother, no."

He tightened his grip on my throat. A shadow fell across the blinding whiteness of his fangs, and I heard him from what sounded like a great distance say, "I warned you not to speak!"

Everything turned gray — his face, the whites of his eyes, even the evergreen trees. The world went quiet, a tunnel of darkness closing in around me like a warm blanket. Then it erupted again with the thunder of his laughter. His fingers loosened. Blood rushed back to my head, and my vision exploded in a rain of sparks.

"I was gentle plucking your cherry. Gentle is not really my preference, so I've been looking forward to getting you alone again."

"We are not alone," I said between gasps.

He shrugged. "Eric won't bother us. What I create, I control. Besides, it will do him good to watch, so he doesn't make this mistake again."

"What mistake?"

He let go of my neck and splayed his hand across the small of my back, drawing me up against him with enough force to knock the wind out of me. "I. Don't. Share."

"I am not your possession, Desollador."

He flipped the knife in his hand. "Wrong again."

Since struggle failed, I decided to give submission a go. What is it they say about bullies losing interest if you don't fight back?

"What do you want? You want to defile me in front of your brother? Have at it."

Whatever it is, they're wrong.

I raised a steady hand to my belt and unbuckled it. I drew it through my belt loops with a pop and handed it to him, heard him suck in his breath as I slid my jeans down and kicked them away. His eyes felt me up from my ankles to my face. Without blinking, I tugged off my shirt and bra and presented myself to him clad in nothing but boots and earrings.

"Do you want me?" he asked.

"I want a bath, a good night's sleep. I couldn't care less about sex, but whatever. I'm too tired to give a damn. Just get it over with."

I knew a brief moment of fear when his jaw hardened and his eyes blackened. I didn't have time to regret my rash taunting before he spun me away from him, and I felt the crack of leather against bare skin, opening a wellspring of pain that drove me to my knees with a cry. The belt came down again across the back of my legs before I could even catch my breath from the first blow.

The leather sliced at my back, my buttocks, my thighs, and the more tender places between them. I didn't have enough hands to cover myself. I heard Eric screaming and wished he would just shut up. The more he pleaded for my release, the harder Desollador beat me. The more I fought to escape the hateful strap, the faster the blows fell.

I don't know how long it went on. I don't know when I stopped screaming and could only sob in great heaving breaths. Or when I started to crawl away and he let fly the buckle end to extend his reach. I begged. I asked him what he wanted from me, promised him anything — everything — he wanted if he would just stop.

He hit me three times before answering. "I have what I want. I want you to hurt, Pet. Just. Like. This." Every word punctuated with a blow.

In desperation, and with a display of will that went against every instinct of self-preservation, I uncurled my spine, stretched my legs, spread my arms, and yielded to my fate, praying my obeisance would count for something. Even as I whispered, "OK, I will. I will hurt for you," I shook in anticipation of his next blow. One that never came.

I still shook, so hard I thought my teeth might shatter, but I couldn't make it stop. Then I heard him mutter "beautiful" and felt his hand on my hip. He rolled me over and used my belt to bind my wrists behind my back. When he caressed a thick red welt on my thigh, I shuddered and asked, "Why?"

"I told you when we met I would break you, Diane."

Fat tears slipped into my mouth, burning my tongue where I apparently bit it during the course of my lesson.

"Fear and lust, I welcome. Even hatred, I'll tolerate, but never apathy. Do I make myself clear?" He punctuated his question with the palm of his hand, bringing it down hard against the welt where my buckle had landed.

Deciding I should have had the good sense to fear him in the first place, I nodded. "I understand! I un...understand. Please stop hitting me."

He curled me into his chest, brushed his hand over my lips and

213

wet a finger on my tongue before seeking out that tender place between my thighs. "You have never been so yielding, Pet. Are you finally afraid of me?"

"Yes. No. Please don't do this."

"Admit it, Diane. You crave my particular affections. Show me you've learned your lesson. I wouldn't want to have to do this to you again."

My emotions were as raw as my skin. My filter wasn't working. So I said, "Liar."

His backhand spun me face-down in the dirt. "You are absolutely fucking right. I want to beat you. Again. Right now. Would you like that?"

He pushed my legs apart, unbuttoning his jeans, his fingers a bruising a pressure on my hips. I sobbed, trying to drag myself out from under him. He spread his knees, pushing my thighs wide around them.

"I could have given you what you craved, Diane. But I guess you'll get what you think you deserve instead." He pushed my head into the dirt, put both hands on my hips to hold them still, and said against my back, "There's one more cherry left on this tree, Pet."

I screamed beautifully for him. The pain lanced me, lifted me off the ground, long enough to see Eric double over.

Desollador pounded his fists into the dirt and roared, "You will watch, brother."

My legs trembled, and my breath came in shallow gasps between screams. "Nononono."

I pushed against his hips. With the belt binding my elbows, it was without any force. He took my wrists in his hands anyway, folded them into the small of my back. "None of that, Pet."

"Please! Don't! Please! Stop!" I begged, horrified that his thrusts matched the cadence of my pleas.

In a husky voice, he told me, "When I'm done."

He used me a long time that night.

After, I rolled onto my side and curled my legs into my chest, racked with breathless sobs I could not suppress. The sound of his zipper made me cry out, even though I knew it meant he put his weapon away.

His hand closed on my bruised thigh. "I am afraid you are not going to like this part."

The knife reappeared in his hand. "Since my brother seems to think you are my dead wife returned to me, I have decided to give you my Crest. We will see if you wear it with more devotion."

"No!" Eric and I screamed together as he started to carve.

He cut too deep at first and tsked me. "I know I've told you I like it when you squirm, but this requires some precision. You are going to need to be still."

The memory came to me unbidden, of Angeline professing to Eric that the night Desollador branded her like a common steer brought her more pleasure than she knew with Eric on their wedding night. *How?*

Desollador laid the flat of his blade against my skin and turned my face to him. When our eyes met, he said, "Do you want to know?"

I just don't want to hurt anymore.

My vision narrowed to a single point of light that became a candle flame. I saw Angeline in the darkness, her hands bound above her head in silk ties, her cheeks flushed and her hair a mess, her chest heaving as hard as mine.

"Do you trust me?" Desollador asked. Her or me, I wasn't sure which.

She said yes. I said no.

"It is not safe for you here without my protection. Anyone could steal you, claim you as a war prize."

"Let's not speak of war. No one would dare steal anything of yours, husband." She craned her head to take his lips, but he pulled away, teasing.

He lifted a small box from the windowsill and touched it to her breast.

She squealed. "So cold!"

His lips covered her skin, hot breath against her navel. "I intend to make sure any who dares to covet your body will know you belong to me."

She tested her bonds. "How could they not?"

He lifted the lid off the box to reveal a slightly curved piece of metal with a round shape cut out of the middle. "This has been beneath the ice since sunrise yesterday."

"What is it?"

"Mercy, darling. This is mercy."

"Hmmm, that is most kind of you."

He pressed the metal against her hip. "What—oh!" He kissed, sucked, nibbled while she squirmed under him. I could feel his desire rising.

After a while, she said. "Husband, I cannot feel my leg."

He nipped at the inside of her thigh, then a little higher. "Do you have feeling here?"

"Please."

"Please what?"

"Stop tormenting your bride so."

"I have not begun to torment you." He picked up a small bit of glowing metal from the brazier. One end of it was a carved wooden grip, but the other was metal, delicately forged into the shape of two facing crescent moons, a downward facing arrow between them.

"That looks like—"

"Do you trust me?"

She relaxed, stretched her leg out on the bed, tilting her hip to him. "Of course."

He placed the chilled metal against her thigh again and smiled. "You are mine."

She nodded. He kissed her lips, her neck, lower, and then he pressed the glowing brand into the matching cutout in the freezing metal. Somehow he managed to do all this without ever taking his eyes off hers.

Only they weren't her eyes, they were mine. And I now wore his mark, only one carved, not branded, into my skin. Desollador licked my wound clean until only a white ribbon of scar-tissue remained. No longer sobbing or averting his gaze, Eric glared at his brother.

Desollador noticed and said, "Fail to honor this one, brother, and I will not spare you."

"Spare me? You made me a monster!"

"I could have ended you."

"Like you ended her?"

Desollador's thoughts were still wrapped up with mine, and I saw her through his eyes. Even more, I smelled her, and smelled Eric on her. His brother had fucked his wife. She had *let* him. I felt Desollador's rage at that scent, saw his fist slam her face into the table, and heard the sound of bone breaking loud as the ice-sheets cracking in spring. Then he hitched up her skirts, took by force what she once freely gave him — this night reminded him so much of that one — and then finally cut his mark off her thigh. Blood in his mouth. So much screaming…until there wasn't.

The memory played in jolting bursts, like a firecracker exploding. In the midst of it, Desollador shoved himself off the ground, plucked Eric up and hurled him into a tree so hard he tore its roots from the earth. "Enough of this. Where is the Athame?"

"I don't have it."

From one tree into another. "I could compel you to tell me, but this is so much more satisfying." To another.

"Either way, it is pointless. I do not have it."

"Who does?"

"Desollador, he will kill her if you find it for him. Don't you see that? I know you feel something for her. If he gets the Athame, he will end her."

Desollador looked at me over his shoulder. "If he can take other souls, he won't care about hers."

"He needs hers so he never needs the Athame again. Did you miss that your Pet has the power to take souls too?"

"It doesn't work like that. He has never claimed any power from a soul he consumed."

"He thinks Diane's will be different."

"How would you know?"

"He will kill her if he gets the Athame. That's all you need to know."

Desollador stalked back over to me, crouched down and picked up my belt. I couldn't help it; I flinched. He wrapped it around my neck and pulled me up from the ground. "Are you worth saving, Pet?"

I felt a pressure in my head and heard static. He grasped for my will, but I pulled it away. I wanted to tell him I would end him when I got the chance, but knew that was probably not the wisest threat to make just then, so decided to just keep my mouth shut. He pulled me against him and kissed me like he owned me.

You are mine. No one will end you, save me.

I will not wear your Mark.

You will, or I will kill everyone you love. You are mine, as slave or mistress. Betray me, and I will take my mark back and bring such pain down on you that you will think I was merciful with my wife.

Betray you? We are enemies!

No man will touch you but me. You allow it at your...and his...peril.

I grasped the belt and ducked out from under it. "No man will ever touch me again, not you or anybody else. Are we done here?"

"We are far from done." He looked from me to Eric. "Where is the Athame?" The silence dragged out for minutes, but eventually Desollador smiled. "Clever."

"I swear to you, he will kill her."

"And I swear to you no one will ever take what's mine again."

I lasted about fifteen seconds after Desollador left, presumably to chase the Athame—whatever that was—before I hit my knees. Blood smeared the backs of my legs. The most intimate parts of me burned as if he'd rubbed salt in them. My skin throbbed with dozens of angry red welts. My shoulders clicked when I moved my arms, driving pain from the tips of my fingers to my neck. Bits of dirt and pebbles pockmarked my belly and breasts. I didn't even think the vampire knew how much he had hurt me. Then it occurred to me that Angeline's death had been accidental. The thought chilled me. I wondered if he mourned for her.

Eric took a step towards me. "I can help."

"Don't." I scrambled away. "Don't touch me." I didn't want him to look at me either, still naked and too vulnerable.

My shirt was ruined and felt unclean now. My uniform, the last vestige of my comfortable little world wherein I had just killed vampires and pretended to be an artist.

Wherein I dreamed of what it would be like to live a normal life and have even one single friend to share it with. Wherein my only drive to continue living was the desire to atone for the sin of letting my parents die when I was just a girl who didn't know any better. A girl brought so low by the shame of allowing herself to be defiled by a monster, she doubted she was even one of the good guys anymore.

I am NOT that girl now.

I felt the impact of my decision like the concussive force of a bomb exploding. I would not be shamed again. I wore a patchwork of bites, bruises, welts and the bright red wheels stitched by Desollador's belt. Every mark bore evidence of my atonement.

Didn't I have a battle-dress of scars to prove my rank? Some of them already long-healed, I knew each by the memory of its creation. One by one, I traced those scars, teeth bared against remembered pain as I coaxed them up from my flesh. Thick bands of white, like fine leather, like the ribbon of his Mark, rose on my skin. Here were garments that should strike fear into the heart of my enemy. See how much I can take, what I can suffer, before I break?

Then I started on the bruises, saturated with rich blues and purples that bloomed into supple panels of armor that reminded me of scales. They stretched and contoured to cover my breasts, thighs and groin, most of my legs. Welts and wheels transformed into a tight chainmail across my torso, storm-gray and red so dark it was almost black against the violet and indigo brilliance of my bruise armor. All of it fastened with the deep rivets that had been punctures.

I wondered if I was dreaming again, if this was how I imagined I looked in my sparkly swimsuit and purple pantaloons on that long, lost Halloween. Or was I really a warrior princess? I hurt too much to be dreaming.

With that thought, like the transformation of my wounds into garments, the deliverance of shame from my flesh, my pain slid from my skin and took shape. Lethal, wondrous shape.

Agony became a dagger slung low on my hips, its blade fierce and mercurial, awaiting necessity to determine form. Heartache became a staff across my back, tension coiled within it in intense anticipation.

The twin crescents of the Mark formed into a hilt, while the arrow lengthened into a narrow blade, double-edged and barbed at the end, forged of the same otherworldly metal that made Heartache and Agony.

I knew that underneath my armor, my flesh would be unmarked because my mind was clean again, unhindered either by suffering of body or soul. When I decided I would not be shamed, my will imposed the decision on me down to my marrow—so thoroughly I didn't even find it very strange to have grown a wardrobe from my injuries like some bizarre comic book character.

"What on Earth?" Eric's voice sounded far away and full of wonder.

"Eric, go and find the others. I need a minute."

"Why don't you tell me what happened?"

"I just figured out what I am."

Desollador raced the length of the Serpent, as fast as four legs would carry him from the maddening scent of sex, sweat, blood and sticky-sweet heat. As far as he ran, he carried with him her scent and the memory of her apathy. Her audacity still tasted bitter on his tongue.

He growled into the silence, his voice reverberating through the trees, pacing him in the darkness. He snarled again in answer to his own fury. The bitch was lucky he hadn't decided to finish her off for her defiance. His mercy was the only reason she was alive.

Mercy! He roared this time. He had meant to whip her into unconsciousness. Then she submitted…and he caved. Even as he craved the ruined din of her sobs. Even though her suffering thrilled him. It was a headier provocation than even her naked flesh, and still he spared her the worst of it.

A loblolly pine stood too close to his headlong trajectory. His forequarters impacted with the gray plates of its trunk with an echoing crack. The forest heaved a great breath and then, with a slow whoosh, the tree fell.

The destruction felt good, at the same time fueling and giving outlet for his rage. Another tree went down. And then a third. But it angered him that they were so stoic in their deaths. Where was the screaming? Where was the blood?

A stranger's growl rose up to meet his. Throaty and mechanical. The scent of exhaust flooded his senses, crowding out Diane's scent. His vision went red. All thought of forest flew from him, his ire redirected entirely at the gleaming intruder in his path.

A dark rope of pavement curved before him, a slash of metal separating him from the incomer. He vaulted, hind legs pushing off guardrail. The Dog hit the sleek, black machine headfirst, snarling. The crunch of metal satisfied him vastly more than a crack of lumber, and the chaotic, tumbling destruction that followed was a thrilling diversion. Then the sharp gasoline tang of the stranger's blood filled the air, fusing rage and thirst into a singular pulsing Hunger. Finally, the Vampire would be sated.

Kylie cursed the GPS for the ninth or nineteenth time since the sun went down. How was a winding two-lane road with no passing zones and a 25-mile-per-hour speed limit possibly the fastest route anywhere? Every radio station she could pick up played gospel music or static, and there hadn't been a gas station in miles to ask directions. She checked her cell again; still no bars.

Some jerk in a muddy pickup truck with no tailgate and oversized tires pulled out in front of her, and she swore in three different languages. Apparently for him the speed limit was too ambitious an aspiration, so she trailed behind him doing all of twenty. Her ride sputtered its dissatisfaction. The motor had been in danger of vapor locking for miles. What she needed was a good straightaway to step on it and blow the carbon out of the engine.

"Come on, asshole." She flashed her high beams at the redneck in the lifted truck and revved the motor, more to keep it running than anything else.

She wished, not for the first time, that her Caddy was out of the shop. If anything happened to Tommy's precious Mustang out here in the boondocks, he would kill her, baby sister or not. He'd been restoring it since he was a teenager. Now he was married with a wife, two-point-five kids and a regular nine-to-five.

Kylie saw that life for herself, not so very long ago. Thought she was well on her way to living it. But that was before two years of infertility treatments and an affair that gave her husband the one thing she couldn't.

Up ahead, the truck pumped its brakes and hit a gravel pull-off to let her pass. "About time!" She threw up her hands, but felt a little conscience-stricken by her misdirected temper.

Kylie went into the next curve a little fast, making up lost time, but the Mustang wasn't much better than the pickup on these mountain roads. She was made for the straightaways, as the song goes. Aside from the fact that drum brakes sucked and should be illegal, the thing was a chore to steer, and its high beams were no brighter than driving lights on modern cars. The seatbelt had been cutting into her neck for hours and...

She sighed, chiding herself again for being ill-tempered and ungrateful. She was lucky Tommy even let her drive his car, much less take it out of state. But he knew she wouldn't last much longer in her hometown, watching another woman's belly grow with her husband's child, a child she wanted so damned badly. So she'd sent her resume out to every hospital in North Carolina—the state's healthcare field was flourishing and RNs were in high demand—and finally got a call back. She'd been all set to head out this afternoon, make the half-day's drive, then get a good night's sleep so she'd be well rested for her morning interview. That was *her* plan, anyway. The Caddy had others.

Now she found herself running hours behind, lost and exhausted.

The road curved around a forest that went on forever, without a single street sign to prove she may be closer to civilization than she had been a half hour earlier.

Maybe it would have been wise to stay behind the truck, she thought.

Her eyes scanned the trees for movement. The last thing she needed was to hit a deer. With Tommy's car.

So she was watching when the first tree fell. It looked like a shadow—black on black—stretching across the woods. She felt more than saw its impact. Then another came down like thunder. The third was close enough she could see the trunk falling, but not where the branches would land, so she stood on the gas, her only thought to get out of the way before it came down on her head.

Boom!

The impact hit the passenger door so hard, Tommy's precious Mustang launched from the pavement, rolling in mid air so that Kylie had just enough time to see the blacktop rushing up at her before landing on the driver side door.

"The tree hit me!" and "I should never have taken Tommy's car," were all her coherent thoughts before sheer panic set in. She felt the car rolling in slow motion, the awful sense of being upside-down, then right-side-up again, a brief moment of relief, then disbelief as it started a second roll. When the car went into the third, gaining momentum, she thought she might puke. The world tumbled by so fast, she couldn't distinguish up from down. Couldn't tell if the car was tumbling down the road or the mountain or about to launch off a cliff.

The steering column broke under her grip. The seat-back snapped. She flopped and lurched, tried bracing her hands on the roof, pressing her feet into the floorboard to hold herself in place, but couldn't overcome the momentum. She felt her forehead hit something unyielding, next a blossoming pain across her temple and cheek, then a sharp jab in the top of her head. It was all caving in, she realized, crushing her.

And the noise!

The passenger compartment of the Mustang sounded like the

interior of a trash compactor. With each crash, thud, crunch, and screech, she felt the walls of her cage closing in on her.

"Please stop! Please!" She sobbed, begged in between a litany of "No's" that roughly marked each rotation. She cried "No!" many, many times before the car finally stopped.

In the silence and stillness that followed the crash, Kylie raised her hand to her head, her temple, her throat, and brought her fingers up to her eyes. She could just make out the color of blood, a lot of it. Head wounds bleed a lot, she told herself, but she had the shakes on top of it. Shock. Maybe concussion. She took inventory of her injuries. Her face felt ruined. Her mouth felt crunchy, like her teeth were shattered, or maybe full of broken glass. Her shoes, both of them, had come clean off her feet at some point during the crash, but her legs and arms seemed to be in working order. The seatbelt wouldn't budge.

When she managed to finally look at the car, bile rose in her throat. The driver's seat had shifted to the center of the car during the wreck, the sun visors overlapped each other, and the dash was a crumpled mess. Jagged gashes ran through the roof in a dozen places.

And a man sat on the hood of the car.

Had she hit him? "Are you...are you OK?"

He smiled at her and, she was sure of this, he had fangs. She clicked her seatbelt release over and over again in quick succession, but it did no good. Ignoring her question, he stood, placed both hands on the roof of the car and pushed. The roof peeled away, just opened up like a pop-top. Kylie screamed until he reached into the car and squeezed her windpipe closed.

The seatbelt gave him no trouble. The vampire uprooted it like a weed.

"Please don't hurt me," Kylie begged as he pulled her from the wreckage.

He smiled again, but the expression offered her not one iota of comfort. He propped her up against a tree and pressed his chest to hers. "I'm going to kill you."

His nostrils flared when she cried, "Please no. What do you want?

I'll do whatever you want."

Another smile. Whatever his reason for wanting her dead, her reaction pleased him. Then a darkness flooded his eyes, a hardness, and he snarled, "You don't have what I want."

Without further warning, those fangs ripped at her throat, piercing, tearing. It hurt worse than the accident, but the assault on her mind, oh, that felt like being in the car all over again, spinning, falling into crushing darkness.

Almost before Kylie fully understood her fate, the vampire stopped, pulled his head away from her throat and growled. He seemed to study her a moment, then drew back his fist and slammed it into the tree beside her head. No. *Through* the tree. He roared in her face, looking like a horror movie creature with black eyes and bloody teeth.

Over his shoulder, she caught a glimpse of headlights up on the road. The vampire saw them too. He released her, and she crumpled into a ball at his feet. Then he laid his hands on the mangled Mustang, hefted it over his head, and hurled it at the lights. It smashed head-on into the pickup, the one with over-sized tires and no tailgate, the one she should have just stayed behind in the first place.

The vampire roared again, this time with words. "Mercy! Again! The bitch is still in my fucking head." He turned those eyes on Kylie again. "A word of advice. Keep the baby; the brat just saved your life."

She gasped.

He knelt down, pressed his thumb to her jugular and said, "Two heartbeats."

She shuddered and closed her eyes, daring to hope she might survive, that she might emerge from all this with something to live for. When she opened them again, the vampire was gone and the redneck in the pickup was limping toward her.

Silhouetted in the truck's headlights, she couldn't make out his features, but he had a kind voice. "Miss, are you OK down there?"

She nodded, then realized he couldn't see it and said, "I think I'm pregnant."

CHAPTER 10

Sodomite. That is what the Lord called men who coupled like beasts. Kayin considered it possible Desollador's unpure form, the Dog, had corrupted the vampire's mind, as much consuming meat with its life-blood still inside corrupted his soul. Diane, on the other hand, disappointed him, flaunting her nakedness before Desollador and his brother. When the vampire took up her strap, Kayin believed he would chastise her for the temptation of her flesh, but he succumbed to it and ravished the proffered body instead.

Realizing the err of her lewdness, she cried out to be spared, but the vampire would not relent. She beseeched him to cease their relations, but he knew her until he was spent. She cried loud enough to bring her companions to her rescue, but Salvion held them behind the wind, blocked the sight of her from their eyes with a maelstrom of soil and leaves as locusts around their heads so she would not be further debased. They pushed and railed against it like gnats at his back, but he paid them little mind as he studied Diane's plight.

This would be her breaking. If she was truly His chosen, this would be her remaking as well. That is, He would bring her up from her nest and multiply her days like the Phoenix. He would make her garments to hide her nakedness as He made them for the first people in the Garden. He would give her mighty weapons— Kherev and Khanit, sword and spear. He would give her the power of Will to remake her world and, it was Kayin's greatest wish, to remake him as well.

Kayin wore his true flesh again, having left the poacher shell behind to make haste for Benevolence. It would have started to go to Earth by the time he returned to it, and if Diane and her companions were unable to set him free, he would be forever reliant on the Eater of Souls for such form that would allow him to walk among man without condemnation. In this flesh, only the One who made him could look on him without fear, the One who Marked him in Earth's first days and whose face had been turned from him since.

Kayin went to his knees before Him, there on the good earth that bore witness to Diane's desecration, even as Desollador carved his own Mark upon her thigh. The position of supplication felt alien and uncomfortable in his less than human form, yet achingly familiar. He hid his face under his wing, ashamed that he'd waited so long to cast off pride and beseech his creator. How could it be that Kayin chose this night, when he would bear witness to such terrible violation, to make his first supplication to the Lord who Marked him thus?

"Would it have made a difference, Hashem, had I prayed sooner? Would thou have granted unto me entrance to Sheol? Would thou have granted unto me that my flesh return to Earth so my Spirit could rest?"

No answer, only the soft cries of the wounded warrior down the hill and the steady beating of her companions' fists against the wind. Kayin beat his own upon the ground. "How long, LORD? Wilt thou forget me forever? How long wilt though hide thy face from me?"

Kayin watched his tears skim over the earth, condensation like dew on grass. "Be gracious unto me, LORD, for I languish away. Heal me for my bones and my soul are affrighted." Still the soil rejected his tears. "LORD, how long? Return! Deliver my soul! Save me for Thy mercy's sake and, according to the multitude of Thy compassions, blot out my transgressions."

He uncovered his eyes, tucked his wings back against his spine, and lifted his face. "For I know my transgressions; and my sin is ever before me. Restore unto me the joy of Thy salvation."

That is when he saw her coming into her glory. Diane with blood upon her thighs, but not bleeding. With a decision in her eyes a breath before transformation. Before He smelted her bruises into armor. Before

He bestowed upon her her Kharev and Ahtum and Matteh, Sword and Dagger and Staff.

Kayin held his breath in awe of His work, then let it out in a ragged whisper of praise. "We are…fearfully and wonderfully made."

Kayin waited for me at the top of the hill. As I ascended, the wind came full circle around me and, with it, a wall of particles that looked like coffee grounds. It blotted out everything, even Eric, except Kayin.

He had discarded the old poacher's form for one I had seen in my dream. My eyes narrowed. "You were watching? Did you enjoy the show?"

He shrugged, wings rising and falling at his shoulders. "He gave you your armor and your weapons. That is all that matters."

So my rape was incidental, a catalyst for my change. "Why did you watch?"

"I wanted to see what would happen. Edward warned me to stay away. You know we can only be stopped, any one of us, by stopping all of us."

"Yet you are here."

"You have something of mine."

I folded one sock down over my boot laces, both of which had been unaffected by my transformation, and retrieved the juju box hidden there. "I don't understand what this is."

"That is Edward's power over me."

I opened the box and withdrew the tip of a horn tucked inside. "This binds you to him?"

Kayin nodded.

I connected the dots in my head. "Natalie took the box from Edward too, didn't she? In the end, she bound you to her."

"She bound my soul to her bones."

"Why didn't you wake when she died?"

He shrugged. "I was bound to her *bones*. She laid opened her breast and fused that little chip of me to her own rib. She lost too much blood doing it, but her death did not allow me release."

Jeez, why couldn't she bind him to a finger bone? A toe? Why the hell a rib?

Reading the confusion on my face, Kayin answered, "A binding is only as strong as that to which it is bound. Bone to bone, what one could be stronger than that which He took from Man to create life?"

"How did Edward get it back?"

"Edward and I are bound by more than bone. I have his birthright. Wind, to call my body back from dust. When those boys brought Edward back through the veil, the wind came to me again. It returned to dust the bones that bound me and put my own back together again." He looked wistful. "Edward tried to give me earth, but that is forbidden to me."

"The horn?" I reminded.

"I gave it to him. What good is a body that cannot be looked upon without fear? Without Edward, this form is the only one I have. It is not enough."

"Would you give it up, Kayin?"

"I would not choose to live as a thief in someone else's body for eternity."

"Would you give up the wind?"

"How would I call my form from dust without it?"

I held out my hand, offering him the fragment of horn Edward had taken from him. It turned to dust in his hand before reforming on his forehead, strong and whole again. "If you give up the wind, I will give you shadow."

The wind died at once, and a circle of earth a foot wide and two feet tall fell down around us. I saw Eric come through the trees first, then the others. So many things happened at once. Bree shoved Kayin away from me with a thought. He became dust in defense of her power, while Mace became shadow. Both reformed a moment later, Mace as the Wolf, Kayin as the demon.

"Stop," I barked. "All of you will stand down."

"Is he one of them?" Renn asked.

"He looks like of them, doesn't he?" Bree answered.

"As opposed to the werewolf and whatever the hell Diane is supposed to be right now." Roger kept his distance from all of us.

"He is Kayin." I could see a pattern laid out before me. "And I am going to free him."

Pretty sure everyone asked "Are you crazy?" at the same time.

To Eric, I held up the box that used to have a piece of Kayin inside.

"Natalie bound Kayin to herself, then laid down in your coffin with this damn thing around her neck so he would stay bound. Forever. *That* is why she died with you."

As if it could make up for his loss, Kayin said to Eric, "She made a great sacrifice to rid the world of us for a time."

"How?" Eric asked, his voice barely a whisper.

"Bone to bone."

Eric choked down an anguished cry.

"Is that what I was supposed to do?" I asked, more to myself than to Kayin. "Bind you to me and lie down and die?"

A shrug.

"Fuck that."

I drew the Mark. Agony seemed too cruel for a surrender. How long had Kayin yearned for a form of his own, to take the shape of one of His creatures again? To Kayin, I said, "Show me the thread that connects you to him. Show me the wind."

He considered me. "How do I know you will not sever it and leave me with neither wind nor shadow?"

"You are the world's first murderer. I think I'll stay just this side of pissing you off."

I expected it to resemble an umbilical cord, the vortex that coalesced above his heart and extended out into the forest. But it closer resembled a drain, glowing ember and shadow flowing steadily from Kayin's center to oblivion and back again. I watched the tide go out for a short time. It seemed the occasion called for some final words, but I didn't have them.

Kayin did. "I am pleased to have born witness to the making of you, Diane."

I ignored the cumulative weight of my companions' stares and issued a sharp command to Roger. "Tell him to bite the demon. Leg, arm or wing. Just keep clear of his chest."

"What? Why?"

"Because we are going to turn a demon into a wolf."

"How do you know that will even work?"

I looked at the Wolf at my feet. His snout crinkled, showing a flash of fang, but he didn't advance. "I am going to make it work."

I tightened my grip on the Mark and studied the vortex. Almost as wide as the demon's chest and waving like flame, it would not allow a clean cut. I needed a bigger sword; I needed a machete. My blade, still kaleidoscopic until that moment, grew longer than my forearm and glowed quicksilver bright.

Kayin nodded to me and approached the Wolf. Mace swung that massive snout in Roger's direction, then back at Kayin. I don't know if it was Roger's command or the sudden petting motion Kayin made that ultimately spurred Mace into action. With a snarl and a bark, he clamped down on the demon's forearm.

To Roger, I said, "Make him call the change, but don't let him let go of that arm."

"Call the change? You mean to turn back into a human?"

"I mean tell him to try." I wasn't going to let it happen, but the Wolf did not need to know it.

Roger knelt knuckle-to-ground beside the pair and closed his eyes. A cold sweat covered his forehead when the shadows finally converged.

The Wolf and the demon dissolved into the darkness. Only the steady flow of liquid ember connecting Edward and Kayin showed through it. I raised the Mark two-handed and drove it down hard into the stream.

"Now make him stop," I told Roger as my blade hit with a clang and a heavy shower of sparks; the stuff was not as fluid as it looked.

He broke concentration long enough to gape at me. "Stop?"

"Yeah, stop. Stay Wolf. Whatever. Stop the change."

"Jeez, Di, you want me to tell him to bust a nut and then *stop*?"

I winced at the reference. "Think Wolf. Think only Wolf, Rog. I need you to think enough Wolf for the both of them."

"Then why'd I tell him to change in the first place?"

"I needed the shadows."

I brought my blade down through them again, into the vortex. It resisted like metal, and I had no time to hack away at it until it cracked.

The shadows were already starting to fade. In the moment that would have been despair, my blade changed again, glowing brilliant white, emitting a subtle vapor and hiss. Where it touched, the vortex melted. Damn if the Mark hadn't mutated into some other-wordly plasma cutter. I poured my energy into the arc. The weapon took what I offered and more, dropping me to my knees. The arc blazed so bright it looked almost blue, then the vortex split under it. The half not attached to Kayin snapped like a rubber band into the forest.

The half that attached to him gaped open like a sinkhole in his chest. I felt like I would be able to see right down to his soul if I stared into the center of it. *That* half ate up the shadows around them. Shadows of change. Shadows that made wolves of men.

The gaping maw in Kayin's chest collapsed in on itself, shadow flowing into it like earth filling a crater. The shadows that obscured his wings disintegrated, tumbling to the center of him, leaving no flesh behind. The arm still clenched in the Wolf's jaws dissolved too. Before our eyes, the demon turned to dust. Dust that looked like soot.

In fact, it was neither dust nor soot, but particles of shadow. And as they moved, reforming into something new and holy, I realized the shadows were not just a substance of change. They were the substance of Creation.

When the shadows were gone, two wolves stood before me, one tenuously under Roger's control, the other unfettered for the first time in millennia.

The Other Thing (That Looked Like a Wolf But Was Not) smelled of dust. The Wolf That Remembered Being a Man whined—an expression of curiosity—a pensive question that the Other ignored. It regarded the Wolf in silence and stillness. The Wolf stared back, ears flattened, perturbed by the discord between that scent and its physicality.

The Other's fur stayed smooth, relaxed from crest to withers.

Its tail drooped low enough to tickle the damp leaves that blanketed the forest around them, radiating calmness. Yet something seemed off in its eyes. The Other looked like a wolf, but smelled like earth. And looked at him with the eyes of a man. Not the corporal wet orbs of the being, but some awareness they held.

Then there was the woman—so bright. Shining blade. Spirit blazing! The woman looked like flame, but wore the scent of rain and cherry blossoms and swift rivers cutting through high, cold places. In her posture there was at once tension—a coiled, glossy presence—and an ease that proclaimed: *I am ready. We are ready.*

The woman was Alpha.

The Wolf That Remembered Being a Man whined again, this time a question for her. *What am I? Am I Assassin or Companion? Protector or Prey?*

An answering voice deep within the Pack. *Mace, come back!*

Mace. Yes, that had been the Name. The Name at the beginning and end of him. Was it his own?

The woman, the Alpha—his Alpha—walked through the pack, two females and two males. The Wolf bowed his head, teeth bared gently as she passed. Her voice thrilled him. "Roger, it would be better if he was on two legs again for a while."

The voice from the pack again said, "Working on it. He's not listening to me. I can't...find him."

She sighed. "Mace, you must have some choice words for me. Come on, give 'em to me like a man. A howl just ain't gonna cut it."

The Other snickered. Snickered! Her words made no sense, but

233

that clipped snort elicited something like fear or uncertainty deep within his gut. Embarrassment? Were the words supposed to make sense? They hadn't, except for the Name! *She* called him by it. Is that who I am?

"Kayin, why are you still here?" The Other lifted its shoulders and glanced into the Forest in a considering way. Ultimately stood its ground, passive and watchful.

Mace, buddy, you gotta change back.

The Words again, along with the Name.

What was it about that Name? But this time, with the words there was something more, an emotion — a compulsion — just too complex for his lupine brain to grasp.

Another voice, one of the Pack females, the one that smelled familiar, said, "Why isn't he changing back?"

The other male, the one not so familiar, answered, "The Wolf doesn't think like a man. Roger has to reach the Wolf, not the human."

Flashes of images where the words had been. Shadows coalescing. A man with hair black as a crow feather and hard eyes. Mace! Out of the shadows, a Wolf with the same eyes. Me! Again, the man, a stripe of silver, cool against his throat, and between breaths, gone. Shadows. Shadows to hide the transformation.

Now emotion to ride the images. The creature of horn and wing, towering. The scent and then the taste of dust. More shadows. Vortex of fire and the Bright One slamming her blades into it again and again. Shadows fall. The Other that was not a Wolf but looked like one. Still smelled of earth. Shadows. Change!

Shadows...swallowing him. Thick as smoke, crowding out the air. In him. Of him. He was Shadow. What was it about that Name? Mace. Hair black as a crow's wing. Mace. Dark cape of fur. Mace. Me!

Quickly as they came, the shadows found purchase, reworked flesh and blood like clay, and dispersed again. And again he was Man. The Pack let out a collective breath. The Wolf that had been a demon snickered again and finally turned to the Forest, but made an unhasty departure.

Mace, kneeling on the ground, chest heaving from exertion, still shaking that damn earth scent out of his head, growled at the retreating form, "You're welcome, asshole."

Diane laughed, a sound as bright as her blade, as blazing as her spirit. So bright. "And here I thought your choice words were going to be for me."

He turned at the sound of her voice, met her eyes with a fierceness — a wildness — that followed him from the shadows. Her gaze was confident, empathetic, ready.

He bowed his head and bared his teeth in something that looked almost like a smile. She was still Alpha.

Mace didn't look half as pissed as I assumed he must be for his role in Kayin's release. Which is just as well, because I really didn't have time to massage egos. Now that the immediate danger had passed, I couldn't ignore the open-mouthed stares of my companions much longer. I had no explanation for why I turned up looking like one of the X-Men.

Mace surprised me again by swinging that strange, teeth-bared half smile at the rest of the group and suggesting, "What say we save the 'what the hell just happened' for later?"

Roger shrugged, never taking his eyes off me. "That's cool as shit."

I wished Renn had been the one to say it. She had grown so quiet. But I didn't devote any more time to regret until much later, hindsight being twenty-twenty and all. When saving the world, there was bound to be some collateral damage. So what if it was my best friend? I had cut my ties (and losses) years ago. Not one of us mattered now except that, through our sacrifice, every one of the monsters would rot up on that mountain.

With a renewed, if reluctant, sense of duty — purpose — we made our way back to the House from which I had not so long ago rescued us. On the way, I told them just how Catherine's toy soldiers would become an army.

"Did you find him?" Edward asked.

Desollador nodded. "I did."

"How about Kayin? Did you happen to see him while you were out?"

"Am I my brother's keeper?"

Edward didn't crack a smile. "He's gone."

"He's always been gone."

"I mean his link has been severed."

Desollador sobered. "How?"

"Diane severed it."

No question about it, Edward would end her if he got the chance.

"A human girl severed the tie that has bound me to Earth's firstborn for over a thousand years? Where is the Athame?"

"Eric does not have it."

Edward didn't miss the evasion. "That is not the same as not knowing where it is. Don't make me abuse our link, vampire."

"He has hidden it where none without a soul may leave."

"What does that mean?"

"That is all I know. See for yourself." He opened his mind to Edward, showing him the writing on the wall as it were.

"Where is this place?"

He shrugged. "I'm sure it's around here somewhere." In fact, he knew exactly where, but Edward's interests seemed to be at odds with his own for now, so it could wait. "But for the time being I believe we have bigger problems. They're back."

The narrow footpath leading to the House now disappeared into a seamless forest. A forest that should have been obscured by towering columns, thick balustrades with posts kicked out like bad teeth, and windows with more bars than glass.

The House was gone, a thicket of hardwoods in its place. Though they cast all the right shadows, they looked like extras on a movie set. We knew they were an illusion, but that knowledge did not make them disappear. Belief apparently had no effect on Salvion's magic.

I drew Heartache. It remained an ephemeral bō in my hands waiting for need to transform it. Bree pulled shards of duct tape-wrapped mirrors from every pocket, which danced about her windswept curls, reminding me of darting serpent tongues. For all that, Renn saved us.

Eric and I were roughly at the head of the group, with Renn close behind at my insistence. I thought I would have to protect her. Ha!

I swear she jumped to action before I even noticed the Jeep — *my* Jeep — hurtling toward us. It breached the tree line twenty feet above our heads, one-dimensional, doors first, just a likeness of a Jeep against a woodsy backdrop. As it broke through the illusion of forest, it gained dimension. A fender emerged, then bumper and hood. After that, car parts all blurred together.

The instant the vehicle appeared, Renn leapt, driving one foot into my chest, propelling me backward, knocking the wind from my lungs and the bō from my hands. She launched off of me and into Eric, arms encircling his waist, momentum taking both of them to the ground with a loud oomph. The Wrangler sailed past us.

It hit a wall, invisible as the illusion that shrouded the House and dead level with Bree Conner's eyes. Well, not quite a wall because it didn't crumple on impact, just stopped four feet off the ground and not even a car length from her.

Bree screamed into darkness of the false forest, "You threw a fucking *car* at us?"

A growl answered her, followed by an echoing crack, a brief feeling like the mountain was holding its breath, then, through the veil, a tree. A real one. Its trunk was almost as wide as the Jeep, with limbs that could have been trees themselves. This time Bree Conner did not stop the descent. She shattered it. Thousands of branches snapped at once. The trunk and all its many appendages came apart in the air in great splinters.

My Jeep hung suspended in place for a split second after the tree exploded before she totaled it too. I squawked in dismay as every mirror, body panel and otherwise reflective surface on it shattered. Even the rims were toast.

With another scream and a heaving motion, she sent the glittering maelstrom *back*. The projectiles pierced the veil, revealing reality through dozens of narrow gashes. A glint of siding, peeling and shadowed. A window pane draped with a curtain of kudzu. Red brick that may have been part of the chimney.

I swung myself up into what was left of my Jeep, still suspended a few feet off the ground, and fished out a black duffel.

From that, I pulled out a Mossberg 500 tactical 12-gauge and a UTS-15 bullpup—pistol grip, laser sights, 15-round capacity, and every bit as badass as it sounds. One of these went to Mace, the other to Roger. To Renn, I issued my only handgun, the Judge. I hoped these would buy us enough time for all we needed to do. I picked up my bō.

"Showtime," Eric said, and a glow appeared in his palm. "Ladies and gentlemen, we have light." He hurled the glowing orb into the veil.

As we steeled ourselves to cross into the illusion, the Dog leapt through it.

He changed midair. Shadows flowed over the Dog like a cape, which Desollador tossed over his shoulder upon landing. "What happened to you?"

I took a step toward him, holding the bō in front of me with both hands. "You happened."

"Where did you get those?"

He could have been talking about the clothes or my shiny new weapons. Didn't matter. "I *made* them."

I took another step toward him. Eric stopped me with a fist around my forearm. I could have ignored it, an insignificant intrusion, until Desollador warned, "Brother, do not touch her again."

"Get over it," I said. "I told you that you don't own me. After tonight, you won't even be real anymore."

"Not real?" He looked thoughtful, then asked, "When did you start believing in vampires, Diane?"

"You know the answer to that."

"Yes. When one killed your parents. Their deaths set all this" — he waved a hand to indicate me and all those behind me — "in motion. You and I might have never met, except for two deaths that happened in a place more than a year after I left it."

"Christopher," Eric said in a way that sounded like a plea.

Desollador ignored him. "Yet somehow that event set you on *my* trail. I was bound to notice you, Pet, and either take you apart or make you mine. It was only a matter of time."

I drew the Mark. "Careful, vampire. You might give me more weapons than wounds."

"And you never even saw me coming." Desollador pointed at Eric. "I've been trying to figure out why Diane has only killed vampires that I sired. But she didn't even know they were mine, did she? She was just doing as she was told. Was that the plan you cooked up with your witch friend, brother? To send her after my breed so I would take an interest in her?"

Eric answered, "When you came for her, you were bound to bring the rest of them down with you."

Desollador nodded, as if to himself. "How could she turn down the calling after such a loss? But then to kill every vampire *except* the one that killed her parents. That's a strange vengeance."

Heat flared like an itch at the back of my neck. "Eric?"

"Or didn't you ever wonder about that, Diane?"

I had. I had always wondered.

"Why them and not *him*?"

"He got away. I went back to sleep," I said, parroting words I had heard from my prophet too many times.

"He did not get away, Pet. Did you know vampires are territorial? In a city, there are enough warm bodies to split between a sire and his progeny, but out here? Not enough population to hide more than one.

239

How long have you claimed this territory, Eric?"

I shifted the weight of Heartache from one hand to the other. It coiled like a whip at my feet, a cool liquid amethyst. The Mark glowed violet too, so I drew it for good measure. What I really wanted was a shotgun with rounds that worked on Desollador. Even as I thought it, the sword morphed into a phantasm of my cut down 12-gauge. Dream-things made real. I pointed the Mark at Desollador and whipped Heartache in a wide arc at Eric's throat. He dodged, though I never saw him move.

"I can explain," Eric said, as if I gave a damn.

"How long have you been in Benevolence, Eric?"

Out of the corner of my eye, Desollador twitched, and I fired, and violet brimstone shredded his abdomen. My otherworldly ammunition proved a hell of a lot more effective than buckshot.

"Did you feel that, vampire?" I asked with teeth bared. He clutched his tattered shirt and grunted. "Or did it just piss you off?"

He leveled me with his eyes and replied, "I felt it."

I didn't like his tone, so I fired again. "Then stay the fuck down," I advised. "I don't think this thing runs out of bullets."

I swung again toward Eric. "I said, how long have you been in Benevolence?"

I'll give him credit for not bullshitting me. "Long enough."

I would have shot him then and there, but didn't want to leave Desollador an opening for retaliation, and despite my bluff about ammunition, I guessed my own endurance determined when it ran out. I felt like I was doing ninety miles an hour, fueled by caffeine, sugar and adrenaline. Eventually I was going to crash.

"Long enough to what?" I wanted, no, I *needed* to hear him say it.

"Long enough to kill your parents."

I lashed out at him again, and this time he didn't duck. Heartache left a deep slice down his left cheek, laying him bare down to his jaw bone. "Why?! You lectured me about giving my virginity to Desollador when you murdered my *family*! What was it, Eric? You took away my childhood as vengeance for leaving you with a rotting corpse in another life?"

Desollador started to laugh. He got to his feet again, but rubbed his chest like it itched where I shot him. "That's pathetic, little brother."

So I shot him again. "I said stay down!"

To Eric, I said, "Tell me why."

"We needed you motivated. We needed to give you a cause."

"Who's 'we'?"

Eric did not answer. He didn't have to. Catherine needed me motivated.

"That bitch!"

"You have to understand. This war is bigger than two people, Diane."

I sheathed Heartache because wielding it exhausted me. "Understand what? Catherine created this war. Catherine made the monster. She was selfish and stupid and paid for it with her daughter's blood. She did not need to take my family's too. She had no right. You had no right!"

He had the gall to justify. "Yet you are here. Because of that tragedy. Your parents died to save the world; can't you see that?"

"The world? Come the fuck on. You know what? That motivation—that cause—that has been driving me these years? That was guilt, you son of a bitch! I thought I was supposed to save my parents, that she tried to help me save them, and I failed. I have spent every day despising myself for that failure."

"Then guilt made you an Assassin."

And then I shot him too. But his wounds healed as quickly as Desollador's. I thought of the plasma cutter that severed Kayin's link, and the violet shotgun changed shape in my hand to match it. "Show it to me, and I might let you live."

He didn't pretend to wonder what I meant by the demand, but refused me anyway. "I am the anchor."

"You are the deadweight! I told you I would find another way. I don't need you. Show me the link!" Eric risked a quick glance behind me; I read danger in his expression.

The rest happened so quickly. Desollador charged, the veins in his neck and shoulders straining with rage. He was good as new and, true to his word, pissed.

I drew Heartache, the ephemeral bō, again. He had always been its intended. Standing the bō into the ground as he leapt for me, I envisioned a spearhead, barbed and monstrous, before the vampire impaled himself on it—through the cold, black center of him.

Even this could not kill him, but I saw in his eyes that he felt my pain at last. Throbbing ache and bitter disappointment. Lost innocence and twisted yearning. The breaking of me.

The vampire succumbed with a convulsive wail, fingers clutching at the bō, lacking the strength to draw it out. That is what I'd made Heartache to do.

"Show me the link, Eric."

A swirling trail of the same blue flame that Catherine favored appeared, leading from Eric's heart into the veil. "I'm sorry."

I severed it in one stroke. "Run, Eric. I will give you that much head-start for helping us here. When this is finished, I am coming for you. I kill no other vampire until I see you dead."

He shook his head. "I won't run. Someone needs to watch over your body."

I didn't argue. That too had been the plan. But I shrugged. "You get no points for chivalry now, Eric."

"I told you this war is bigger than two people. This isn't chivalry. It's strategy."

I let him lay his hand on the back of my neck and find the pressure points that would put me to sleep. I vowed to myself I would kill him as soon as I awoke.

Renn never saw the Dog come through. She and Bree were already on the other side, poking at the illusion of forest now riddled with holes in search of the House. They found the front entrance by pure accident. Inside, the deception ended, like a door opening from the woods of Narnia into a mid-century foyer.

Mirrors banked the entrance—set above matching console tables—shards hanging precariously in their ornate frames and glittering on the floor beneath. When they turned back toward the false forest, Bree called more glimmering fragments of reflection to follow in their wake. Here and there, through slashes in the veil, there were windows, some with remnants of glass still intact. Not for long. Bree shattered them as well, and pieces of these joined the growing maelstrom of mirrors surrounding them.

Where they walked, where the mirrors spun, the illusion fell to tatters.

Renn scanned the glowing lawn through a sparkling funnel of reflections and ever-thinning ribbons of fantasy in search of flying cars, trees and anything else that might break the veil to destroy them. Where Bree walked, she collected more bits of ammunition, calling back her duct tape-handled daggers and myriad of Jeep pieces. Even the raindrops began to form a fluid surface of reflection that sliced through the make-believe.

Here and there, vaguely manlike shadows moved through the trees that weren't trees, suggestions of monsters that set Renn on edge, sending her reflexes into overdrive. More than once she shoved Bree out of the path of an imaginary threat, prompting a string of vulgarity and earning herself a dozen nicks and cuts from the ever-spinning tornado of glass.

After two trips around, they cleared the illusion from ground level to about twenty feet above it, so the house appeared to be cut off at the second-story windows, disappearing into an awning of floating trees. They peered into the blackness where the roof should be.

Finally, Bree said, "He's up there."

Renn eyed a crumbling trellis of roses. "Do we climb?"

"I'm telekinetic. No, we don't climb. We float."

Renn's stomach rolled as her feet left the ground. With the tornado of reflection shredding the path ahead of them, they made their way toward the roof to find Salvion.

He didn't make it easy. Images of trees collapsed on top of them, through them. Far below, the house crumbled away, falling into the depths of a fiery pit that had the classical appearance of Hell. Winged demons rose up to terrorize them. When the first one appeared, Renn fired at it, remembering too late that the creature wasn't real. For every illusion Bree destroyed, another replaced it.

They were lost now. Fumbling about with fingers splayed, feet stretching for solid ground, like searching for a light switch in the dark. With no anchor in reality to get their bearings, they wandered, Bree's breath coming in heavy sighs, raspy from exertion.

Then the winged demon appeared inside the tempest, claws descending inexorably toward Renn, and she raised the gun again.

That's when the pillow of air holding her aloft went dead. Renn fell fifteen feet onto a banked surface, shingles peeling under her as she started to slide. She lost the gun in a frantic grab for purchase, rolled onto her stomach and split her nails in the soft wood.

Finally her feet and then her fingers found a thick net of vines that stopped her descent. No way to tell how close she was to the edge because the illusion was seamless here. She yelled up into the darkness. "Bree! The roof is straight below..."

A two-handed blow to her torso drove her back into a brick pillar she figured had to be a chimney. A scrape against the shingles signaled that her attacker was advancing, so she scurried to the backside of the pillar, sliding down to a defensive crouch. Listening intently to his every footfall, she waited until she judged him to be no more than a few feet in front of her before bracing her hands against the chimney and kicking both legs out at knee level.

Salvion hit the roof with a bellow, but immediately took hold of a length of kudzu to secure himself. Renn's eyes were wide, the whites of them bright against the night. Bree joined her and Salvion on the roof, following the sounds of their struggle, that whirlwind of debris surrounding her—a pervasive virus eating his fantasy bit by bit.

He rushed again. Renn scrambled away, but this time he caught her by the ankle with one hand and slung her back. The last thing she heard before blackness was the crack of her head against the bricks.

Bree saw Renn take aim…at her. She considered for a moment the possibility of stopping a point-blank spray of birdshot in midair. Not a chance. Not when the spinning mirrors were starting to make her dizzy. Not when she could feel the entire weight of their two bodies in her head. She didn't even think she could muster the jolt of energy to knock the gun out of Renn's hand. Only one option left. Bree dropped her.

She heard her hit down hard, then a scrambling grab for purchase before, "Bree! The roof is straight below…"

She followed her voice and, through thick ribbons of illusion, watched Salvion scoop up Renn's unconscious form and toss it off the roof, too far away for Bree to catch. She tried—felt Renn slip through her proverbial fingers—and managed only to break her fall. She hoped that would be enough.

Salvion reknit his illusion behind her. Her mirrors shredded, and he mended. She advanced, and he retreated. *This isn't working*, she thought. She flung a pair of daggers at him, but he became insubstantial and dodged before they hit.

The forest dissipated like fog when he abandoned his solid form. Though she was glad for the ability to see again beyond the scope of her mirrors, his lack of substance made him hard to catch. She needed to give him an incentive for flesh.

That's when she saw Renn's gun. On a hunch, Bree sent the tempest of mirrors surrounding her to surround Salvion. With an imperceptible closing and widening of the circle, she steered him to the place where the gun lay not quite buried in the kudzu.

Salvion saw it, took the bait. She'd made a temptation worth risking the maelstrom. He crouched down, laid a transparent hand on the revolver, took form and raised his hand to fire.

In that moment, Bree pulverized the mirrors, leaving not one of them larger than a spec of dust. She funneled the particles down Salvion's throat, shoved them into his ears and up his nose, dusted his body like glitter until he was a near-solid reflection.

Trapped in his flesh, she held him there by trembling, steadfast resolve...and hoped she could hold on long enough.

Mace felt Roger tense at his back when they found Edward. He was in the sitting room, straddling a chair, elbows resting comfortably on its back, staring at the now-defunct white chalk circle.

He spoke without making eye contact. "It's true I can't feed on your souls anymore—Catherine made sure of that—but I can still feel them."

He reached a hand out, palm up. Mace took a cautionary step back, though it galled him to retreat. "Right there, pulsing like a heartbeat."

Now he met Mace's eyes. "I didn't lose my taste for it. I didn't lose my...hunger...for it. That bitch created me un-whole and left me that way, then took away the only thing capable of making me feel human."

"Human? Killing people to steal their souls is not human."

"Not to steal." He stood, tossing the chair aside. "What is it you people say about hunting? It's cruel to hunt for sport, just for the pleasure of killing, but justifiable if you plan on eating the meat." He put an obscene emphasis on the last word.

Mace ached to change, to charge, but Roger forbid it. *Only as a last resort. I almost lost you that last time. And anyway, I got this.*

There is this old adage about a bull in a china shop. Point in fact, a bull is actually a careful creature. *Mythbusters* proved it. As long as the aisles are wide enough for its considerable girth, a bull in a china shop will do such minor damage that even filing an insurance claim would be a waste of time. Even six bulls in a china shop are comically graceful. But a deer...a deer will topple every shelf that's not nailed down like a stack of dominoes.

Roger called a family of deer, two does and one monstrous buck, into the House. Hooves designed for the forest scrambled to find purchase on the hardwood floor. They reminded Mace of Bambi on the frozen pond, not at all the regal protectors Roger described in his plan. The buck charged, just missed Edward, and skidded into the wall.

Roger was concentrating so hard, he looked like he needed to take a shit. The buck regrouped and charged again; this time powerful hooves shoved Edward through the doorway into the dining room, where he landed on his back in the middle of the threadbare rug. There!

Edward launched from his back to his feet without so much as a grunt of effort. The rug caught fire where he knelt.

The flames did scary things to eyes when he said, "Thing is, I really do enjoy the sport."

The room exploded. Ceiling, walls, floor — everything flammable — caught in that moment. In response, Mace unleashed a hail of buckshot, which sent the deer scrambling, Beastmaster be damned.

The bullets hit Edward's center body mass with a thud, like impact with wet earth or wax. The force of it, though, slammed him back against the far wall, giving Roger space to crawl in and open the hatch. Then he drew as well, but another flashover sent flames rolling in thick, black clouds overhead. The gun seared his hand with an audible sizzle.

Edward closed the distance between them, reached into Roger's chest and tore the still-beating soul from his body. It came out like a paper doll version of him, precariously connected, thin and fragile. Roger's eyes widened. His mouth formed a perfect "O" shape, and he started to fall. The delicate link between his body and soul sundered in aching slow motion, but not slow enough for either of them stop it.

Mace tore the silver from his throat before Roger hit the floor, knowing full well that his sacrifice would not save his friend and accepting that he would never find his way back from that wolfen state without him. So be it.

Edward's whole body smiled as Roger's collapsed. He shredded the disembodied spirit into a ghoulish confetti and tossed the pieces into the flames. As Wolf, Mace crashed into the monster, his momentum taking both of them down into the earthen pit that had been prepared for Edward beneath the floorboards. The Wolf That Remembered Being a Man held fast in his mind one task, one singular purpose for existing: *Hold him inside the circle.* As the flames spread above them, he pricked his ears forward, bared his teeth and snarled. He would hold the monster until his Alpha came...or until the world burned down around him.

CHAPTER 11

Is this Hell?

I saw many horned beasts fleeing a house on fire, hooves and antlers kicking out the posts of crumbling balustrades. Rolling plumes of black smoke chased them out. What was the rule about smoke? Crawl low, stay under it. Well, that was just fine, as I appeared to be out cold on the damp earth, limbs askew, naked except for boots and earrings.

Why am I naked? I remembered having clothes...a costume of some sort.

A vampire crouched over my body, and I had the impulsive urge to Gather him, but could not remember why. What was his name? Eric. Eric killed my parents. My arms didn't quite work right, in fact did not quite seem to be arms at all, but I managed to crawl onto his back and peer over his shoulder at my body. I saw but did not feel him shiver. The shell of me seemed to be breathing, unharmed in the presence of the traitorous bloodsucker.

A livid, pulsating spear caught my attention and, still crouched on one vampire's back, I shifted my gaze to another, this one writhing on the ground not far from me with a blazing staff of light staked clean through his heart. Desollador. I had a flash of awareness at the sight of him, a moment of lucidity. And in that moment, I heard myself say: *How do you like it, asshole?*

Well, some part of me said it. Certainly not the part of me passed-out on the ground, or the part crouched on the traitor vampire's back trying to discern meaning in the chaos. Some bitter part of me took offense to the intimacy my enemy and I shared. One that secretly yearned for a closure wherein he would feel a modicum of the shame, loneliness and heartache that had plagued me for so long.

I had a growing feeling there was someplace I needed to be. The more I thought about it, the more I suspected there were, more accurately, several places I needed to be. And I needed to be in *all* of them now.

How can I be in so many places at once?

How long had I compartmentalized myself to deal with the war Catherine tricked me into fighting? Since the first time I killed? Since I discovered my parents dead in their bed? Or had it been a slower process, a coping mechanism developed over time, as my world shrank, as the friends and connections of my youth and of the whole mundane world fell away, and I stopped seeing people as friends and loved ones and started seeing them as potential victims or monsters? Or had my other selves — the Dreamer and the Assassin — always been with me? Another latent talent for Catherine to exploit.

That reminded me. I would kill her too after I finished with Eric. If her ghost could die. But first, I had some places to be! So many places at once. Too many places for just one of me. Like a breath I had been holding, I let them out — the Dreamer and the Assassin. Me, but so, so different.

The Assassin, with her battle dress of wounds-made-armor. She held no fear or regret, almost no humanity at all. In truth, I was in awe of her. The Dreamer, ephemeral and transient. At times, she was formless. At times, she held the shape of the entire world in her womb. Shadow-born, she recognized no boundaries between will and being, past and future. She had been liaison to Catherine and held the most regret for having failed to see the true nature of her ghost. The witch ultimately would be hers to end. But these traitors could wait. I had places I had to be! So many places at once. Good thing there were three of me.

The Assassin

It felt good to finally have some space, to be separated from the moonstruck flower-child and the pathetic, depressed teenager living inside of me. Even so, I wasn't crazy one little bit about the circumstances. The dream fabric felt viscous and sticky against my skin. I wanted to be back in the real world, but this was the only space where I — we — could put all the necessary pieces in place, where all worlds touched, where not one of the bastards could hide from us.

Not even *her*.

Catherine had betrayed me, and I hated her for it. But I needed her more. *Bitch. Where are you?*

Yeah, maybe the insult was petty and poorly timed given our urgency, but it felt good to say it. *Catherine, I need some direction here. Where is Salvion?*

I admit feeling relief seeing her face. But she did not answer my question. What she said was, *It was the only way to set you on this path, Diane. They died so you could save the world.*

Bullshit. I'm not saving the world…not from these guys. There are serial killers with higher body counts. Why not set me after them?

There are things you still don't understand.

No shit. And I don't have time to be enlightened now. Where the hell is Salvion?

She pointed at the roof of the burning house. No sooner had I wondered how I would get myself up there than I found myself standing on it. Bree leaned against the chimney, drenched in sweat, either because of the heat from the flames below or the effort of maintaining her hold on Salvion. Well, at least I thought it was Salvion. He looked more like the Silver Surfer.

I debated how to get him from the waking world into the Dream. I wasn't too fond of the flower-child's 'let's hug and become one' method. But I had the Mark and Agony. The former became a whip in my hands again. I aimed for the barrier where the worlds touched and, being forged of ectoplasm or something anyway, the whip sliced right through, encircling Salvion's torso in a glowing manacle.

I braced my feet — or set firmly in my mind the idea of bracing my feet — and pulled. Salvion erupted from his reflective shell and lurched through the barrier. On the other side, his form burst into a cloud of fairy dust. Bree let out a loud breath and collapsed on her hands and knees.

"Diane, if you're listening, whatever it is you need to do in this house, you better do it fast. My best friends are in there, and I am about to tear the place down to get them out."

I couldn't tell her that I heard her or even that she was talking to the wrong Diane.

At any rate, I could feel the other me, the flower-child, in the house already, and *she* heard. Well, that was that then. Now to deal with the pissed-off dead guy wriggling like a fish on a hook at the end of my...lasso.

Desollador hasn't killed his little toy yet, I see.

I hefted Agony in my hand. I kind of liked the way it felt as just a dagger as I slipped it under his ribs. Well, he didn't have ribs so much as the dream of bone where ribs should be, and the pain he felt was whatever he imagined a knife in the ribs would feel like. I hoped he had a nasty imagination.

Nope. You thinking of giving it a go, Salli?

He stayed wisely, and surprisingly, silent. Which was just as well because holding him was difficult enough without the distraction of banter. Where the world felt syrupy before, now I felt like the landscape tried to suck me down with every movement. I knew if I lost my grip on it, if I sneezed, if I so much as blinked, it would drag me down. I would lose my hold on it and him. The dream would control me, and Salvion would be let loose in the world again.

So we took the long way down. With really no alternative, we jumped off the roof. First there came an awful stomach-churning falling sensation. I struggled to keep my wits through it. We fell past one story, then three, then ten. Salvion laughed, still with Agony in his ribs so that he made a whistling sound when he exhaled, like the thing had pierced a lung. I wondered if his dream-body actually had organs. While I was busy wondering, we almost missed the ground, dove right past it and ended up waist-deep in muck. I could feel the world hanging empty and cold right below my knees.

Not for the first time, I wished we could do our fighting awake. Flower-child could have this dream shit!

Painstakingly, I pulled myself out of the earth and Salvion with me. When we started to walk again, our feet made sucking sounds with every step, though when I looked down, I couldn't actually see any mud...or any feet for that matter. The dream fought me hard, harder than Salvion, who seemed content for the moment to just follow.

I wondered if it was possible he was more afraid of the Dream than me or if he just hadn't guessed our destination yet.

In the waking world, the path from the House to the cellar was a short one, but covered in kudzu. I wished I didn't know that. Maybe then the dream path would have been clear...or at least hospitable. Unfortunately, I grew up in Benevolence, and I knew a thing or two about kudzu.

It's not called the 'vine that ate the South' for nothing. In ideal conditions, it grows as much as a foot every day. Herbicides just make it grow faster. It chokes trees, pulls down power lines, violates houses and swamps entire valleys. It is invasive, suffocating, and downright evil. Here in the dream, the kudzu was alive. It coiled around our ankles and climbed up our legs, making every step a battle. Between the mud and the weeds, the dream was winning.

Though I was loath to do it, I pulled the dagger from Salvion's rib wherein it reformed into a scythe. It seemed like the only solid thing in the whole world, and I focused on it. Poured all my energy into it. And started to swing.

The vines split, dissipated, scattered even. This mastery gave me a renewed strength. I had some place I needed to be. Now. The ground beneath us solidified or disappeared entirely. I did not look down to confirm. I could move freely again and didn't want to jinx it.

There was only one way to accomplish the next part. Walking had always been a stupid idea. Once we got to the cellar, I didn't exactly have a key that would open the door to a locked room. And even if I could open the door, how would I seal it again when I finished? No, there had only ever been one way. The dream had been trying to tell me that all along.

Wrapping the whip around my wrist again, I closed my eyes, let go of my grip on the landscape of kudzu and mud, and gathered an image in my mind of mirrored tile and candlelight. At once, the room solidified around me, as if we had always been standing in it.

Now, seeing this, Salvion started to struggle. First a frantic charge to the end of his leash. Then a futile swipe at my selectively insubstantial form.

Neat trick, huh, Salli boy? Learned it from you, you know.

I steadied myself for the final move, the make-it or break-it moment. As I had pulled him into the Dream from the rooftop, I reversed the arc of my whip and launched him—body and all—back to the other side, to the waking world, into a room filled with mirrors, all virtually unbreakable, and with just enough light to see his own reflection.

The Dreamer

The wallpaper melted, miniature damask roses turning first liquid orange, then black, in the inferno. Flames rolled upwards, trampling each other to gain ground, to be the first to plant their seed in hardwood floors and wainscoting yellowed from hundreds of years of disuse.

I heard a groaning sound coming from three stories above the flames. A wooden grumbling that reminded me Bree was coming. Roger lay in the middle of the room, untouched yet by the blaze, with one leg folded under him, eyes and mouth open in twin expressions of surprise, his soul scattered about like macabre party streamers.

I snatched wildly at the fragments, gathering them in my arms and between my fingers, finally spreading them out on the floor beside his body. I couldn't patch it together seamlessly. Like a jigsaw, oddly shaped pieces interlocked, the structure gaining strength as I solved more of the puzzle. How long had it been? Three, four minutes? I had to work quickly. But there were missing pieces, small as Chiclets. Holes where they should have peppered the entire fabric. Who would he be without them?

Better than dead, I decided, and stuffed the thing back into his body. He came to with a gasp, and I Gathered him inside me even as the groaning above became a breaking roar. Damn, she was fast.

Down in the pit, the Wolf held the Soul Shredder at bay. Blood ran in deep rivulets down his fur, what had not been burned away. Edward charged the door. The Wolf clamped down on his calf and pulled him back, marks in the dirt suggesting not for the first or even the fifth time. The Soul Shredder bled flame, and the Wolf screamed as he let go.

Still, he would not relent, shouldering and clawing the monster back against the wall.

I Gathered them both, releasing Roger and the Wolf as quickly as possible on the soft, wet earth outside as the second story disintegrated and flames consumed what remained of the first. Edward roiled inside me like bad seafood, but I needed to see if the patchwork quilt I made of Roger's soul would suffice to make him whole again. Bree landed beside him, embracing, touching his forehead, his hair, as if to assure herself he was still all there. If only she knew.

The Wolf whined, half-collapsed before them. Bree sat back on her heels and covered her mouth to gasp, "Roger, you better bring him back. He's hurt bad...and I don't know how to patch up a wolf."

Roger trembled, his eyes suddenly wet and glassy. He reached a hand out toward the Wolf That Remembered Being a Man and dropped it again. "I...can't. I can't feel him anymore. I can't feel any of them anymore."

I looked back into the flames, wondering what vital piece of confetti I had missed. *I'm sorry, Mace. I am so, so sorry.*

With that, I let go of the scene and the Dream that overlapped it. Our destination was such a long way back, with only a faded map — a memory — that Catherine left to guide me.

I spent *years* in the blackness with him, with his blackness inside me. I wanted so much to just puke him up, but it was too soon. I don't know how much of my soul he burned and blackened trying to get out. I only survived because it was *my* dream. Still, I felt like Atreyu sludging alone through the Swamps of Sadness, the Nothing on my heels and the Gmork in my belly. I wanted him out of me. Would it ever be time?

A wavering light appeared, reminding me of one of those crime drama TV shows, a dome lamp swinging over an empty interrogation room. Except the light came from candles, ugly coils of beeswax wrapped around thick white wicks. They cast long shadows over a circle of chalk on the dirt floor. A woman knelt in the center of it, with dusky red hair braided to her knees, the barest slivers of silver at her temples, and a gown of fragile cheesecloth thin enough to reveal small breasts and narrow hips.

Slender arms, the color of smooth bleached river stones, and bare feet were all of her the gown did not cover. Well, those and her face, round with wide green eyes and heart-shaped lips.

The dream held just this circle and nothing more, an island of time in the very moments before Edward's creation. I spit him out of me and into it and held my breath. Was I right about this place?

Then it happened; the circle ate him. Here, Edward was just a terrible ambition in a stupid, selfish woman's mind. This was more than Purgatory, this awareness of self where one does not even exist. I hoped this was Hell, or as close as a being with no soul could get to it.

The Girl

It wasn't the first or even the second time I had possessed someone. Unlike that first time, I climbed into Desollador's body willingly. The Vampire, however, was not a willing host. I crowded him as thick as earth over a casket, with him trapped inside pushing and raging, nails scraping against his confines. Turnabout's fair play. How many times had he supplanted his will for mine?

The spear was an inconvenience. I didn't feel the sharp agony I inflicted on the Vampire, more like the cringing shiver—an empathic perception—you feel when someone describes an injury or you see a wound on someone else's skin. Still, it was constant and made me ache to rub my palms against my thighs for distraction. Even as I thought it, the Vampire buffed the rough denim of his jeans in a strange syncopated fulfillment of my desire.

Did it feel this way when he was inside my head?

Yes. Desollador's voice thrummed through my consciousness, a dissonant chord in my awareness.

Refusing the goad to converse, I forced him to his feet in the same way I executed the unpleasant thigh-rubbing occurrence. This instigated much bucking and rattling against the ever-shrinking space where his will resided.

He surprised me by managing such rebellion while enduring the pain of Heartache.

You know I told you over and over again that it didn't have to hurt. Forget what I said. I am going to hurt you in ways I haven't even thought of yet.

Yeah, yeah. He's made me regret this, made me wish I had never been born. Heard it all before. I focused on putting one size 13 foot in front of the other.

Bitch, get out of my head!

At least he stopped calling me 'Pet'. I think I preferred this new moniker for its lack of intimacy. It kept our relationship in perspective.

I had to hold onto Heartache to keep it from touching the ground, wherein it ran the risk of bracing against forward movement. The Vampire ceased the brute rush on my habitation and focused every bit of his will on his right hand in a single-minded effort to dislodge the spear, so I had to use the left to keep the thing in place. A step, then tightening or adjustment of my grip on the shaft, repeat. It felt like trying to scratch my head and rub my belly at the same time. A skill I had never been able to master.

The stairway did it. There, I had to master more than putting one foot in front of the other; I also had to manage a descent. That required balance, coordination, and still I had to hold the spear. Only I couldn't.

It fell with a clatter and the Vampire rushed up from his confinement like a dam breaking, sweeping me along in the deluge. I clung to the banks of his being for dear life. One foot already over the falls. If I went over, we'd all die. All of me.

There were so many places I had to be. And I had to be in them all once because *they* had to be in them all once. In desperation, I took Heartache back into me—not the object but the affliction that created it. Throbbing ache and bitter disappointment. Lost innocence and twisted yearning. The breaking of me.

I would be the spear.

I let go, surrendering to the force of the Vampire's will as it swept me into the cold black center of him, where he thought to bury me. I dropped like a stone, sinking with the molten weight of lava.

I felt his soul cry out from the agony of me. The deluge receded as quickly and desperately as it came.

His body was mine, as if he had vacated it entirely, and not so awkward when I was not fighting him for control. The cellar door swung in effortlessly, but the hatch in the floor behind the ladder was a different matter. Its underside was inlaid with amethysts, zapping the Vampire's energy like Kryptonite. His nails were bleeding by the time I completed the task.

Staring down into the darkness, I could feel the Vampire's conflict, the anticipation of relief from the awful pain I sunk in him warring with the fury that I turned him into a puppet.

He spoke to me in scraps of memory: the belt landing on my thighs, my hymen breaking as he tasted my blood on his tongue, the way he brutalized me in another woman's body. *Tender foreplay, Diane, compared to what I will do to you.*

I ignored the desire to remind him he was in no position to make such threats as I lowered his body into the narrow scuttle at our feet, battling claustrophobia and a creeping sense of pity for the monster. Then I forced myself to close the hatch, completing the circuit of amethyst that surrounded it, sealing the Vampire inside, awake and alive, hopefully for all eternity.

Finally, I replied, *No, it was tender, Desollador, compared to what*

I'm about to do to you. With painstaking care, I extricated myself from his body, but I left Heartache behind. The Vampire had earned it, and I had no need of it anymore.

&PILOGUE

I came to with an immense headache. *So that's what it feels like to split myself apart.* I was no longer naked, but clothed in a man's shirt which covered me from neck to thighs. I told Eric that chivalry would win him no favors, but I was glad of his attempt. From thigh to ankle I found myself wearing fur, a large wolf—his coat matted with blood in places and burned away entirely in others—crouched over me.

"He's been like that for hours."

"Jesus, how long have I been out?" I asked Bree.

She shrugged. "Hours?"

"Where are the fire trucks? Surely someone saw the house burning."

She shrugged again. "What house?"

I sat up too quickly and immediately regretted it. I clutched my temple and squinted against double vision. Two of everything, except the house. There wasn't even one of it. "What the...?"

"I buried it," she explained.

I stared at the newly turned ground where the house had stood and just said, "Oh."

Roger hadn't said a word, just stared at the Wolf without blinking. I prodded gently, "Still no luck reaching him?" His eyes watered. He shook his head, opened his mouth to answer, and closed it again.

Did he remember dying?

"It's not your fault, you know," I offered.

He sobbed.

"Edward tore you apart in there. I put you back together as best I could, but I didn't have a lot of time. You'd already been dead for several minutes. The pieces were so small and, well, I don't think that power is within you anymore."

Bree gaped at me. "Dead?"

I nodded.

She grasped his shoulder as if to assure herself he was actually in one piece, and asked, "What exactly was torn apart?"

I met her eyes. "His soul."

She swallowed, looked at Roger and then the Wolf — the casualty — and drew a ragged breath. "Thank you for bringing him back."

I nodded again and looked around me. I didn't see Eric anywhere, not surprising since I'd promised to kill him, but....

"Where is Renn?"

Bree winced. "He took her."

I leapt to my feet. The Wolf nudged the back of my legs. "Which way?"

She passed me a scrap of paper. "I didn't see. He left this."

A note...the vampire left me a note!

I know you will never accept my apology for what I did to your parents, but I hope you can forgive me for what I must do to your friend. It is the only way to save her life.

Yours,

Eric

ABOUT the Author

B.K. Raine lives in North Carolina with her husband, teenage daughter, two dogs, and a cat she insists isn't actually hers because every cat she's ever owned has died a sudden and gruesome death. Raine works as an advertising executive in the media and publishing industry, but has been an author since she was 16, penning her first book on wide-ruled paper with a No. 2 pencil. Her first editor told her she couldn't write but had some great ideas, and if she was willing to leave her pride at the door, he'd teach her the rest.

Blood Toy is the debut novel in her dark urban fantasy series. Look for Book 2, *Kindred Shadows*, Fall 2015.

You can learn about B.K. Raine, read her blog and stay tuned for upcoming books at https://bkraine.wordpress.com/.